ADAM

LIGHTHOUSE SECURITY INVESTIGATIONS WEST COAST

MARYANN JORDAN

Finally Home
Kris Michaels
5/28/24

Cover by: Graphics by Stacy

ISBN ebook: 978-1-956588-58-3

ISBN print: 978-1-956588-59-0

❀ Created with Vellum

ABOUT THE AUTHOR

I am an avid reader of romance novels, often joking that I cut my teeth on historical romances. I have been reading and reviewing for years. In 2013, I finally gave in to the characters in my head, screaming for their story to be told. From these musings, my first novel, Emma's Home, The Fairfield Series, was born.

I was a high school counselor, having worked in education for thirty years. I live in Virginia, having also lived in four states and two foreign countries. I have been married to a wonderfully patient man for forty-two years. When writing, my dog or one of my cats can generally be found in the same room if not on my lap.

Please take the time to leave a review of this book. Feel free to contact me, especially if you enjoyed my book. I love to hear from readers!

Facebook

Join my Facebook group: Maryann Jordan's Protector Fans

Sign up for my emails by visiting my Website!

Website

1

The rhythmic percussion of his footsteps over the dirt path created a cadence more familiar to Adam than any song. His mother often quipped that he came out of the womb running, never wanting to walk first. She might have been right.

Beads of sweat dripped down the sides of his face, and he lifted the bottom of his shirt to swipe at the moisture across his forehead.

The first light of dawn unfurled over the horizon, adding the illusion of warmth to the chilly early morning air. Cumulus clouds blanketed the peaks of indigo mountains rising in the background. Below, the surf chased the sea foam along the sandy coast in a never-ending dance.

Adam had dabbled in other sports during middle and high school but always returned to distance running, finding cross-country more satisfying than laps around the track. The sport was the perfect melding of teamwork while always striving for his personal best, which meant the most to him. While feeling the burn in his muscles, the solitude allowed his mind to wander, escaping the chaos of everyday life. And it offered him the unfettered time to make lists.

The mental inventories were Adam's way of organizing and prioritizing the constant changes. *Call Mom and Pop this evening. Confirm with Stella that she can pet-sit Charlie while I'm gone. Buy cat food on the way home today.* Unlike most people who jotted their lists down on paper, their phone, or a calendar, when Adam had committed a list to memory, he retained it until he mentally crossed it off.

During his time in Army Ranger school, his memory and fleetness earned him the nickname of Hermes, after the messenger of the gods known for his speed. Having never studied Greek mythology, Adam was pleased to discover that Hermes was swift and blessed with cunning intelligence. As a Ranger, speed and memory were essential during numerous high-stakes operations where his team succeeded.

Transitioning from Ranger boots to high-end athletic footwear had been a guilty pleasure when he'd transitioned to civilian life. Now, running along the trail overlooking the California coastline in his favorite pair of running shoes, his feet were light as he pounded the dirt. With his elbows bent and arms pumping in rhythm, he inhaled deeply as he appreciated the passing scenery.

He crossed paths with another early morning runner, exchanging a nod as the universal greeting for runners who don't waste their lung capacity on a verbal greeting. For Adam, running wasn't a social exercise. It was the physical challenge, the mental cleansing, and the chance to bring order to the start of his day. He didn't have the opportunity to run every day but found he faced whatever was coming his way more clearly on days he did.

His trail was lined with low-lying scrub brush, acting as a visual break while offering a clear line of sight to the surroundings. Having purchased a home not too far from the trail, the view was becoming familiar since he ran the path often.

He continued creating a mental checklist of what he needed to accomplish once he got home before heading to work. Grinning, he thought of his *work...* Lighthouse Security and Investigations West Coast. Hardly a stuffy office with cubicles filled with people who hated their jobs. His employment wasn't just a place but a way of life for those like-minded individuals.

Rounding a curve, he was careful of the loose gravel while maneuvering easily along the path. *Only two miles to go until I reach home.* He lifted his shirt again, peeling it upward before whipping it over his head. Wiping the sweat from his face, he slowed his pace and allowed his body to cool in the early morning air.

His boss had informed him of an upcoming

assignment, and he was anxious to receive the information today to finalize the plan. Coming to the last part of the trail that would take him to the back of his property, he thought of his boss. *Man, I'm a lucky fucker.*

Carson Dyer started his business several years ago when he partnered with Mace Hanover, who established the first Lighthouse Security Investigations business in Maine. The West Coast branch handled much of the same business as the original LSI, but when physical location made a difference, having an LSI on each coast was beneficial.

And while Carson had not made an official announcement, it was well-known that he and Mace were in discussions with one of their former Special Forces buddies who already had an investigative business in Montana.

While the work they did could be based anywhere appropriate as long as the boss was the right fit, they'd laughed at the idea of a lighthouse in Montana. Carson had only grinned and responded, "You never know what you might find when you need to."

Mace and Carson had filled their business with men and women from the various special forces of the military, CIA special ops, or those serving in the intelligence or law enforcement community line. They were known as Keepers after the lighthouse keepers of old who were tasked to guide people to safety. Their missions were more complicated now, but the ideal still stood.

When Adam had sat across from Carson for his interview with LSIWC, he'd grappled with nerves, an emotion he rarely experienced. He wanted the job more than any other security job around. What LSI had to offer in the way of equipment, safety, missions, and, most importantly, the camaraderie among the other Keepers, Adam desperately wanted to be included.

When Carson offered him a position at LSIWC, it was as triumphantly confirming as when he'd graduated from Ranger school. Carson's efficiency and no-nonsense approach to running his business reminded Adam of the days when he was in the Army and a new mission came through. But back then, as a Ranger, he always went out with his team. Here, he occasionally had solo assignments, which he never minded.

By now, he'd turned onto his property, his small house coming into sight. On the back porch, he stretched, feeling the familiar pull of his muscles. Then he entered the security code into the keypad, used the thumbprint pad, and stepped inside. Bending to pet his less-than-patient feline, he acknowledged Charlie's complaint. "I'll feed you in a few minutes."

Continuing to his bathroom, he turned on the shower, stripped, and stepped under the steamy water flow, once again breathing deeply. He rarely indulged in long showers, feeling the need to use the hot water to take care of the functional basics of washing his hair and body. Once dried, he dressed in his typical black cargo pants and long-sleeved black T-shirt. Clothing choice was also something he didn't spend much time on.

Dress clothes when needed. A few pairs of jeans to swap out with the cargo pants. And black shirts. An ordered life didn't involve wasting time on choices that weren't important.

As Charlie wove through his legs, he grinned down at the black-and-white cat demanding breakfast. He hadn't planned on getting a pet so soon after moving into his house, but Charlie had shown up on his back deck one day and didn't seem inclined to leave. Each day, Adam discovered the small feline pronouncing ownership of the place. Opening the door the first time, he was uncertain what the cat would do, but Charlie had walked in, sat in the kitchen, and stared up with large eyes. And just waited. Adam had fed him some of his lunch, and from that moment on, Charlie ruled the roost. Now, cat food was on the weekly supermarket mental list.

Once the cat food was in the dish, Adam drank his protein drink while stirring the hot water into his oatmeal. When he and Charlie were fed, he poured a travel cup of coffee and hit the road.

Thirty minutes later, he turned off the road and onto a lane that twisted toward the coast. After clearing multiple security gates, he continued toward the decommissioned lighthouse that overlooked the area. Parking alongside other SUVs, trucks, and a couple of cars, he grinned at the one minivan. At the rate his co-workers were getting married, he figured minivans might one day outnumber the trucks.

Once inside, he greeted their office manager, Rachel. She was retired from the Navy. Her Naval pilot husband was killed many years ago in a training exercise, and when her two children became adults, she eagerly accepted Carson's request to be the administrative assistant for LSIWC.

Walking past Rachel's desk, he entered the labyrinth hall, which led him deeper into the compound. Welcoming chin lifts were offered and received as he greeted his co-workers.

"Your mission has been uploaded to your tablet," Jeb called out. The former SEAL was a cybersecurity expert as well as a software engineer. He handled most of their computer systems, and like all the other Keepers, Adam hadn't met anyone better suited for their position. "Let me know what you need once you've had a chance to review it."

Settling at the large table, he looked down at his tablet. Carson had already informed Adam that his next job would be as a security detail. It sounded straightforward, although several of those missions had become much more complicated than initially thought. But that was why they were hired—Keepers planned for anything.

LSIWC didn't offer bodyguard services for the wealthy or entitled. When they provided security, it was usually at the behest of the US government. In this case, their FBI liaison, Landon Summers, had recommended LSIWC for the international think-tank assignment.

He was to accompany a university professor and academic assistant to a RAND meeting near Washington, DC. Looking at the information, he quickly scanned through the basics. RAND was a research and development think tank. The meeting focused on global warming and how climate change impacts poorer countries. It seemed the professor also had written papers on how climate change affects the plants grown by drug cartels. *What the fuck?*

Dr. Paul Mendez. Fifty-nine years old. Born and raised in Colombia until the age of ten, when his family immigrated to the United States. He attended the University of California San Diego, majoring in climatology. He continued his educational journey in botany. He was one of the foremost leaders in the study of global warming's effects on crops and, recently, had specifically studied how climate change would affect the drug cartels' cocaine production. Adam scoffed. *They can let the cocaine crops burn in the fields... That'd be better for everyone.*

He stared at his tablet, no emotion on his face, but his mind filtered through the continued information. Dr. Mendez. Black hair liberally sprinkled with gray. Five feet, nine inches tall. Slight build. Silver-rimmed eyeglasses. Brown eyes. He traveled often, especially to his birthplace of Colombia, to study the plants and visit relatives. Adam filed away that information, wondering if it was significant… or suspicious.

He continued to peruse the photograph of the professor, his mild-mannered appearance seeming congruent with his grandfatherly image. He pulled his bottom lip inward, pressing down with his top teeth as his gaze continued to assess. Not willing to jump to conclusions, he moved on to the assistant accompanying Dr. Mendez to the meeting.

Valerie Clemens. Thirty-one years old. Her photograph was from the university faculty ID. Brown hair pulled severely back from her face. Dark eyeglasses framed hazel eyes. She'd smiled toward the camera, exposing straight teeth except for one slightly crooked incisor, giving her face character. Undergraduate degree in environmental science. Masters in botany. She'd traveled and worked with Dr. Mendez since her early days in college, assisting him with research.

Little else was provided about the two, and he shifted to the meeting details just as Carson settled into the seat next to him. Lifting his gaze, he waited.

"You're probably wondering why this requires a security escort," Carson began.

Adam remained quiet. He would never question any assignment but simply waited to see what information Carson wanted to offer.

"RAND Institute is a think tank based out of the DC area. They have offices internationally, including here in California. They study and research a multitude of societal concerns."

Adam tried to hide his wince but was unsure if he'd been successful.

Carson continued, "The fact that Professor Mendez specifically studies the climate effects on crops, including the crops that drug cartels grow, could also make him a target of others who want that information. Although, according to the institute, the likelihood of danger to the professor is small. It's a short assignment. One day there, then the full day of the meeting. They will have morning meetings the next day, and then you'll escort them back. Basic security detail."

"Sounds simple, but who knows how these conferences end up," Bennett said from across the table. The former Ranger sniper had recently spent time escorting a visually impaired explosives expert to a conference in Las Vegas. When that mission morphed into a kidnapping and rescue, Bennett had to call on the rest of the team for assistance.

Adam nodded, acknowledging the veracity of Bennett's statement while inwardly glad he wouldn't be in Las Vegas. "I'll be ready to leave first thing tomorrow morning," he said. "I assume unannounced flight arrangements have been made?"

Natalie looked over her shoulder and grinned. "You got it. I'm sending all that information to you as well." Natalie was a logistics expert who had been recruited from the Deltas. Married to Leo, another

Keeper and former Delta, Adam knew that Natalie would have no problem getting whatever he might need during the mission.

He offered his silent thanks with a nod, then continued to look over the meeting schedule as the other Keepers went about their business.

"I hesitated to assign this to you," Carson said, drawing Adam's immediate attention. Before he had a chance to respond, Carson continued. "The work the professor does assists the government in knowing what the cartels' responses might be in light of their major source of income."

A muscle ticked as he tightened his jaw. "Makes me wonder why we give a fuck if their drugs dry up before harvest."

"I know this is close to home, but—"

Adam shook his head sharply. "No. No problem. Security detail only. Got it. Don't make this into something it's not."

Carson held his gaze for a moment, then nodded. "Okay. Let us know if you need anything." Standing, he walked back over to a computer set up at a nearby desk.

He looked over as Chris, a former SEAL, said, "Stella said to remind you that she'll be in to feed your cat while you're gone."

"Tell her thanks, man," he said, nodding. Chris and his free-spirited artist wife lived close to him, and Stella was always eager to pet sit for any of the Keepers when they were out of town.

Adam ignored everyone else and looked back at his tablet, memorizing all the information. Finally satisfied, he offered goodbyes, then headed to the equipment room down the hall. Met there by Teddy, their equipment and facilities manager, he reviewed the weapons and necessary items that might be needed.

"You good?" Teddy asked. Theodore Bearinski had retired from the military but was bored out of his mind until Carson offered him a position in their equipment, supplies, and physical compound. The former sniper was exceptional at his job, and his friendly demeanor belied his astute perception of everything that affected the Keepers.

"Yeah, thanks," Adam said after signing for the equipment he checked out. "It'll be an easy assignment… there and back."

With goodbyes said to Teddy and then to Rachel as he left the building, he stowed everything in his SUV and headed home, already making mental notes about the trip. Multitasking when he got home, he fed Charlie and called his parents.

"Mom? Hey, I just wanted to let you know that I'll be on a trip this week. I leave tomorrow, but if you need me, you can reach me by my cell phone."

"Oh, Adam, I hope it's somewhere nice." In the background, she called out to his dad. "Adam will be gone this week. Do you want me to put him on speaker?"

"Of course. I have no idea why you ask, Martha. You know I want to hear what he has to say."

Adam grinned at the familiar banter. It wasn't the first time he'd heard their side conversation when he called, and he sure as hell hoped it wouldn't be the last.

"Son!" his dad called out, always thinking he needed to shout when Adam was on speaker. "Where are you off to? Or can't you tell us?"

"It's just to the East Coast, Pop. Washington, DC, just for a few days. It'll be an easy trip."

"Oh, you should go see the Smithsonian. The one with the big dinosaur bones." Excitement laced his mom's voice.

"That's the Natural History Museum," his dad added.

"Yeah, I know. I still remember our family trip when I was in middle school," Adam said.

His parents were silent for just a few seconds, then his mother laughed. "My, my, I had forgotten about that. We walked our legs off on that trip. Up and down the mall, going into every museum we came to."

"I doubt I'll have any time, but who knows? I might have a chance to do some sightseeing," he admitted. The possibility was slim, but the idea seemed to give his mom some pleasure.

"Oh, I hope so, sweetheart. You always work so hard."

He chuckled. "It's all good, Mom. Anyway, I can't

talk long. I just wanted you to know I would be traveling. I'll call you when I get back.

"Love you," his mom said.

At the same time, his dad called out, "Stay safe."

"Love you both. Talk to you soon."

Disconnecting, he looked down at Charlie. "You get to have Stella come feed you for the next few days."

Charlie sat on the kitchen floor, licking his whiskers. Looking up, he gave a soft meow, then continued his grooming.

By the time Adam ate dinner and finished his trip preparations, he ended his day with Charlie curled up at the foot of his bed. Turning out the light, he was ready for the assignment.

2

Valerie walked briskly past the closed doors along the third-floor hall of the academic wing of the university's botany program. The building was old, but she never entered without imagining the countless scholars who had walked the halls before her. A grin slipped out as her comfortable flats barely sounded on the worn but polished tile floor. Camera crews had recently been on campus filming a recruitment advertisement for the university, focusing on their newer, shinier buildings and athletic fields, so she was sure they hadn't visited this hallowed hall. Shaking her head as she continued walking, she knew the quality of education was in the instruction, not the age of the lecture rooms. While the department conducted world-class research, the building it came from certainly wasn't.

She finally stopped at the last wooden door, not surprised to see a light shining from the bottom, indicating what she already knew—the professor was working late. Knocking, she twisted the knob and opened the door, allowing her gaze to drift over the familiar corner office. Tall bookshelves filled with a motley collection of old textbooks intermingled with newer ones. A wooden desk was covered in papers, looking like a scene from years ago, except for the sleek laptop in the middle. A narrow bench sat in front of the window, holding pots and planters overflowing with greenery. Those were not part of any botany experiment but were lovingly grown by someone who wanted to bring life to the otherwise stodgy office.

Her desk was in the corner, near the window overlooking the lawn. Not pristine, but her papers were certainly in neat piles.

The man sitting behind his desk looked up, pushed his glasses farther onto his nose, and offered a familiar and affectionate smile. "Ah, Valerie. How did you know I would be here?"

"The evening before you leave for a conference? Where else would you be, Dr. Mendez?"

He opened his mouth, but she quickly threw her hand upward. "I know, I know. But it's an old habit too hard to break." Through the years she had served as his assistant and academic partner, he'd insisted she call him by his first name, Paul. She did when they were in a casual setting, and even though it was just the two of them here now, she still maintained using his professional moniker at the university.

"What time is it?" he asked, looking at the vintage watch on his wrist.

"Late enough that Ellen called to make sure you would get home at a decent hour. She wants you to eat well and rest tonight since we leave early tomorrow morning."

At the mention of his wife, Paul smiled again. "Between my Ellen and you, I can pretty much stay on schedule, can't I?"

As brilliant as Paul was, she affectionately thought of him as the quintessential absent-minded professor. His mind was perpetually engrossed in his research, but eating meals at a regular time and going to bed at a decent hour often never made it past the studies, governmental task forces, writing professional papers, and lecturing that filled his time.

"Before you ask, I have all your notes, our flight arrangements, and the information from the conference. Your notes are uploaded to my laptop but also printed out for you."

"Oh my," he said, shaking his head slightly. "When you were in my freshman environmental science class years ago, not having a clue what you wanted to major in but desperately needing a job as an assistant, I truly lucked out."

She smiled with genuine affection. "I'd say we both got lucky." She stepped over to his desk, glanced at what was on the screen of his laptop, checked to make sure it was saved, then powered it down. Because he wanted to ensure he never deleted anything, his notes, research, mail, calendar, and all lectures automatically synced with her laptop. "Well, you won't need this until after we return from the trip. I'll have everything with me on my laptop."

"Excellent!" Standing, he looked around his office and frowned. "I always feel as though I'm going to forget something when I take a trip."

She looked around as well but shook her head. "I promise you have everything you need for the conference."

They left his office, locked the door, and walked out of the building to the faculty parking lot. He stopped at his old car, which had seen better days, and turned to her. "What time do we leave tomorrow?"

"I've already talked to Ellen to ensure she understood your schedule. I will come by and pick you up at six o'clock. We'll go to the airport, where we will meet the man providing security during the conference."

He huffed slightly, shaking his head. "I hate that we have to have someone…" His voice faded slightly, then he added, "But there are those who would like to stop the information coming out of the meeting." He sighed. "Oh, well. Better safe than sorry."

Her lips pinched tightly together, and she nodded. "I'll see you tomorrow." Watching him leave, she climbed into her car and drove to her apartment, continually glancing in the rearview mirror. Being the assistant to a man who had research that interested law enforcement and drug cartels, it was hard not to have an overactive imagination.

Once at her two-story townhouse rental, she reveled in having a garage. On nights when she got in late, it was nice to drive in and close the door, feeling secure before heading inside. But then, she loved everything about her residence. Throughout college and graduate work, she'd lived in small apartments, so the larger space offered more of a homey feel. The garage level led into a small laundry room and then straight into the kitchen. With a wide bay window, her living room overlooked the park across the street. The kitchen and dining room overlooked the small, fenced backyard. On the second floor was her bedroom and en suite bathroom, and two smaller bedrooms with a bathroom between. Since the owner's bedroom was in the front, her window also overlooked the park.

Typically, she would have arrived home earlier, fixed dinner, and watched TV or read while having a glass of wine before bed. But getting home later than usual and knowing she would have to rise earlier for their flight the next morning, she opted for an easy dinner of a scrambled egg sandwich.

While eating, her phone rang. Grinning at the caller ID, she swallowed, then answered, "Hey, Mom."

"I know you're traveling tomorrow, and I didn't want you to fly without telling you I love you."

Her heart squeezed as her smile remained. "I love you, too, Mom."

"So I'm sure you're all packed and ready. Did you manage to get Paul ready, as well?"

Her mom had met Paul and Ellen numerous times over the years and knew his penchant for forgetting things. "I've done all I can. He's in Ellen's hands now."

"Well, good. I wanted to let you know I briefly talked to Tim earlier today. He said he's coming home on leave in a couple of months."

Her heart leaped at the idea of seeing her brother after his long deployment. "Thank God! As soon as you know when, let me know, and I'll schedule time off." After a few seconds of comfortable silence, she asked, "How are you doing, Mom?"

"You know me… staying busy. My boss is retiring, and I'm thinking I might not be far behind."

"Really?" This was the first she'd heard of her mom thinking of retiring from her job.

"I don't know. So many things to consider. I thought when you and your brother are here at the same time, we could talk and maybe look over the finances to see what you think."

"Whatever you need, Mom, we'll be there."

"I know, baby girl," her mom said, using the affectionate pet name Valerie had never grown out of and didn't mind. It reminded her of when her dad would come home and call her that even when she was a teenager.

"Well, it's late, and I need to get up early."

"Can't wait to hear about your trip. Call me when you're home."

"Love you, Mom. Good night." Disconnecting, she moved over to the table near the front door. Ensuring her carry-on case had her laptop and necessary papers, she turned out the lights and headed upstairs. The familiar squeak in the hallway was strangely comforting as she continued into her bedroom. She double-checked her already-packed suitcase, then got ready for bed and climbed in after setting her alarm.

Just as she drifted off to sleep, her phone vibrated with an incoming text. A shiver moved through her as she grabbed the phone and looked to see Unknown as the caller. Hitting the button, she saw the message.

Ready?

Letting out a long breath, she typed the simple one-word reply. **Yes.** She set her phone back on the nightstand, knowing no other message would come in or be expected. Rolling over, she punched her pillow and willed her body to sleep.

Driving to the professor's house, she felt the familiar pre-flying anxiety filling her gut as she drummed her short fingernails on the steering wheel. Glowering toward the red traffic light that seemed to have been holding interminably, she felt the band of nerves tighten. Glancing at the dashboard clock, she sighed, reminding herself to calm down. Considering she added extra time to the schedule, she wasn't late getting to the professor's house.

While she wasn't generally late for anything, it also wasn't one of her virtues to be early. But knowing Ellen, she felt sure the professor would be ready for their trip as soon as she pulled into their driveway. Walking to the front door, she smiled as she spied Ellen peering out the window, offering a wave.

"I don't know why I'm hurrying," she said, entering their foyer. "We have plenty of time, but flying always makes me feel like I have to get to the airport before anyone, or I won't make it through security!"

"I know how you feel," Ellen agreed as she welcomed Valerie inside. "But Paul is all ready, and I think you two have plenty of time." She leaned closer. "I made sure he had nothing in his carry-on that would hold you up with TSA."

"Good thinking," she whispered in return, smiling. She still remembered the time that Paul had bottles of liquid plant food in his briefcase, causing quite a delay at the security checkpoint.

Glancing to the side, she spied him shoving a few more papers and files into his already stuffed briefcase. "Don't worry," she assured. "I know we have everything we need."

She nestled his luggage into the trunk of her small car, glad that both she and the professor packed lightly. As she climbed behind the wheel, she waited as Paul turned and offered his wife a sweet kiss. They had been married for almost forty years, having met in college. Watching the two of them easily express affection after all these years made Valerie wish once again that she'd be able to find a lasting connection. A subtle pang squeezed her heart, and she winced, turning to give them another moment of privacy.

Soon, he was buckled at her side, and with a final wave toward Ellen before she stepped back inside their house, they headed off to the airport.

"Once we get to the airport, we're supposed to meet the person traveling with us for security," she reminded.

"Do we have his ticket?"

Her brow furrowed as she shook her head. "That's not our responsibility. If he doesn't, he'll have to figure out what to do."

"If we've never met them, how will we know who they are?"

"I guess it'll be like the movies where someone will hold a sign?" It dawned on her that she honestly had no idea. Seeing a crease through the professor's brow, she added, "But that's not for us to worry about, either. I'm sure the institute pays them very well, so they can sort out their own flight arrangements."

"I hope it's not like the last people who provided security for that climate change conference."

She laughed softly and nodded. She and Paul had traveled to another university hosting a conference on climate change. Outside the lecture hall, a group of protesters gathered, seemingly made up of fear-mongers and conspiracy theorists fighting against anything scientific. Valerie's patience for willful ignorance was thin.

A counter group of college students relishing the idea of protesting the protesters were ready to join the melee. She, Paul, and the others at the conference barely made it through the throngs before punches were thrown.

The only security available was a few mall-cop archetypes who were either too old or too slow to be able to keep the lecture hall from being overrun. She'd wished for a backup plan. Thankfully, no one was injured, and she and the professor were able to slip out a side door when the presentation was interrupted.

Dismissing her memories of that fiasco, she asserted, "I'm sure whoever has been hired by the institute will be more than adequate." She had no facts to back that statement, therefore making it more of a hope than a conclusion.

Finally arriving at the airport, she pulled into a parking spot and grinned. "Made it with time to spare!"

Once her trunk was unloaded, and she ensured nothing was left behind, she slung her briefcase bag over her shoulders, made sure he had his briefcase, and then they rolled their suitcases toward the airport entrance. Approaching the main doors, she turned to ensure Paul was behind her as the doors slid open. "This is the way we go—oof!"

Her directions were cut off as she slammed into something large and hard. Hands grabbed her shoulders, and her head whipped around at the touch. Staring at a chest, she lifted her chin further until she was staring into the blue eyes of a tall man. A very tall man. With exceptionally blue eyes.

Heat flooded her body as she rushed out her apology. "Oh, I'm so sorry! I wasn't watching where I was going! I'm really, very sorry—"

The man still had hold of her shoulders, offering steadiness. Her eyeglasses were askew, and she reached up to straighten them so she could see clearer. *Yep, he's just as attractive as I thought.* She felt heat moving from his hands to her arms, and then the flush continued throughout her body. Surprised by her reaction, a multitude of thoughts slammed into her, each vying for attention. *He's tall. He's gorgeous. Black hair and blue eyes. Midnight-black hair. Mesmerizing blue eyes... like the Centaurea cyanus flower. Why are his lips moving? Why do I hear my name?*

Jerking, she realized his lips were moving because he was speaking to her. Feeling ridiculous, she blinked as she shook her head. "I'm sorry? What did you say?"

"Ms. Clemens?" His gaze stayed on her face before moving slowly next to her. "And Dr. Mendez?"

Still locked into place, she felt as though her mind slogged through molasses, unable to process the simplest reply when she heard the professor reply, "Yes. That's us. Are you our security?"

Blinking as her chin jerked back in surprise, she couldn't imagine this man was their security after the lackadaisical previous security types she'd seen. This man was fit... more than fit. And there was an intelligence in those blue eyes that she would normally respect, but now it made her wonder what he saw as he stared back at her.

He released his steadying grip on her arm to reach inside his pocket, then pulled out a leather ID holder. "My name is Adam Calvin with Lighthouse Security Investigations West Coast. I will accompany you two to Washington, DC, where I will be responsible for your safety until we return to California."

"How nice to meet you, Mr. Calvin," Paul said, pushing up his glasses as his broad smile beamed. He reached out, and the two men shook hands.

"Likewise, Dr. Mendez."

Still lost in the deep voice that managed to cut through the cacophony of the airport chatter, she was barely aware of the professor as another deep rumble came her way.

"Dr. Mendez, if you and Ms. Clemens will follow me, we will bypass this part of the airport and get to our plane."

He reached for her suitcase, and before she had a chance to insist that she was perfectly capable of rolling it herself, he inclined his head toward the left, and the professor immediately started that way.

Having no recourse except to follow them, she quickly caught up and said, "I'm sorry, but I think you're going the wrong way. We haven't been through TSA yet."

"It'll all be taken care of," he replied.

Used to overseeing Paul when they traveled, she wanted to continue to argue that they weren't going in the right direction. But then the professor leaned over and whispered, "Isn't it lovely that we don't have to stand in the long line at security?"

While Mr. Calvin certainly had a high-handed way about him, she had to admit the professor was right. She just hoped Mr. Calvin knew what he was doing and where he was going.

Suddenly, she realized they were stepping back out of the airport and being led straight toward a large black SUV. Alarmed, she called out, "Wait! Wait!"

Mr. Calvin stopped and turned his head ever so slightly over his shoulder. The blue eyes that had captured her immediate attention were now hidden behind a pair of reflector sunglasses. The barrier rendered his gaze inscrutable, and she had no idea if he was humoring her or irritated at the interruption of his directions. She'd just met him yet felt a twinge of loss at not seeing the blue eyes focusing on her.

"Yes?" he asked, his voice devoid of emotion.

Clearing her throat, she said, "I'm not trying to be insulting, but you do realize that the airport is behind us?"

"I've made alternate flight arrangements."

Jerking, she shook her head. "Excuse me? What alternate flight arrangements?"

"If you'll follow me, you'll see."

"No," she protested. "I make all of our travel arrangements, and our flight leaves from here—"

Mr. Calvin opened the back of the SUV and set her suitcase inside. She rushed forward and started to grab it as he picked up Paul's luggage and placed it next, trapping hers in a way that she couldn't pull it out.

"Mr. Calvin, stop!" she fumed.

"Is there a problem?"

His words were softly spoken, not showing even a hint of irritation, which simply served to make her more irate. Taking a breath, she attempted to calm down as she emphasized, "Yes!" Even as she spoke, Paul had opened the SUV's back door and was climbing inside. "Professor, stop."

With her hands planted on her hips, she turned and glared upward at Mr. Tall, Dark, and Glowering– okay, technically, with his sunglasses on, she couldn't see if he was glowering, but it served her purpose to imagine that he was. "I wouldn't be very security conscious if I just got into a vehicle with a man I don't know, would I?" She rarely spoke in *snark* but felt the situation called for it. Emphasizing her point by tapping her foot on the ground, she refused to move, making it impossible for the back door of the SUV to be lowered. Of course, she was well aware that he could move her rather easily, but she kept up her pretense at bravado, nonetheless.

"Do you ever get into a taxi or an Uber?"

She blinked, instantly realizing he'd made his point with only one question. Sighing, she felt her shoulders slump.

He stepped closer and pulled his sunglasses from his face, peering down at her.

"Your caution is well advised, Ms. Clemens. The RAND Institute hired my company. You may call the head of the institute if you would like."

Slowly shaking her head, she sighed. "No, I believe you, although I don't understand why different flight arrangements were made or why I wasn't informed."

He didn't answer, but she stepped out of the way as he lowered the SUV's back door. He walked to the back passenger door and waited while she peered inside to see the professor sitting calmly inside, smiling at her. Climbing next to him, she buckled as her door was closed. She forced a smile toward Paul, then leaned forward slightly, curiosity taking over as she attempted to batten down the interest in where they were being driven.

3

It only took a few minutes for Adam to steer into the secluded tarmac designated for private jets, but he felt the prickle on the back of his neck where he was convinced Ms. Clemens was still shooting invisible laser beams at him.

When he'd first laid eyes on her, the element of surprise had him questioning his usual keen intuition. Approaching the pair, it had been easy to spot Dr. Paul Mendez. The eminent scholar was exactly as the photographs Adam had viewed. Poised to introduce himself, Adam felt his world tilt when Valerie Clemens looked behind her, and her pivoting body collided directly with his. Instinctively, he shot his hands upward to keep her from falling over, and the moment her startled, wide-eyed hazel gaze met his, a current hummed between his hands and her arms, sending an electrical charge through his senses.

He didn't know why he expected her to be meek

and mild, but she was a complex mosaic of intelligent questioning, a little snark, a protective shield for the professor, and analyzing the situation for danger and then acceptance. She was not overly short, but at six feet, five inches himself, he towered over her by a foot. He tended to gravitate toward taller women, but something about her appealed to him that he refused to ponder. *It's a job, not a dating site.*

Irritated with the direction his thoughts had wandered, he focused on the task at hand as he parked next to a small hangar. The shine of the metal walls was a testament to the building's newness, and he was impressed with the accommodations. Climbing out, he opened the door behind him and waited for her to alight.

Her head was busy swinging back and forth—her gaze first on him, then the hangar, and then back on him—as if seeking hidden answers in the air.

"Is this where we get out?" Dr. Mendez asked, a bewildered expression on his face.

"Yes," Adam retorted, the word clipped.

Seemingly taking Adam's answer in stride, Dr. Mendez threw open his door and stepped down from the vehicle, leaving Ms. Clemens still seated and speechless, with her mouth opening and closing several times.

Finally, regaining her voice, she snapped, "Why are we *here*?"

Stating what should have been obvious, he sighed. "We're boarding a private jet to Washington, DC.

That is, we will, once you have managed to exit the vehicle. Do you need assistance?"

Her eyebrows arched. "But why are we taking a private jet?"

"Because those are the arrangements I made."

Now, her brows snapped together, and she huffed. "I don't understand, Mr. Calvin. Part of my job for the professor is to make his travel arrangements. This is nothing like the arrangements I made."

Torn between continuing to stand and debate with her or moving to the back of the SUV where it sounded as though Professor Mendez was trying to figure out how to open the door to retrieve his luggage, Adam decided to multitask and do both. He walked to the back and pushed the button so that the door lifted. Glancing over at Ms. Clemens, he sighed. She was messing with his pre-flight mental checklist.

Dr. Mendez stretched his arm out for his luggage, but Adam pulled both of the suitcases out. As he reached back in to get his own bag, he continued the explanation. "This will make the trip much more enjoyable for all of us instead of being stuck in a tin can with a bunch of other people. It also allows for only us to be on board in case you want to rest, have something to eat, or review your notes. It also makes the security arrangements easier."

"That's sounds excellent," Dr. Mendez agreed. "This will be a delightful treat."

Ms. Clemens was still sitting in the back seat,

emitting an audible huff. Adam suppressed the smile that threatened to escape.

"I still don't know why we have to do this," she mumbled, her voice tinged with reluctant acceptance.

Just when he wondered if he'd have to haul her out, Dr. Mendez moved around to her side and beamed. "Isn't this wonderful, Valerie? I can't wait to tell Ellen! Do you know where my phone is so I can take a picture?"

As Adam secured the back of his SUV, Valerie jumped into her assistant duties, ensuring the professor had his luggage and briefcase. She found his phone and had him stand beside the plane before snapping a few pictures indulgently. "I'll send them to Ellen and let her know of our flight changes."

Adam noted that her agreeability factor rose once Dr. Mendez acquiesced to the change of plans. He led them through a side door into the hangar, where a sleek Cessna awaited them. The pilot walked over, and Adam grinned while shaking hands. "Good to see you, Robert." He asked about Robert's wife and children, then introduced Dr. Mendez and Ms. Clemens.

The pilot greeted them. "The weather is perfect, and we'll make good time. I'll have you in Washington, DC, by midafternoon."

Adam allowed Robert to take them aboard and give them a quick tour of the onboard amenities, including a fully stocked bar, refrigerator with various juices, sodas, water, and a variety of snacks and sandwiches.

Dr. Mendez, no longer seeming befuddled at the change in plans, rubbed his hands together, eliciting a smile from his intrepid assistant. Considering Adam hadn't seen her smile before, her beautiful expression snagged his attention.

Soon, they were all buckled into the plush cream-colored leather seats. Once the plane leveled, Valerie unbuckled her seat and walked to the small kitchenette. Looking over her shoulder, she asked, "Dr. Mendez? Mr. Calvin? Can I get you something to drink?"

She was the professor's assistant, but she certainly wasn't required to be his. He stood and walked over, standing next to her. "Thank you, but I'll help myself. Please get whatever you and Dr. Mendez would like." He opened the refrigerator and pulled out a bottle, snagging a plastic-wrapped tray of fruit, cheese, and nuts. "Help yourself to any of what they have here."

"Thank you, Mr. Calvin." Her voice was softer this time as she held his gaze.

"Adam."

She blinked, then jerked slightly. The corners of her lips lifted slightly as she inclined her head. "Okay, Adam. Please call me Valerie."

The professor struggled with his seat belt, then stood and walked over, accepting a soda from Valerie, then turned toward Adam. "Please call me Paul."

Adam replied, "All right, but when we're with others at the meeting, I'll refer to you by your professional title, Dr. Mendez." Out of the corner of his eye, he watched as Valerie's eyes widened slightly, and he could have sworn his decision impressed her.

"That's what Valerie always does," Paul said, still smiling.

They retook their seats, and he swiveled to face them. Pulling a small table between them, Valerie and Paul marveled at the convenience.

"I usually travel economy." Paul chuckled. "I remember the days when we got a soda and a bag of nuts. Now, we don't get anything at the back of the plane."

Valerie smiled as she nodded. "Yes, and even then, sometimes, the university barely reimbursed us for the costs. This is... well, this is an extravagance," she added, looking at Adam.

Adam couldn't help but watch as she meticulously unwrapped the plastic covering from her snack and appeared delighted by the simple treat. She seemed such a contradiction, and he'd only been in her presence for a short time. *She's not fitting into my mental catalog of what she would be.* Staring at her, lost in thought, he almost missed her question.

"Adam, since you changed our flight arrangements, do I make the assumption that we have the same hotel arrangements that I've made, or have those also been changed?" She held his gaze and seemed to steel herself for his response.

"We will stay in the Hotel Washington, close to the White House, Washington Memorial, and National Mall. I think you'll find it a much more enjoyable environment, and the views from the upper terrace are outstanding."

"A hotel with a view." Paul nodded as he looked at Valerie. "How nice!"

"A bit out of our compensated price range," she said, a crease settling along her forehead.

He was sure she wondered about the price difference between the high-end choice and the budget hotel she'd booked. "All paid for by the RAND Institute," Adam assured.

Pulling her lips inward, she leaned back in her chair, now playing with the remnants of her snack. Paul, oblivious to her concerns, reclined his seat and soon drifted off to sleep. Valerie yawned several times, and her eyes held a glint of weariness. Soon, her eyelids drooped and stayed closed.

Adam breathed a sigh of relief, his gaze soft on the enigma before him. Valerie Clemens was a paradox. She was certainly more beautiful than her employee photograph, but also with a backbone and spirit he hadn't expected. Prettier and pricklier. And she was obviously loyal and protective of Paul.

His knowledge of the professor's work was peripheral at best, but then it wasn't a requirement for him to fulfill his role as a Keeper. It was about surveillance, not engaging in conversation.

Glancing over at Valerie, he noted her head had

rolled to the side, and her face at rest was stunning. Her chest slowly rose and fell in a deep rhythm as she slept, and he found he enjoyed the view more than his consummate professionalism should allow. Shifting restlessly in his seat, he scrubbed his hand over his face, struggling to harness his thoughts.

He would be an idiot to ignore that most of his fellow Keepers had fallen in love with someone on a mission. Right now, he and Jeb stood as the only last unattached Keepers. He wasn't looking for love and didn't figure it was in the cards for him. One day, maybe, if he was lucky. *But not on a mission—too much drama. Too much heightened emotion.*

A soft, almost comical snore escaped from Valerie's parted lips just then, causing him to stifle an involuntary grin. *Well, maybe this mission won't have too much drama.* The pretty assistant was a passing appreciation only. Even if he had thoughts of more, he could already ascertain that their lives were too different. So his record as a continued unattached Keeper still stood for now.

4

The shift in altitude roused Valerie from her nap, and her eyelids flickered open. Suddenly jolting, she realized where she was—on a plane going to a meeting. Next to her was Paul, also emerging from his sleep. Her thoughts darted immediately to Adam, and her hand flew to her mouth, horrified that she might have drooled while sleeping. Grateful that her chin appeared dry, she glanced around, but he no longer sat across them.

The door to the cockpit opened, and he emerged, appearing just as fresh as when she first set eyes on him. *He could have stepped out of a damn commercial... one of those where the guy looked amazing yet didn't care that he looked amazing.* She felt rumpled and had a crick in her neck from sleeping in an awkward position. He didn't strike her as a man who spent a lot of time on his appearance, so it really should be illegal that he looked so good with so little effort.

Chiding herself for the road her thoughts had traveled down, she shook her head as though to dislodge them physically. She stretched her arms upward to ease the stiffness from her back and then turned to Paul. "Were you able to sleep?"

"That's the best sleep I've had on a trip!"

Smiling, she patted his arm. "I confess, I feel the same. Usually, I'm having the back of my airplane seat kicked, or the person in front of me has leaned back so far, I can't move."

Her gaze followed Adam as he slid back into the seat across from her and fastened his seat belt. His movements echoed her earlier notice of his confident manner. "We'll be landing soon," he said, his words clipped and precise.

A man of little words. She wasn't sure where that thought came from, considering Paul wasn't a gregarious speaker either. But the contrast was evident between Adam and the many verbose professors she dealt with or self-absorbed frat boys from her assistant teaching days who loved to hear themselves talk. She was no longer surprised that she noticed Adam's mature, handsome appearance but also the fact that he didn't seem to be an attention hog. That was definitely a point in his favor. *Perhaps this conference would be enjoyable after all.*

Turning her gaze out the window, she watched as they descended below the cloud canopy to observe Washington, DC, in the distance. As they neared, buildings sharpened into clarity, and the image of the

Washington Monument loomed even larger. She had never flown on a small, private jet but had to admit the experience was far superior to the sardine-can feel of commercial jets.

Having circled around the district, they landed at the National Airport. When the wheels touched the runway, it was a much smoother transition than she'd imagined. She thought of how different the experience would have been if they'd been forced to their original plans. Begrudgingly, she knew the changes Adam had orchestrated were luxurious. Desiring to stretch out an olive branch for her earlier curtness, she offered Adam a smile. "I suppose it's been obvious that Paul and I usually fly commercial and stay in budget accommodations. I was surprised at the change of plans, but thank you, Adam. So far, the change has made for a much more pleasant experience."

He inclined his head slightly in acknowledgment, and if she hadn't been paying close attention, she would have missed the slight widening of his eyes. Her gratitude surprised him, probably due to her earlier irritation at his high-handedness. Wanting to keep the truce extended, she added, "I apologize for my earlier curt demeanor when we met. I... uh... well, I like to have things well planned, and your changes caught me off guard."

This time, his lips twitched upward ever so slightly. The fleeting smile ghosting his lips caught and held her gaze.

"I appreciate your candor, Valerie. In my work, plans are necessary, but I often have to make rapid decisions with little room for discussion. In this case, the modifications were made so I could perform my duties more easily. But I can appreciate how the change in plans was unexpected and jarring. I'll attempt to offer more warning in the future but will say that while there isn't an overt threat on this trip, I have to be ready for anything and will need you to rely on me and to trust my judgment."

Paul chuckled and nodded. "I believe, Valerie, that that's his way of telling us that when he says jump, we just jump."

Adam's smile broadened ever so slightly. "While I don't expect you to ask how high if I say to jump, it would be helpful if you acquiesced immediately with minimal questions."

Valerie felt her spine stiffen at the inferred taunt, but before she had a chance to respond, Adam had unbuckled his seat belt and risen from his seat. The plane had taxied to a stop, and when she swung her head around to look out the window again, she saw that they were inside another hangar.

With a sigh, she realized that this trip was shaping up to be far more interruptive… and intriguing than she'd anticipated. Used to just assisting Paul and helping to present their findings, the trip was now filled with unexpected tensions and curiosities. And at the center of it all was Adam, an enigma who captured her interest despite her better judgment.

Following Adam's lead, she and Paul thanked the pilot and co-pilot, then quickly descended the steps of the jet. Their bags were unloaded, and Adam had them transferred to another large dark SUV. Feeling like a useless appendage, she climbed into the back seat with Paul, checking to ensure he had his brief-case. Paul was thrilled with the accommodations, so she swallowed the snarky remark that threatened to erupt.

When she had made their booking, she had searched for something acceptable within their budget. Her gaze had strayed longingly to a few online listings for more luxurious accommodations, but she had never considered them a possibility. Now, she had to admit feeling a flutter of excitement over being able to stay in a nicer hotel near the monuments. She stared out the window of the SUV, entranced with the sights as they drove along the Smithsonian Museums, monuments, the Capitol, and the White House. They had not budgeted any time for sightseeing but now vowed that she would do so on their next trip to the District.

Arriving at the hotel entrance, she held back a gasp but was unable to keep the smile from her face. Allowing Adam to assist her from the SUV, she waited until he had someone take their luggage inside. Stepping into the marble-tiled hotel lobby was like entering a sanctuary of modern opulence. Wide-eyed, she took in the color palette of gray, black, and red with bold, whimsical illustrations on the reception desk. She hesitated in her casual, travel-worn clothing, feeling underdressed. Several of the guests in the lobby were much more immaculately garbed as men in business suits walked along with women in pencil skirts, designer shoes, and bags. She recognized a few designer insignia on their laptop bags and glanced down at her old leather case and bargain purse hanging off her shoulder.

Normally, she would have advanced straight to the reception desk to take care of getting her and Paul checked in, but since Adam had made the arrangements, she had no idea if she was needed. Feeling out of place, she sidled up to Adam's side.

The pretty and oh-so-perky receptionist flashed a wide smile at Adam that bordered on flirtatious. If Valerie wasn't mistaken, the woman's eyelashes actually fluttered. It took a herculean effort to keep from snapping at the woman, but she settled for rolling her eyes.

Once the elevator doors closed behind them and they began to ascend to the fourth floor, she turned to Paul, an irrepressible chuckle escaping. "I'll have to take a lot more pictures of you to send to Ellen, or she won't believe we're actually staying here."

"I just had the same thought!" Paul exclaimed, laughing.

Adam's brows quirked upward, clearly intrigued by her comment. "As I've indicated, we usually consider a Holiday Inn to be an upgrade with our travel stipends. So I can't deny... this is a nice surprise."

The colors from the lobby carried to the upper floors, and artwork depicting the iconic images of the nation's capital captured her attention. Adam stopped near the end of the hall and pointed at a door across the hall.

"Paul, this is your room. Valerie, you're directly across from him."

"Where will you be?" She assumed he would be nearby since he took his duties so seriously.

"Right next to you."

She didn't have time to respond to her surprise when he continued.

"This way, I will have direct sight of the professor's door and the hallway outside."

Right next to me. Her heart skipped a beat when he revealed he would be so close. She didn't know why it mattered so much, but something about him inched past the professional wall she was used to standing behind. Pushing that thought to the side, she waited as Adam checked out Paul's room first, then she followed the professor into his well-appointed hotel room.

"Paul, let me know if you'd rather rest until dinner or review your notes. If you want to review notes, I'll set up the laptop for you."

"Thank you, but I believe I'll rest for now." He chuckled and shook his head. "Of course, I did rest on the plane, so I shouldn't be tired. Perhaps we could have an early dinner?"

"Absolutely," she agreed. "Anything you'd like to do, I'll arrange." Leaving him in his room, she moved across the hall, surprised to find Adam walking out of her room. She looked down at her key card, wondering if she had the room number wrong.

"This is your room," he confirmed. "I just wanted to check it out and ensure it was secure."

Her brow furrowed as she cocked her head to the side. "I confess I don't understand the need for this level of security. It seems over the top."

"Maybe," he conceded, leaning his shoulder against her doorframe once she'd passed him and entered her room. "But caution has its merits."

She walked to the window and looked out, admiring the view from the fourth floor. "Wow. This is a fabulous view."

"Paul's room will look out toward the White House."

She twisted her head and looked over her shoulder, realizing he stood just behind her, staring out the window as well. "Thank you. He'll like that."

"I thought you might enjoy the view that overlooked the Washington Monument."

Her surprise at his attention to detail beyond just security sent a wave of warmth through her, and her smile widened. Suddenly feeling self-conscious and finding the need to fill the silence, she dropped her laptop bag onto the small table as she turned to face him with her back to the window. "I suppose the concept of an early dinner might seem strange if you're used to eating later. The professor tries to eat breakfast and tends to have a larger midday meal. He finds eating later at night interferes with his sleep. When we travel, I do my best to accommodate his preferences. I know Ellen appreciates the effort." She was babbling but didn't seem to be able to stop the word flow.

"That's fine with me, too."

"Oh... good. Right." Her voice was a bit uneven, finding his intense gaze penetrating and stealing her composure. "Um... where should we meet for dinner?"

"I'm willing to accompany you and the professor anywhere you'd like to try, although there is an excellent steakhouse here in the hotel."

Her laughter bubbled forth. "I can't imagine anything here not being excellent!"

His lips curved upward, and it was the first real smile she'd seen from him. The idea of Mr. Tall, Dark, and Handsome skyrocketed off the charts as he shot straight into the drop-dead gorgeous stratosphere. She held his gaze, forcing her expression to remain only pleasant and not show that her libido had been on hiatus lately.

"Well..." she said, once again feeling the need to end the silence even though she had nothing of substance to say.

He either took the hint or had been looking for an

excuse to leave because he jumped in to say, "I'll be next door. Whenever you and Paul are ready to head down, just knock."

Without waiting for her to reply, he turned and disappeared from sight, but she heard the door of the room next to hers open and close.

She returned to the window and stared at the expansive view. Sucking in a deep breath, she let it out slowly. From the moment they'd arrived at the airport, her careful plans had been obliterated, leaving her to feel off-balance. Well taken care of, but off-balance.

No doubt about it... He's a complication. A complication I do not need. She snorted aloud. *But there's no harm in a little wishful dreaming.*

Too keyed up to rest, she decided to shower before reviewing any of the professor's notes. She had to admit the high-end shower with multiple showerheads, including one setting for just rainfall, was certainly better than the typical drippy faucet standing in a cracked bathtub experience she's had in many hotels. She wondered if Adam was used to these luxurious accommodations.

Despite what many thought, academia wasn't a gold mine. Universities tend to funnel their resources into their sports programs while paying professors a pittance in comparison. And academic assistants were paid even less. Paul's work was now being cited in textbooks and he was sought out as a guest lecturer and conference presenter. His work had even captured the attention of government think tanks who wanted to know more about the effects of global warming on agriculture.

She was also riding the wave to supplement her income by becoming an in-demand consultant in the field since she worked on the research and reports alongside him. Yet she was still needed for administrative duties such as travel arrangements since no one else could assist. *There are ways to supplement income. However, some are akin to selling my soul.*

Stepping out of the steamy shower, she wrapped the thick, soft towel around her as her toes dug into the plush bathmat. Moving to the vanity, she lifted her gaze to the mirror. The reflection of her hazel eyes stared back at her, and a weary sigh escaped.

The sound of running water through the wall met her ears, and she realized it was from the bathroom in the room next to hers. Sucking in a quick breath, the image of Adam taking a shower flooded her mind. As tall as he was, she wondered if he had to stoop to get the rainfall effect. That thought brought a surprising ripple of laughter through her. She shook her head to will away the image of a naked Adam from her mind and focused on the task at hand.

With that thought, she walked into the room, dug around in her purse, and pulled out her phone. After typing the hotel name and her room number, she hit send.

Moving to her suitcase, she cast aside the towel

and pulled out clean underwear and a silky kimono that hung to her mid-thighs. Bought online at a knockoff boutique, it was one of her few indulgences.

Her beauty routine was easy—blow-dry her hair and minimum makeup application. Then she dressed in a green jersey wrap dress. It hugged her curves and hit just below her knees. Still padding around in her slippered feet, she glanced at the clock to see if she had time to kill before she collected Paul and Adam for dinner. Sitting at the small table, she opened her laptop. She knew all the lecture notes for Paul were perfect, so instead, she pulled up the textbook notes she'd been working on.

An hour whizzed by as she was lost in her reading. Her alarm broke her concentration, pulling her back to reality. Lifting her arms over her head, she stretched out the kinks. As usual, it had been easy for her to get lost in the work. She slipped her feet into her pumps and grabbed her purse after double-checking to ensure she had her room key card. Her steps were muffled by the thick carpet when she walked across the hall. She rapped on the door and smiled as Paul threw it open, a rested expression on his face. "I know we didn't set a time, but I was going to see if you were ready."

He patted his midsection. "I did take a nap but woke with my stomach growling. Best alarm there is."

She laughed in agreement. "I'll see if Adam is ready to join us." She turned to walk back across the hall, but a sudden bout of shyness filled her, leaving her wondering if *she* was ready. She was prepared for the academic presentations, but the thoughts about Adam that weaved through her mind left her uncertain. Sucking in a fortifying breath, she barely lifted her hand to knock when his door opened.

She stood still as a statue, her gaze raking over him in unabashed perusal. He wore a navy dress shirt tucked into black pants. His hair was mostly dry and slightly tousled as though his fingers had combed through it when he left the shower. His blue eyes seemed more penetrating as his gaze roamed over her, then landed and stayed on her eyes. Her tongue darted out to moisten her dry lips. Somehow, he'd grown more handsome in the two hours since she'd last seen him.

"Are you ready to go up? The restaurant is on the upper floor with a view."

She startled slightly, realizing that while she had knocked on his door, she'd become lost in her thoughts, leaving him to speak first. "Yes! Absolutely. Um... Yes."

Feeling momentarily awkward, she pivoted on her heels and walked toward Paul as he closed his door. Once on the top floor, they found the restaurant to be in the quiet lull between the rush of lunch and the evening's dinner crowd.

The hostess guided them through the long length of tables, finally stopping at one in the corner with full glass on two sides, offering a panoramic view of

Washington, DC. The dark wood, red leather seat cushions, and soft overhead lighting offered an elegant, modern ambiance to the interior. Deciding to sit across from Paul, she realized when Adam sat at her left and their knees touched, her focus would be more on him than the meal or the outside view.

Something about being in his presence unsettled her. She was secure in her education, knowledge, and subject matter in the academic world. With Paul as her mentor, her confidence in her expertise had grown. As he had included her more and more in his research and travels, she had become as proficient in the subject as he. But once again, in the presence of Adam, she found her thoughts scattering like leaves in the wind.

It occurred to her that she'd spent most of her time in the hallowed halls of academia or out tromping through fields and forests. As she picked up the menu, a sigh escaped. *I really need to get out more!*

Adam's eyes often returned to gaze at her, and she was increasingly aware of the server's constant presence at his side, speaking to him first before turning to Paul or her. But he didn't seem to notice the young woman at all, and she wondered about the stoic man who'd entered her life just this morning and now took up residence in her thoughts. She looked down at the menu, desperate for a distraction.

"The lady will order first."

Hearing him speak, she noted the chagrined expression on the server at Adam's dismissal of the woman's attempts to engage him in conversation. Finding his gaze on her, a warm comfort seemed to fill her. Giving the server her order, she offered him a little smile before returning her gaze to the window, enjoying the vista presented before her.

5

Adam was ensnared by the woman sitting next to him. He had prepared himself for an evening of polite but tedious conversation. He thought the professor and she would be stuffy, spending their time excluding him as they reviewed for their upcoming meeting. He wouldn't have taken it personally, having already assumed he wouldn't know what they were discussing. After all, he wasn't there for conversation but for their protection.

But as the meal progressed, he was quite surprised to find himself wrapped in the unexpected amusing stories and laughter as they told of some of their travels. Asking him about his travels as well, he shared what he could, which was more than he had with any other client. *Not that any other client ever really talked to him while he was on the job.*

He watched as Valerie spoke, her eyes animated and her mouth often curving into smiles that lit her face. The sound of mirth was real when she laughed over some of their travel misadventures.

"The first trip I ever took out of the country was when Paul organized a group of seniors to travel to South America and gain an overview of the research he had completed in Colombia. We were lucky because we also got to visit Ecuador, Peru, and Brazil. I was only a sophomore at the time and felt incredibly fortunate that he allowed me to go. His wife, Ellen, was on that trip, and we became friends."

"It was easy to allow you to make that journey," Paul said, his benevolent gaze resting on her. He looked up at Adam. "She'll tell you that she only took my freshman environmental science class because she needed a science elective and had no idea what to take, but I think it was pure providence, even though that's not scientific. She was one of my star students and quickly became indispensable as my assistant."

She looked down at the perfectly cooked steak and baked potatoes that had just been set in front of her. "I certainly got to go on many trips, but I confess that I'm not very adventurous when it comes to the food." Inclining her head, she sliced her knife through the tender meat. "Whereas Paul would encourage the students to try all the local cuisine, I'm afraid I was a picky eater."

"You always ate the fruit," he reminded.

Adam watched her face light as a smile graced her lips. She caught his eye, leaned forward slightly, and offered an exaggerated whisper, "Bananas and oranges hardly make me an exotic and daring eater!"

Adam chuckled and shook his head as he cut into his steak, as well.

"I would hazard a guess that you're former military," Paul surmised, lifting a bushy brow.

"Yes, I am. Army. Twelve years."

As Paul thanked him for his service, his attention was drawn to Valerie's softly spoken, "Thank you." He never expected thanks but also never threw it back into anyone's face. Something about her voice held his attention.

"When is Timothy expected to come home for a visit?" Paul asked, turning his attention to her.

Her gaze dropped for a few seconds, then she plastered a smile and replied, "Not for a few more months." Turning her gold-flecked eyes toward Adam, she explained, "My brother, Timothy, is also in the Army. He's been in for sixteen years and figures he'll stay until he gets his twenty in and then retire and start a new career. Maybe as a civilian contractor with the military." She shrugged and sighed. "I'll just be glad to have him home."

Something about her wistful voice pulled to him, and he found the connection of the Army felt like a bond and not just a coincidence. It was on the tip of his tongue to assure that her brother would be glad to get home, too. But he stayed quiet since he didn't know if that statement would be true.

Her gaze would lock with his every so often

during the meal, and a surge of something indefinable would pass between them. Each time, she would break the connection first, looking down at her plate or out the window. But he didn't miss how a blush would touch her cheeks or how her tongue would dart out over her bottom lip. He sensed the stirrings of a connection he wasn't used to in his role as protector.

He was pulled back into the conversation when Paul asked him about some of his overseas tours. While Adam couldn't go into details, the professor would launch into various stories about some places Adam had seen.

Valerie even shared photos on her phone of some of their fieldwork. He stared at photograph after photograph of Valerie with her hair in a ponytail or tucked up in a ball cap, wearing jeans and a work shirt, knee-deep in plants or her boots stuck in mud. Staring at the beautiful woman in front of him now, he realized her layers ran deep.

While he didn't mention all the places he'd travel to, he quickly learned to keep the conversation about food, discovering both Paul and Valerie enjoyed his culinary travails as well. "I've had good oxtail, but then I've also had bad oxtail."

Visibly shuddering, Valerie exclaimed, "I certainly haven't eaten good oxtail, but I can only imagine how horrible bad oxtail must have been!" Tilting her head slightly, she prodded, "What's something else you had that was weird?" As she popped another roasted carrot into her mouth, he grinned.

"I'm afraid I can't tell you the most unusual foods I've ever eaten, considering you've admitted you're a picky eater and you're still finishing this meal."

"Wise decision." Paul nodded. "Valerie is an excellent travel companion and is essential to our work. But she is not someone to enjoy truly local cuisine unless she knows what it is and if she likes it."

The server arrived to clear their plates, and the meal ended sooner than Adam would've liked, surprising him. He had felt something inside him shift over the past hour. A crack in his armor allowed a sliver of light to enter, and he had no idea how to suppress it... or if he wanted to.

"Well, Valerie, I should go upstairs and review my notes," Paul said.

Valerie immediately pushed her chair back to join Paul, and Adam stood with them.

"Oh, you young people should stay and have a drink," Paul said.

Under normal circumstances, Adam might have asked Valerie if she'd like to share a drink with him, but he needed to ensure Paul's safety, so it wouldn't be right to let Paul go off by himself.

"I'll need to escort you downstairs."

The three made their way to the elevator and back to the fourth floor. This trip, though, felt different from before. Now, he found he was hyper-aware of Valerie's presence even though they were not looking directly at each other. As the elevator doors slid open, he stepped through first, glanced up and down the hall, and then moved to the side. Paul and Valerie followed and walked side by side until they came to their rooms.

Paul turned and smiled. "Thank you for your company tonight, Adam. It was nice spending time with you, and I'm sure, for Valerie, it was nice to share a meal with someone besides me."

She rolled her eyes and playfully slapped his arm. "Do you want me to help you this evening as you review your notes?"

"Not at all. I have everything well in hand. I'll see you two in the morning."

Adam opened Paul's room and stepped inside, quickly ascertaining it was secure.

"I think I'll order room service for breakfast. So I'll see you about nine o'clock before we go over to the institute."

"That sounds like a very good idea," she agreed. "I'll do the same, and that will save time from having to go to the restaurant."

As the door closed behind Paul, Adam looked down at Valerie as they walked across the hall to their side-by-side doors that seemed to underline their proximity and separation. The silence stretched between them. He fumbled for something to say, not yet ready to say good night.

Valerie inhaled deeply before looking up at him, breaking the tension. "I would also like to thank you,

Adam. I'm afraid I came off as very... um... prickly when we first met."

He half lifted his hand in a dismissive wave. "You were far from prickly, Valerie. Under the circumstances, I thought you were very accommodating."

Her smile lit up the hallway, and his pulse quickened. Her university photograph had not done her justice. It sorely lacked her vitality and warmth. Nothing about Valerie was plain. Not her looks, personality, or conversation. If they had met in a different setting, he would've enjoyed getting to know her better.

Her brown hair glistened with gold highlights. And her hazel eyes were also rimmed in gold. "You wear contacts?" he asked.

"Yes. I wear glasses when traveling because planes make my eyes so dry."

A blush highlighted her cheeks, making her even more beautiful. But duty snapped him back to the present. After she unlocked her door, he stepped in to scan it efficiently, then moved to the side to let her pass through. "Sleep well. I'll see you in the morning."

As her door closed with a final resounding click in the hallway, a sigh escaped him as he moved into his room. He emptied his pockets onto the table. Sitting on the edge of the bed, he faced the wall shared with her room on the other side, keenly aware it was all that separated them.

A strange longing filled him, a wistful ache he couldn't remember having before. She was so close right now, yet still so far away. Falling back onto the bed, he stared at the ceiling, wondering what had come over him.

Reminding himself of professionalism first and always, he finally got ready for bed and sat up reading the latest book but found his attention waning. Eventually, he turned out the lights, but the image of Valerie filled his mind, and he wasn't surprised when sleep remained elusive.

Regardless of how poorly he slept, he woke before his alarm. After another quick shower, he was already dressed when he heard dishes rattling. Stepping out into the hall, he saw three carts, and Valerie was tipping the servers. He stepped forward, and she greeted him with a smile.

"Let me make sure Paul is up," she said, knocking on the door across the hall.

Paul opened it and greeted them both, exclaiming over their breakfast already being served. Valerie wheeled the cart into Paul's room. He was starting an early morning call with Ellen, so she left his breakfast, then walked back into the hall.

Looking up at Adam, she offered, "Since we're both dressed, eating by ourselves seems a little silly. Would you like to have breakfast with me?"

He usually didn't share meals with clients, but now, he'd not only had dinner but also looked forward to joining her again. He easily pushed both carts into her room and over to the small table. She uncovered the plates and laughed as she spied his meal.

"I can tell which one is yours."

He'd ordered a full breakfast, but looking at her plate, he was pleased to see that she also had plenty to eat. "It's good you like to eat a lot."

At that, she blinked, and her fork halted on its way to her mouth. "Excuse me?"

He winced, hearing the words play back in his mind and how they would've sounded to her. "I'm sorry! That sounded so different in my head than how it came out."

She laughed and shoveled in a bite of scrambled eggs. "You're right. I do have a healthy appetite."

His gaze moved down her, then quickly jumped back to her eyes. "I don't see where you put it."

"I like to run," she explained. "Normally, if you hadn't been around today, I would've gone for a run this morning before breakfast. But I figured you might not like that."

"You're right. I would have had to chase you down."

Her nose scrunched. "That means you would have had to leave Paul unguarded."

"Yeah," he said, rubbing his chin. "That would have been a problem."

She sighed, spearing a piece of grapefruit. "Sorry," she mumbled. "The last thing I want is to put Paul at risk."

"Or yourself."

Her nose scrunched again. "I'm not important—"

"Not so," he bit out. He had no idea why he'd spoken so vehemently. Clearing his throat, he shrugged. "The institute paid for security for both of you."

She held his gaze, and he could have sworn a flash passed through her eyes, but he had no idea how to interpret it. She busied herself with eating, and he longed to return them to a pleasant subject. "How long have you been running?"

She looked up and hesitated, studying him. Finally, she offered a small smile. "Since discovering cross-country in high school."

"Me, too," he admitted, surprised at the excitement he felt at their common pursuit. "I run almost every day."

Her eyes widened, and her smile brightened. "I'd suggest that we run together sometime, but as you so rightly pointed out, I know you need to stay close to Paul." She chuckled. "He is many wonderful things, but a runner is not one of them."

At that moment, all he could think about was how much he'd like to run with her. And once again, that thought struck him odd, considering he didn't look for running partners. If he and the other Keepers ran together, that was fine. But other than that, he was a solitary runner. Yet now, he loved the idea of going with Valerie.

"Well, after this assignment, we could go running sometime." He couldn't decide if his invitation sounded like a suave segue to seeing her again or if he sounded pathetic and desperate. His breath held in his lungs for a few seconds until her smile widened once again.

"I'd like that. I mostly run in my neighborhood or on a few trails through a park."

His brow furrowed slightly as he thought about the rougher terrain that he ran on.

As though anticipating his thoughts, she said, "If you run cross-country, that would be great with me. I'm a little out of shape, so I might be sucking wind if there are a lot of hills, but I think I could keep up."

"I'm sure you could," he said. He left unspoken that he would adapt his stride to whatever he needed to for things to be comfortable for her.

By the time they finished eating, rolled the carts out into the hall, and checked on Paul, it was time for them to leave. While he still had little interest in the conference, he appreciated Paul's company and couldn't wait to spend more time with Valerie.

6

So far, this trip hadn't resembled any other trip Valerie had ever taken with Paul, and she continued to feel off-kilter. Over the years of collaborating with Paul, their travels had developed a comfortable partnership. She organized the arrangements since she understood where they were going and what was needed at each stop. She kept Paul on schedule and joined him for most of the scholarly presentations since she had actively collected and analyzed data in his research. She used to type up his dictated notes, but that duty had now fallen to graduate assistants in recent years.

But now, the inclusion of security on this trip had added a layer of complexity, certainly throwing off her schedule as well as encroaching into her comfort zone.

Yet staring at the man sitting in the hotel room across from her, she had to admit that, while his presence still interfered with what she needed to do, she was drawn to the soft-spoken man, who also managed to wield an unspoken authority.

With their breakfast completed, she glanced at the time and hurried to ensure Paul was ready to leave, ticking off the mental checklist of needs for the day. She managed to forget all about Adam for a few minutes, focusing on the professor and the meeting at the RAND Institute.

As they walked down the hall toward the elevator, she glanced up at Adam and sighed as he waited for her and Paul to follow. Adam would certainly make the trip more complex.

She'd had the foresight to cancel the transportation arranged from the other hotel to the institute. Lifting a brow, she looked at Adam as the trio rode to the lobby in the elevator. "I assume you've made arrangements for transportation?"

His lips quirked in a playful grin as he nodded. "It's all taken care of."

"I guess it's good that I'm helping with Paul's presentation, or I'd feel quite useless."

At that, both Paul and Adam chuckled. She grinned as they stepped off the elevator, curious to see what arrangements Adam had made. Another large dark SUV awaited them just outside. Adam shook hands with the driver, then opened the door for her. She slid into the back seat, once again next to Paul, as Adam sat in the passenger front seat. Ten minutes later, the driver pulled up in front of the building housing the institute, and they alighted.

Shouts came from nearby, and Adam immediately stepped in front of her and Paul, guiding them to the steps. His voice cut through the cacophony with a command. "Move quickly."

Hurrying up the steps alongside Paul, she felt Adam's presence. Without turning around, she knew he was directly behind them, creating a shield. It was as though the barricade he created with his presence muted the sounds all around. It seemed strange to be already so aware of him.

At the top of the stairs, her curiosity piqued, and she looked down at the sidewalk, seeing college-age students on one side with signs calling for politicians to make policies to halt the carbon emissions, and on the other was a smaller group of people shouting, "Stop the hoax." Police pushed both groups back to keep them from getting too close to each other.

"Good grief," she muttered, then quickly followed Paul inside with Adam's arm behind her, still providing a protective layer between her and the outside world.

A woman walked toward them, her heels clicking smartly on the tile floor. Her gaze swept over the trio, landing on Paul, passing over Valerie in dismissal, and then pausing on Adam. A smile curved her perfectly painted lips the closer she got, but Valerie could easily discern that the smile was for Adam alone. Heaving a sigh, Valerie thrust out her hand. "This is Dr. Mendez, and I'm Valerie Clemens." She specifically didn't introduce Adam because he'd cautioned both her and Paul not to emphasize anything about him.

The woman snapped out of her Adam trance and focused on Paul. "Welcome, Dr. Mendez. I'm Penelope Rogers. I work for Dr. Marchess. I'll take you upstairs. Since others will be joining your presentation, we're using a small auditorium with stepped seating. I think you'll find it to be adequate."

"I'm sure I will," Paul agreed. "You will need to coordinate with Ms. Clemens once we get there. She handles all my presentations."

Penelope's gaze drifted over Valerie, her gaze assessing. Seeming to find Valerie unworthy of more interest, she simply offered a curt nod and then turned her attention to Adam. Unable to keep from looking, Valerie glanced to the side to see that Adam had stepped back and was speaking with one of the building's guards.

"And who is—"

"Here are your security badges," Adam said, stepping back to Paul and Valerie. As he handed them out, his gaze held on Valerie, and she grinned. It was a ridiculous response, yet it felt good to have his attention.

As soon as that thought hit her, she thanked him and then turned to walk with Paul. *I don't need a man for validation.* Yet as they entered the elevator and Adam's attention had not drifted to Penelope, who seemed to preen more in a desperate attempt for him to notice her, Valerie was struck with another thought. *I don't need a man for validation... but that doesn't mean I can't just want a man.*

She inhaled deeply as the elevator doors opened, pushing aside all other thoughts. The RAND Institute began in 1948 to connect military planning with research. Eventually becoming an independent, nonprofit organization, the newly formed company was dedicated to furthering research and promoting scientific, educational, and charitable purposes. Completely nonpartisan, they used fact-based analysis to tackle society's most pressing problems. With an office in California, she and Paul were often called in to share their research. This was her first trip to the Washington, DC office, and as they entered the small auditorium with stadium seating, she breathed easier. Just like being in the field, this setting was also like coming home to her.

She and Paul moved to the low stage and began the pre-presentation preparation. The institute had one of their technical employees there to hook up her laptop containing presentation notes. Within a few minutes, he was ready.

No longer feeling Adam nearby, she looked around as the meeting attendees filled the seats. This meeting included not only RAND employees but other guests, as well. Her eyes were drawn to the back, where she saw Adam leaning against the wall, his arms crossed over his chest as he stood in the shadows. That seemed safer for him to be so far away… less disconcerting. Her gaze moved over the attendees, barely stopping on one in particular but holding just long enough to see his barely perceptible nod. Moving to sit next to Paul, she smiled at her mentor and friend. "Ready?"

He chuckled and nodded. "Thanks to you, *we're* ready."

"Years ago, the prediction that climate change would affect the already vulnerable populations has come true. Farmers in many countries that have already learned to survive by growing plants used by drug cartels find their land less productive.

"In 2019, half of the Mexican bean crop wasn't planted for lack of water. Many villages were already taken over by threats of violence or the economic security to grow crops for cartels. Now, those crops are not flourishing.

"And whereas some say their country's government officials should bring in resources, those fighting the drug cartels find that if they don't send more support into the most vulnerable communities, they risk losing those people completely. Yet to do so fuels the drug cartels."

Usually, Adam had no difficulty ignoring all other stimuli other than what he needed to stay focused on the safety of who he was with. Yet, while his gaze traveled over the people in the room, his focus continually drifted to the professor's words and the charts, graphs, and images projected on the screen behind him.

In both his missions during his tours as a Ranger and as a civilian Keeper, he knew life was rarely just black or white, good or evil, right or wrong. He was already aware of the difficulty poor farmers had in many countries where they could only stay alive and take care of their families to grow whatever crops would pay for them to survive. He never considered how the poorest of the poor were affected when little precious water combined with higher temperatures made whatever crops they attempted to grow die on the vines.

Paul continued to speak, and Adam's attention shifted back to the stage as Valerie continued the presentation.

"As someone who has studied the effects of global warming and climate change on plants, and recently, specifically on the cash crop of coca plants, which has become vital to many countries' basic economy, there are trends that others are studying. When it is predicted that coca production into cocaine could decrease by as much as forty percent due to the changing land suitability, drug producers will have to respond to the changing environment. For example, the opium poppy used to produce heroin farmed in Afghanistan recently resurged when it was discovered they were harnessing solar power to drill down into the earth to find water. With only a few solar panels, they are able to pump water to increase productivity.

"While this is not our area of expertise, I will mention that cartels could possibly turn to synthetic drug production. As long as they have the resources, they will have the manpower from the farmers, who could no longer grow crops.

"And we have just started working with others in the field to share information on the increase of violence in poorer societies due to the economic devastation from global warming. We offer our written reports to be available, and Dr. Mendez and I look forward to talking with you during the breaks."

Adam was fascinated with Valerie's clear voice, animated enough to keep the attendees riveted as she proceeded through her lecture portion.

At this point in the presentation, Adam's interest waned slightly as the professor's lecture moved to empirical studies, followed by charts and graphs on display. He now thought about Paul's background, knowing he'd come from Colombia and wondering if traveling back and forth for research was easy.

As his gaze moved over the attendees again, finding nothing to warrant his concern, they drifted off to where Valerie sat to the side, quietly watching Paul, ready to leap up and assist if she was needed. Suddenly, imagining her traveling with Paul to some of the world's worst areas where poverty and criminal activities rule the land caused him to shudder.

When the lecture was over, Paul and Valerie stayed to answer numerous questions, managing calm in the face of multiple calls of "Dr. Mendez, Ms. Clemens!" Valerie moved to the front, taking care of Paul's laptop and notes, and began answering questions directed to her as well. With her part of the presentation and her name just under Dr. Mendez's on his academic papers and articles, Adam realized that she was also professionally sought after.

As the crowd thinned, he lost sight of her. Pushing off from his position against the wall, he felt his chest tighten when he discovered she was nowhere to be seen. Just as he was about to move closer to the back, a side door opened, and he watched as she slipped through and walked back to the stage. The air held in his lungs rushed out. *Bathroom break. She must have needed a bathroom break.*

While his focus and mission were on both Paul and Valerie, he needed to keep them together as often as possible. In the RAND building, with security and a process for entering through guards and a metal detector, he felt that they were safer. Yet he couldn't shake the feeling of uneasiness he'd experienced when she was out of his sight. *At least, I need to tell her to let me know when she takes a break.*

When the group surrounding them finally left, Penelope reappeared to guide them to a room where lunch was served for those attending the meetings.

Valerie approached Adam and smiled. "Please, get

something to eat. You can't be with us all day and not eat anything."

He smiled at her concern. "Don't worry about me. I had a big breakfast and will eat a big dinner tonight. I'll be fine."

Penelope seemed to appear at his side magically. With her predatory smile wide, she leaned close. "If you'd like, you may certainly come and have lunch with me in the employee lounge."

"Thank you, no. I'm right where I want to be." He spoke to the irritating assistant, but his gaze was on Valerie. He meant the words… with her was not only where he needed to be but also where he *wanted* to be. Glad when Penelope moved on with a loud huff, he turned to Valerie.

She appeared to be holding back a grin. Clearing her throat, she asked, "So, um… what did you think of his speech this morning? Bored to death?"

"Not at all. It held my attention more than I thought it would. Probably more than it should."

Her brow scrunched, and she tilted her head to the side. "I don't understand."

"I found it interesting that a climatologist and botanist would have anything to do with predicting what the cartels might consider a viable source of income in light of global warming. To be honest, I've never thought of that."

She nodded slowly. "At the risk of sounding like I don't care because I assure you I do, the cartels are not going to give up their positions of power and wealth. Preying on those who become addicted to drugs will not go away even if they have to change the drugs they sell. Power usually wins out."

"We talked last night about the many places you visited—"

"Yes, and my appreciation of excellent cuisine," she said, laughing.

He chuckled and rubbed his chin as he looked down at her. "I suppose you go to Colombia a lot since that's where Paul is from?"

He didn't know why he asked the question, but as soon as the words left his lips, he spied the way she tried to hide the wince.

"Yes, fairly often. While he has focused on many areas in Central and South America's agriculture economy, he certainly cares about his country of birth."

There was more Adam wanted to ask, but for now, he remained silent. He had a feeling that voicing his concerns would not be well received. *Not part of my mission, anyway.*

The afternoon session was set up the same as the morning, with Paul and Valerie at the podium. At one point, after she had presented for the last time, she moved to the back to sit.

While the morning session held his interest, Adam felt unsettled during the afternoon but couldn't ascertain why. The audience members appeared to be scientists like the professor, whether they worked in a university or at various think tanks.

No overt threat erupted, and while Paul and Valerie's company proved to be pleasant, it was becoming apparent to Adam that their safety was not threatened. But knowing that anything could happen at any time, he remained vigilant.

The door in the back occasionally opened as someone left or entered. His attention would gravitate to the area before swinging back to Paul. Near the end of the afternoon session, as the questions began, his attention was snagged by a young, dark-haired man in a suit who came in and sat in the empty chair next to Valerie. Her forward-facing gaze never changed as she continued to watch Paul, but the man leaned ever so slightly toward her, mouthing something.

Valerie never took her eyes off the front, but Adam's interest was piqued. Turning away from her, he focused on the front as more people moved forward to speak to Paul. Shifting slightly behind some attendees, who were now leaving, he chanced a glance to the back, just in time to see Valerie also lean slightly toward the man, her mouth barely moving while shaking her head. With an almost imperceptible nod, the man stood and left the room. Valerie then moved toward the front, smiling to greet someone she knew and answer questions.

A cold snake of suspicion slithered through his veins. Then he immediately chastised himself. *She's at a professional meeting and knows many of the attendees.*

Of course, she'll have people speak to her, and she'll speak to them.

But like the prickle he would feel on the back of his neck during a mission alerting him to something not quite right, he couldn't get rid of the idea that the short interlude with the man sitting next to Valerie was not to be dismissed.

7

Valerie smiled at Paul as they climbed back into the dark SUV Adam had arranged to take them back to the hotel.

"I thought it went very well, Paul. What did you think?"

"I agree. The RAND Institute certainly knows how to showcase those of us in research. I confess that I like these smaller meetings better than the large conventions."

The ten-minute drive back to the hotel gave Valerie a chance to look out the window as they passed some of the iconic landmarks of Washington, D.C.

She was unable to keep from glancing toward Adam as he sat in the front seat. As much as she would love to walk down the National Mall and wander inside the Smithsonian Museums with

Adam, she had other obligations that she couldn't ignore. Sighing heavily, they were soon let out at the front door. Adam got out first and opened her door, a chivalrous gesture that seemed second nature to him. His eyes met hers, lingering longer than necessary before he turned to Paul. Escorting them both inside, they once again entered the opulence of the hotel.

Deciding to go to their rooms to freshen up, then meet for dinner, she stood in front of her door as Adam checked Paul's room and then walked over to hers.

"I thought you would've been front and center with Paul during his lectures," Adam said.

He scanned her room with a practiced eye and stood at the doorway as she walked in past. At the nearness, she inhaled the scent that seemed woodsy and very masculine—and uniquely him. Dropping her briefcase on the bed, she turned, still unable to keep her appreciation of his looks hidden as a blush crossed her face. Sucking in a deep breath, she focused on his words. "Sometimes I am, and other times, I like to go sit near the back."

"Gives you a chance to disappear a little bit?" His gaze seemed to question her much deeper than his words indicated.

Chuckling lightly, she nodded. "Neither Paul nor I are attention hogs. He would much prefer being out in the field, studying."

"And you? What is your preference?"

For a heartbeat, her imagination spiraled into the realm of personal. *What would my preference be with your hands and lips—*

She snapped back to reality and forced her thoughts to her professional preference. Clearing her suddenly dry throat, she said, "I enjoy the chance to travel, and I enjoy assisting him with his research." The words felt rehearsed and mechanical, but they were the safest ones she could offer.

He started to turn but paused and cast a lingering look at her. "There was a man who sat next to you near the end of the afternoon session. He seemed interested in talking to you, but I have a feeling you didn't share that interest."

Caught off guard, she blinked, unable to hide her startle. "I didn't recognize him and don't know who he was. He sat down next to me and, after a few minutes, asked if I would like to have dinner and drinks with him. I told him no and then ignored him when he tried to continue the conversation." She shrugged. "He finally gave up."

Adam was silent for a moment, the quietness no longer comfortable. His gaze penetrated, and she fought the urge to squirm. Finally, his lips curved upward. "I have a feeling that probably happens a lot to you. I'm sorry."

Letting out a shaky breath, she continued to hold his gaze steadily. "You don't have to apologize for all men."

"No, but I'm sorry all the same."

The unspoken connection hovered between them, so tangible she had to keep her hands to her sides, or she was afraid she would give in to the urge and reach out to touch him. Clearing her throat again, she nodded. "I assure you, it doesn't turn my head. Climatology and botany are professions often filled with men. While more and more women are getting into the field, there are times when I'm the only woman in the room or out on one of our research trips. It wasn't the first time I've been hit on, and it won't be the last."

"Once again, you shouldn't have to put up with that at any time. I am sorry."

She inclined her head, still holding his gaze. "Thank you. Well, I better freshen up quickly, or Paul will be out here ready for dinner before I've even brushed my hair."

He dipped his chin before turning and entering his room. His retreat also gave her the mental space to breathe as she leaned her back against the door for a moment. Moving with haste, she quickly headed into the bathroom. A few minutes later, refreshed, she grabbed her phone and stood by the window, no longer focusing on the view. Sending a text, she tossed her phone onto the bed, not waiting for a reply as frustration filled her.

Staring out the window, she focused her gaze on the cityscape and filled her lungs deeply before sighing heavily. A knock on her door jerked her back to the present, and she shoved her phone into her purse and stepped out into the hall where Paul and Adam waited.

Dinner was very much like the previous evening, with an air of normalcy settling around them. This time, the three immediately fell into comfortable conversation, laughing while sharing stories.

"I'm sure you must have been very bored today," Paul said, looking at Adam.

"I wondered how you were able to see what threat there might be in a room with dim lighting and so many people," Valerie added. "I assume you've learned to tune extraneous sounds out?"

"I can usually focus on just what I need to," he agreed. "Although, today, I found it more difficult because I was listening to part of your lecture."

Valerie was surprised, and Paul perked up at that comment.

"I've been to many areas where the locals had to do whatever they needed to survive. I can't blame anyone for the crops they grow to ensure there's food on the table and for the safety of their family. It made sense that the cartels will just move into the production of something else."

Nodding, Paul agreed. "As I'm sure you've ascertained by now, I'm not into politics or making policy, not for our country or anyone else. I'm a scientist. I research, and I study. Then I can advise governments and politicians on results and trends with what I learn. Today, for example, representatives from the academic world attended, as well as other think tanks like our hosts, the RAND Institute. They are the ones who take my data and then present it to governments, politicians, and other groups that would benefit from it."

Valerie looked over and was impressed at how Adam listened carefully. She often found that if a subject didn't directly affect someone, they simply blew it off or dismissed it as unimportant. Adam seemed to be taking in what he'd heard today and wanted to learn more.

"I am curious, though, about the relationship of losing the cartels' cash crops and moving into synthetic drugs. That doesn't seem tied directly into your study of climatology and botany."

"You're right." Paul agreed. "That was merely a byproduct of some research we've done in other areas. We're interested in ways to continue to produce crops in light of global warming, whether it's corn or beans in the middle of Nebraska or in the middle of Afghanistan. Other scientists and researchers can take my conclusions and figure out how to create viable ways to continue to grow various crops."

"Like the example you gave of the solar panels that they're using in Afghanistan to keep growing poppies."

"Exactly. And because I've focused a lot of recent

research on Colombia since that country is close to my heart, I've had the opportunity to figure out what some of the cartels are doing. From a purely economic standpoint, farming certain crops will no longer work for them. And they will find other avenues to make money, and violence ensues."

As the dinner ended, the trio returned downstairs. Paul bid them good night, and once again, she and Adam walked across the hall. He checked her room and hovered at the door for a moment.

She wanted to be spontaneous. It had been so long since she'd given in to the urge without overanalyzing, weighing pros and cons, and then finally giving up. Turning, she gathered her courage and blurted, "I thought about ordering dessert from room service in a little while, maybe with a glass of wine. Would you... are you... I thought maybe I could order for you, too... if you were interested."

She felt her cheeks heat as the words that she'd just said played back in her head. Instead of sounding like a mature woman on the other side of thirty, she sounded like a bumbling teenager, and she could only imagine that he would like to get away from her. Just when she was ready to pull back the invitation to salvage whatever dignity she could, he spoke.

"I'd love to. Whenever you want, that'll be fine."

"Oh. Good. Um... wine, beer, or liquor?"

"A beer is good. Dark. Guinness, if they have it. And I'll pay."

"Oh, no. Please... um... my idea, so... um... my treat." Not giving him a chance to argue, she rushed, "I just need to review the notes for Paul's meeting in the morning. It's not going to be in the lecture hall. It'll just be in a smaller conference room with some RAND employees who are directly interested in the subject. So maybe in an hour?"

His lips slowly curved into a smile, and she couldn't help but notice that it wasn't a wide, full grin but a slow-burning, hard-to-earn-but-easy-to-appreciate smile.

"I'll be ready."

"Good, then. You can just come over when you're ready." As her door closed, and she heard him enter the room next door, she let out her breath, feeling lightheaded. Realizing she'd been holding her breath, she was glad she hadn't passed out while both waiting for his answer and admiring his smile.

Not knowing how long it might take for room service, she called and placed an order for their sample dessert platter, a glass of wine, and a Guinness.

She found it difficult to focus on the notes she was supposed to review. Finally, after twenty minutes, she gave up and headed into the bathroom. She brushed her hair and touched up her light makeup, then hesitated. *I want to look nice... but not desperate. I want him to notice me... but not look like I was trying to get him to notice me.* Dropping her chin to her chest, she closed her eyes. *This shouldn't be so hard.*

A knock sounded, and she hurried over to the door. Throwing it open, she expected to see the server, but it was Adam standing behind the rolling cart. Furrowing her brow, she leaned out and spied the server, walking down the hall toward the elevator. He looked over his shoulder and shrugged. Jerking her gaze over to a smiling Adam, she stepped backward, allowing him to roll the cart inside.

"Did you pay for this?" she asked.

"Guilty."

"It was supposed to be my treat."

"Having you invite me to share this with you is treat enough."

She opened her mouth, then snapped it shut quickly. What could she possibly say to such a sweet sentiment? Smiling while she hoped she was hiding the horse-race beat of her heart, she moved to the small table. He followed with the cart, and she set the domed tray in the middle of the table while he reached for the drinks. Napkins, forks, and two small plates were next. "I had no idea what you might like, but they had a dessert sampler platter that simply sounded too good to pass up."

With a flourish, she lifted the cover and gasped at the selection. The platter was filled with small servings of tiramisu, bread pudding topped with caramel sauce, cheesecake with raspberries, and small cookies with an almond slice pressed into the middle. Around the edge of the platter were small chocolate truffles. "Wow." She looked up quickly and laughed.

"I was expecting to surprise you with this, but I'm the one overwhelmed."

A deep chuckle erupted from his chest, and she could swear his blue eyes twinkled in the dim light.

"Don't think I'm not overwhelmed."

As the words left his mouth, she was aware that his gaze was still on her, not the culinary delights on the table. Clearing her throat, she reached for the Guinness, setting it on his side of the table. He uncorked the bottle of wine, poured a glass, and then held it out for her.

With the delicate glass in her hand, she tilted it slightly toward him, and after he poured his Guinness, they tapped the glasses together.

"Here's to a successful trip," she said.

"Here's to meeting someone new," he added.

Their eyes held, and as though she had no control over her expression, she felt her lips curve upward into a wide smile. Feeling daring, she added, "Yes... here's to meeting someone new."

"Here's to someone new who I can hopefully see again when we're back in California."

Her breath hitched. "Perhaps, here's to a new running partner," she ventured.

Now, his smile was as wide as hers. "I like the sound of that."

Laughing, she sat in the chair and waved her hand toward his side. "If we keep toasting, this delicious, calorie-laden loveliness will go to waste."

"I would hate for any of this loveliness to go to waste."

Her breath hitched once again. Swallowing, she pushed down the thoughts his words brought to mind and busied herself, placing a variety of small desserts on both plates.

For several minutes, their conversation centered around tasting and the difficult process of choosing favorites among the desserts.

"You've only had one truffle," he noted.

"Are you keeping track?"

Chuckling, he shook his head. "No, but I was curious what your favorites would be."

"I love chocolate, but only in small quantities. Even when I buy a box of chocolates, I only have one a day."

His eyes widened. "That is admirable restraint. I'm impressed."

"Well, that's only for chocolate, which is pure decadent candy. For other desserts, I can enjoy more."

"I would have to say right now, based purely on observation and the sounds you make, it's a tossup between the cheesecake and bread pudding," he said, his gaze on her.

She blushed, now wondering if she'd embarrassed herself. "What do you mean, the sounds I make?"

"It's just that when you bit into the tiramisu and the chocolate truffle, you didn't make that particular *groaning-in-ecstasy* sound that you made when you had a bite of the cheesecake with raspberries and the bread pudding with caramel."

Her face heated even more, and she scrunched her nose. "Now, all I can think about is how I must sound while eating!"

He reached over with his fork and scooped up a bite of the bread pudding from her plate. Holding it out, he brought it toward her lips. "Don't think. Just taste to enjoy."

She hesitated for only a second. She wasn't worried about eating off someone else's fork. Someone she'd only met the previous day. Someone she knew very little about. Considering she longed to kiss him, taking a bite off his fork seemed simple at that moment. Her mouth closed over the tines as her lips closed over the bite. When she pulled back, the moist bread pudding, with its sweet caramel sauce, was as near to perfection as she could imagine. Giving over to the enjoyment of the bite, she closed her eyes as she chewed and swallowed, the flavors melting together in sweet harmony.

"And that, right there, is what lets me know it's the winner."

Her eyes snapped open at the tenor of his voice, deep and resonating. His blue eyes were no longer twinkling but seemed darker. Perhaps, as she stared into his face, it was because his pupils were now larger. She once read that pupils dilate when someone is sexually aroused. Since she'd never had a real occasion to ascertain if that was true, she now thought it must be. *But before I can state that definitively, I need to gather empirical evidence.* And staring at his lips, she knew exactly how she wanted to gather the data.

8

Adam had leaned forward, almost absentmindedly, when he'd held the fork with a morsel of dessert out to Valerie. He had no idea what came over him. He'd never been a man who could be described as an accomplished flirt. He was barely a conversationalist. He was more comfortable with bullets than bouquets, so he often preferred danger zones to dinner dates.

The longest previous relationship he'd had occurred many years ago. He'd never found anyone who desired more than a quick physical relationship when he had been in the Army, and his schedule had been chaotic at best. Canceling plans without being able to tell the other person that he was flying to a Third World country to rescue someone, or was needed to infiltrate a regime, or to provide backup on a military offensive were surefire ways to stay single.

Since he'd been out of the service and working for LSIWC, his life had taken on more steadiness. Still, he simply hadn't met anyone captivating enough to hold his interest for longer than an evening of shared physical release. And even those encounters had become fewer and farther between.

Valerie was an enigma. He'd known her for only about thirty-six hours, yet he was drawn to her in a way he hadn't felt in years. She was intelligent without arrogance. She was loyal and caring yet fiercely independent. She radiated beauty, whether dressed in her professional attire or like the photographs he'd seen where she was knee-deep in an agricultural field among crops and Indigenous people of a Third World country.

Seeing her stare at him from across the table, he felt the electricity crackle, so no doubt the sexual chemistry was swirling. But the last thing he wanted to do was rush something, ruining the chance of getting to know her better. Steadying his breath, he wanted to approach cautiously.

Clearing his throat, he looked down as he finished the desserts on his plate, leaned back in his chair, and stared at his beer bottle as though it would indicate what he should say. Suddenly, he looked up and simply asked, "Tell me something about yourself."

For a brief instant, her eyes widened, and then a crinkle formed between her brows. The air grew thick with the force of the silence. "Uh…"

He continued, "Paul mentioned when you were a

freshman, and in one of his classes, you didn't know what you wanted to major in. Tell me what made you decide."

She snapped her mouth closed, covering well if she seemed surprised at his turn in the conversation. Looking down, she took a sip of wine as though she needed the fortification. "Well, in my freshman year of college, I had no idea what I wanted to do with my life. I always scored high in math and science, yet a number of the possible professions I had researched while in high school just didn't appeal to me. Medicine. Engineering. Computer science. I wasn't interested in teaching. I just felt a little... well, let's just say that high school left me feeling a little lost."

Drawn to her, he wanted to ask more but decided to let her give him only what she was comfortable with. Nodding, he remained silent, giving her the freedom to decide what to divulge.

"I had to take a science class during the spring semester of my freshman year. Horror stories about biology and chemistry abounded, so I took an environmental science class. I'd heard good things about Dr. Mendez. Of course, as you now know, that changed my life. I had some money with an academic scholarship but was also eligible for financial aid. I worked in the cafeteria at the college, but when I discovered he needed an undergraduate assistant, I jumped at the opportunity to apply for the position."

She smiled, staring off to the side as though miles away or perhaps years in the past. "Dr. Mendez and I got along great. He needed someone to type up notes and some of his research. He had a graduate assistant, but they were starting to research independently and had less time. So through him, my eyes were opened to the world of climatology and botany." She laughed. "Of course, I had to take biology and chemistry, but by then, I was a more secure student and did well. After finishing my undergraduate degree, I continued working for him and earned my master's."

"And you're still with him, now. It seems like a very successful partnership."

She laughed, and he loved the sound. "I surprised myself on the first trip he allowed me to accompany. He and Ellen let me come along when they went to Colombia. His cousins received us warmly, and then I was fascinated as we went out into the farmland and saw how resilient the farmers were."

"And the first time you saw what some of them were growing?" As soon as the words were spoken, he spied her hazel eyes darkening and hurried to explain. "I'm not judging. It's just that I can imagine it must've been... well, thought-provoking?"

"To be honest, less so than you might believe." She leaned forward, holding his gaze after taking another sip of wine. "As a scientist, I'm not passing judgment on what crops a farmer plants and cultivates. I'm interested in how crops change, how farmers adapt, and what crops do better in different, ever-changing environments. Whether it's corn, beans, coffee, cacao... which, by the way, made this lovely chocolate."

He laughed and nodded. "Thank God for cacao."

As their mirth slowed, she continued. "Or the coca plant. Just like the poppies in Afghanistan. Cocaine and heroin drive those economies."

"So the scientist in you is purely interested in the research and data."

"Yes, but I'm also a human with emotions. I understand what the farmers are doing to survive." A wince crossed her face. "Once, we were out in a field, and a Jeep of men came along. We were blindfolded, and I was terrified. It was just Paul and me. We were taken to a cartel's crop field that was planted closer to one of their compounds—"

Adam was startled, and the air rushed from his lungs. "Fucking hell, Valerie!"

"We weren't harmed in any way other than just being scared. And while we weren't on the direct compound, I could see a difference in how the cartel members dressed and lived. The money they make off the drugs they sell makes you realize their system has huge economic inequity."

She shook her head and re-focused on him. "Okay, that was a crash course in how Valerie ended up in her chosen profession. What about you?"

He rubbed his chin and stared for a moment. He had no doubt there were layers and layers to Valerie, and he wasn't close to discovering her deepest part.

But it seemed her sharing was over, so he allowed the conversation to shift to him.

"You already know I was in the military. Special Forces with the Rangers. And with that comes a great deal of training. We had to be able to pick up and go at a moment's notice and have the desire to see a mission through to the end. We learned to plan and then to be flexible. I don't consider myself an adrenaline junkie, but I enjoy the ever-changing scenery and the camaraderie of a team. But that kind of career doesn't have the longevity Paul has discovered."

She nodded slowly, her attention riveted to him.

"People get injured and medically discharged. Some people crack under the strain. Some people stay in and then become teachers at the Ranger school. Some move on to desk jobs. And others of us stay in until we make the decision to get out before it's made for us. I know soldiers who get out and work in family businesses, go to college, work for companies, or go into security like me. Working with Lighthouse Security Investigations has given me more training. It allows me to continue doing what I love the most... providing security for those who need it and investigating criminal activity."

"Oh... I understood the security aspect of your job but never really thought about the investigations."

"We're sometimes tasked with investigations from the FBI, local law enforcement, or even the justice department. Our work is... less constrained than government investigations. And whatever we turn up, we hand over to the appropriate law enforcement personnel."

"Well, I'm impressed! I had no idea."

"It's an easy assumption to make when you meet one of us on an assignment like this. What we don't do is security to the stars."

She laughed again, and he realized how quickly he could become addicted to that sound.

"Are you saying I'm not a star?" she teased.

He was quiet for a moment, then said, "Oh, I think you're a star. Absolutely."

Her smile faltered as her gaze never left his face. "This has been an interesting trip, Adam."

He agreed with her spontaneous confession but wasn't entirely sure of her meaning. He nodded slowly but remained silent.

"I've never been around someone in your profession," she admitted.

"If I recall, you thought I was high-handed yesterday morning."

"Yes, I did, but then, you have to admit, you were bossy."

They both laughed, and taking a chance, he stood and held his hand out to her. Her gaze dropped from his eyes down to his hand and back again, and he held his breath. She reached out and placed her hand in his, and he slowly drew her to her feet.

He wanted to kiss her. He desperately wanted to kiss her. Stepping closer, with her hand still enveloped in his, he waited, barely breathing. He was prepared to give her space if she needed it, never wanting her to feel trapped.

She lifted her free hand and placed it on his chest. The touch was so light, yet he felt the heat as though it were a brand on his skin. With her head leaned back, she held his gaze.

They bent toward each other, then halted. The few seconds seemed to stretch into eternity before she lifted slightly on her toes, and he met her half-way. He touched his nose to hers, then nuzzled the side as he twisted his head and sealed his mouth over hers. It was as soft and full as he imagined. When she opened up underneath him, his tongue glided over hers. The taste of sweet wine and desserts blended perfectly to create a unique essence, and he knew in that instant that he would always associate those tastes with her.

He curved one arm around her back, pulling her flush against his chest. Slipping her hand from between them, she let it travel over his shoulder, scraping her fingers lightly along the back of his neck.

He'd enjoyed sexy kisses before but had never once felt as though he wanted to drop to his knees and worship the woman ensnaring him. *How can this be? How can I crave more than just her body so quickly?*

A kiss was all he allowed himself, though. He was still on an assignment and wouldn't give in to the urge to indulge more and possibly compromise

Paul's or her safety. But for now, he gave himself fully to the kiss, including soft nibbles over her lips. He dragged his tongue lazily over hers, memorizing the tastes and textures of her delectable mouth, craving it more than any dessert.

His body was very aware of hers plastered to his front. Soft breasts pressed against the hard muscles of his chest. His erection, trapped behind the zipper of his pants, pressed against her soft belly. He allowed his thoughts to drift to another time and another place when they would be in a similar position without the confines of clothing.

He knew beyond a shadow of a doubt that he wanted to get to know her better. One more day, and they'd be safely back in California. She would no longer be an assignment but would be free to become a woman he wanted to spend time with.

An alarm sounded, and he felt her jump slightly in his arms. He lifted his head to see her flushed and dazed, appearing as moved as he was by their kiss.

She looked to where her purse lay and sighed heavily. "I'm so sorry for the interruption. I set my alarm earlier as a reminder to pack everything this evening since we wouldn't return to the hotel after the morning meeting. And to ensure that I have Paul's notes."

As much as he hated to admit it, she was right to be reminded that they were both there for a job. He inhaled a ragged breath, then let it out slowly. "Thank you, Valerie. Thank you for the dessert. The drinks.

Sharing some of your life with me. And for the kiss. You've made this a memorable couple of days."

Their gazes never wavered, but he could swear he saw questions moving through hers. Hoping to answer them before they grew insurmountable in her mind, he quickly added, "I was serious when I said I wanted to see you again, and I really hope you do, too. Friendship. Running partners. Or a chance to share more than kisses… I want to see you again."

Her kiss-swollen lips curved into a beautiful smile, and her fingers slid to his biceps, digging in slightly. "I'd like that, Adam. I'd like that a lot."

They placed the empty dishes back onto the cart, and he rolled it outside, leaving it in the hall next to her door. She had followed him, and when he turned, she lifted on her toes again, placing her lips near his. Not about to turn down the invitation, he encircled his arms around her, pulled her flush against his body once more, and kissed her in a way that he hoped would let her know how much he was looking forward to being with her as a man and woman, not as part of an assignment.

And if her kiss was anything to go by, she felt the same way.

9

The instant the door closed behind Adam, Valerie peeked through the security hole and waited until he had gone into his room. Closing her eyes, she felt as though she were standing with each foot in a different world.

Retreating to the bathroom, she hastily gathered her hair into a ponytail, locked eyes with her reflection, and inhaled a long, shuddering breath. Then she counted down a full minute to steady her nerves.

Striding back into her room, she grabbed her phone and looked down at the message. Grimacing, she vowed this would be the last time. Then she breathed deeply again and shoved her hand into her briefcase to pull out a thumb drive.

Cautiously, she checked the hallway through the peephole again, finding it still clear. Her hand gently turned the door handle and pulled the door open.

Still seeing no one around, she kept her hand on the door as it shut, allowing it to ease closed with a barely audible click. Holding her breath in anticipation, she didn't hear anyone coming. Nimbly tiptoeing down the hall toward the elevator, she pressed the down button and waited.

Come on... Come on. Impatient, she felt a surge of relief when the elevator arrived, and the doors slid open, revealing no one inside. Stepping in, she moved to the side, pressing one floor down while staying out of sight of anyone who might have stepped into the hall. When the doors slid shut, she let out a sigh. *This sucks. Christ, this sucks.*

One floor down, the elevator stopped, and the doors opened. A man stepped in, his demeanor as polished as his expensive shoes. He turned to face the doors in the elevator rider's universal stance of anonymity. Pressing another button, they began to descend.

She'd watched him get on as she continued to face forward, but the brass walls of the elevator gave a muted reflection. She noted his black hair was neatly trimmed and styled into place with gel. He wore a dark suit, undoubtedly expensive. A white dress shirt and navy tie made him look like almost any other young professional in the DC area. His voice was tinged with a slight Hispanic accent.

"Any problems?" he asked, still not looking at her.

Her response was instantaneous. "No, no problems at all."

"You and the professor have a companion on this trip."

Swallowing deeply, she spoke in measured tones. "Yes. I informed you of the hotel location change as soon as possible. I was unaware of what the institute had planned."

"Do you have the information we require?"

She felt what little bravado she'd managed to corral slipping away. "Yes. Do you have the money?"

His lips curved into a smile, and a gold cap glistened on one of his incisors. "Of course."

He reached his hand into his jacket's inside pocket, pulled out an envelope, and handed it to her.

She forced her fingers not to shake as she took it from him, and again, with more bravado than she felt, she looked inside and flipped through the money. Realizing too late that she should have brought her purse with her, she folded the envelope as best she could and shoved it into the front of her pants pocket.

Reaching into the other pocket, she wrapped her fingers around the thumb drive. Blowing out a breath that sounded more ragged than she'd wanted it to, she pulled it out and handed it to him.

"You know, there's very little on there that you couldn't have gotten from going through his works and studies. I mean, the institutes have the same information."

The man scoffed, his eyes narrowing. "Ah, academics," he drawled. "I know it well. Always drowning in a sea of papers and data. You doing the legwork is what makes this relationship so valuable." He grinned again, flashing his gold-capped tooth. It felt like a wink, letting her know she was out of her depths in this clandestine world.

The elevator had descended to the lobby level. The doors parted, and he stepped off with a grace that belied his predatory nature. He walked away without so much as a glance, allowing the doors to slide shut.

She exhaled deeply as if releasing a breath she'd been holding for years. Then she steeled her spine and hit the button for her floor. Suddenly, the doors opened again, and several men stepped on. They'd obviously spent too long at the bar as the smell of liquor permeated the elevator immediately. Not willing to be the only woman alone with the inebriated men, she darted through the doors and into the lobby, ignoring their catcalls and invitations.

She spied her contact walking over to a man, neither looking her way. Not wanting to be seen while waiting for another elevator, she darted behind a tall potted plant. She recognized the game she was playing was risky. *But it's no game.* Remaining still, she waited for them to leave. The taller, older man, dressed similarly to her contact, turned her way, and while she remained hidden, he was completely visible to her. Unable to drag her gaze away, her heartbeat pounded against her ribs. *This* man oozed danger.

Her contact handed the thumb drive to him, and they continued to talk for a moment. Then he turned and walked briskly out the door with an air of status and his back ramrod straight. Her contact followed soon after, and it wasn't until they were out of sight that she felt she could take a breath.

The elevator doors opened, and she hurried inside. Once on her floor, her shoulders slumped in relief at not seeing any activity in the hall.

With soft, hurried steps, she quickly tiptoed back to her room. Holding her breath as she stood at her door, her eyes flipped nervously toward Adam's door. She pressed her key card against the entry pad, wincing as the tiny beep seemed loud in the silence of the hallway. Clutching the handle, she pressed down gently, then pushed the door open slowly and slipped inside. Holding the inside doorknob, she allowed it to close softly.

Turning, she leaned her back against the metal door. The steel barrier felt as thin as paper, barely keeping her safe from the dangers outside. She released a long but silent breath, her heart drumming a frantic rhythm. Once again, moving with haste but staying as quiet as possible, she grabbed her phone. Her fingertips glided over the digital keyboard as she composed a terse text and hit send.

Done.

She removed the envelope filled with cash from her pocket and shoved it into her purse. Finally alone and unobserved, she sat on the edge of the bed. Her body fell back, hitting the mattress with a soft thud. *How long can I keep this up?* She stared at the ceiling, its blank expanse offering no respite.

10

Adam stared at the screen on his tablet, disbelief flooding him. LSIWC was able to monitor the cameras in the hotel. Still, he'd also placed a hidden security camera in the hallway to ensure he would be alerted if anyone tried to enter Valerie's or Paul's rooms while they were gone.

When he returned to his room, his mind was stuck on the memory of the kiss he'd just shared with Valerie and the tantalizing possibilities of the plans he was making for when they returned to California. When he heard the soft alarm, he jerked back to the present. The chime alerted him to her door opening, and he first went to the peephole, expecting to see her placing something else on the room service cart to be taken away.

Opening his tablet, he watched the security feed, seeing her hurry down the hall. His instincts, honed from years in covert operations, screamed that something was off. Her movements weren't natural, indicating an attempt at subterfuge.

She entered the elevator. *Where the fuck is she going?* He called the compound, getting ahold of Leo, who had the night shift. "I need visual and audio on elevator two in the hotel ASAP."

No sooner had he slipped out of his room to navigate the carpeted hallway in case Valerie was in trouble did Leo send the elevator security feed to his tablet. He stood, staring at the screen, shock reverberating as he watched and listened to the conversation. *She accepted money from the man... she gave him information. What the fuck?*

Not used to giving into emotion on the job, a fury he hadn't felt in years ignited within him. His fingers gripped the tablet so hard it was a wonder it didn't crack. Realizing she was coming back up on the elevator, he darted into the stairwell and continued to watch, but she didn't return. He called Leo again. "Goddammit, I lost her."

It didn't take Leo long to say, "She got off in the lobby."

"I'll go—"

"No, she's getting back on the elevator," Leo said. "Elevator one." As he waited, Leo added, "I don't have a fuckin' clue what she was doing, but you'll want to see the feed. I'll send it. And I'm working on an ID of both men."

"Both men? She met with someone else?" His voice betrayed his incredulity.

"No. But the man she met in the elevator had a rendezvous with someone else. You watch the feed, and we'll get IDs."

His mind raced through possibilities as he watched Valerie step off the elevator and hasten down the hall. His gaze stayed trained on his tablet, seeing her carefully open the door to her room and let herself in.

He stealthily slipped down the hall and entered his room in silence. As soon as he was there, he watched the feed from the security cameras in the lobby. His eyes immediately snagged on the two men talking and then passing something between them, but when he spied Valerie hiding behind a plant, he nearly lost it. "You gotta be fuckin' kidding me."

"I take it you've watched it," Leo said. "If it weren't so fucked up with those men, I'd think it was funny. But Jeb and Ian are with me tonight, working on the IDs. We should have something soon… what? Oh, hang on. We've got a hit."

Adam swiped his hand down his face and waited. Each second found his patience waning and his anger rising.

"Arturo Perez is the man in the elevator. From Colombia, but now a graduate student at George Washington University. Goes by Art. No record. The older man in the lobby is Joseph Perez," Leo said. "He's in the country officially as a visitor from Colombia, having checked in with the Colombian embassy. He's been in the country for three days. Due to leave tomorrow."

"Anything else on him?"

"Art headed back out. Caught a taxi. Joseph left soon after, but a driver picked him up. More notes are coming your way. I'm checking with Carson right now."

As the visual of the man came across his tablet, he read the notes Jeb included. It appeared that while it had been suspected that Joseph Perez worked for the Colombian cartel that flirted with bringing the mighty Sinoloan cartel into his country, he'd never been officially labeled. Just a *fucking person of interest.* And Valerie was secretly passing information to them. Pain filled him, then slowly leaked out as rage replaced the void. Drugs. He could have forgiven almost anything but her dealing with drugs.

Jeb got on the call. "We got in touch with Carson, and you're not going to like this, man, but he says to stand down. You stay there and finish your assignment, and we'll alert Landon of the concerns."

Landon Summers was their liaison with the FBI. Landon often skirted on the fringes of the governmental restraints placed on him, making him a friend of the Keepers and a worthy accomplice.

Adam let out a long, slow breath, his emotions churning in his gut. He understood what Jeb was saying… Joseph Perez was fucking untouchable. Carson had given him an order. *Let it go, and just continue the mission as assigned.*

Standing in his room, he thought of the next day spent with Paul and Valerie. He had no problem escorting them back to California, but he'd be damned if he was going to let her get away with thinking he was interested in her.

With grim resolve, he strode to her door and took out his master key card designed to unlock any door. Pushing it open, he slipped inside. Valerie sat on the edge of the bed, still in the clothes she'd worn earlier, a portrait of innocence. She looked up in fright, eyes wide, as she jumped to her feet, her hand clapping to her chest.

"Adam? Oh my God, you scared me! Did you forget something? Wait a minute, how did you get in?"

At that moment, Adam knew there was no going back. No matter what happened, their relationship had irrevocably changed even before it had a chance to grow into something more. "Does Paul know?" The three words were growled, almost unintelligible.

Her chin jerked downward slightly. "Does he know what? About us? Of course not!"

"Oh no. I'm not talking about us. There is no *us.*"

Now, her whole body jerked as though slapped, but he continued. "I thought there could've been. I hoped there was. But that was until you took a little stroll down the hall and into the elevator."

Her eyes widened even more, and the gasp flew from her lips. "Wha... how did you... how do...?"

"I'll ask the questions. How long have you been a

traitor? Selling the professor's research and knowledge to the cartels? How much did you get paid? And maybe more importantly, are you just a heartless bitch, or do they have something on you? I swear to God, I hope they have something on you because at least that would help me understand why you're doing what you're doing."

Her face paled, and her mouth hung open as though all the oxygen in the room had fled. Shaking her head rapidly, she finally sucked in air but remained ghostly white. "You have no idea what you're talking about," she barely whispered, her voice shaking with emotion.

"I can't believe you're stupid enough not to realize that elevators have cameras and microphones."

Her chin lifted as she held her body rigid, her arms wrapped tightly around her waist, warding off his verbal blows. Her gaze never left his eyes. "Don't assume what I do or don't know."

He had to admit he was surprised. He thought she would dissolve into tears, but her spine of steel would've been a turn-on if he wasn't so pissed at her betrayal.

Her eyes narrowed as her hands shifted to land on her hips. "I can't believe you barged in here… no, not barged… you snuck in, invading my privacy to sling accusations. Guilty before even having a chance to prove innocence, right?"

"This is not a trial, Valerie. This is just me knowing what I saw and what I heard."

"And I'll say it again... you have no idea what you're talking about."

"Then maybe we'll just go across the hall and knock on the door. Perhaps Paul would like to know what's happening with his research. Or maybe he's in on it too—"

"Stop it! He doesn't know anything that's going on. And if you keep this up, you'll ruin everything."

"Oh yeah, I can see that. I might end up ruining the wad of cash you've grown used to collecting. Do you always meet with Art Perez? Or do you sometimes get to hand over the goods directly to his uncle Joseph? You know, the one who's on a suspected cartel watch list but manages to use his pull at the embassy to move around freely." He scoffed as her eyes widened even more. "Maybe instead of Paul, I'll just make a call to one of my friends at the FBI. Let you explain what's going on to them."

The air between them was thick with tension, filled with accusations and secrets. His words hung heavy in the room.

Her chest heaved, and her hazel eyes spit fire, giving evidence to her emotions. "You're sabotaging everything! Dammit, Adam, you leave me no choice." She whirled and stalked to her briefcase, digging into the bottom.

Uncertain if she was pulling a weapon on him, his muscles tightened, and his hand inched toward the gun concealed at the small of his back. He would use it if he had to, but hated the idea of aiming it toward her.

His surprise continued when she stepped away again and flung a small leather wallet onto the bed. Unease moved through him, but her actions indicated she wanted him to see what was in the case. Moving cautiously, he reached down and picked up the slender wallet. Flipping it open, he saw a card with a name and a phone number.

He stared at the name. Agent Robin Sellers. DEA.

His gaze jumped back to Valerie's face as confusion warred with the anger in him. "What the hell is this?"

"She's my handler. My contact." Her voice was hard, but she was unable to mask her body's visible shaking.

His gut now told him that whatever she was doing, she was not the hardened criminal he thought. No longer trusting his instincts, he kept his hard stare on her. "What do you mean, your handler?"

"Oh, come now, Adam. I'm sure you're familiar with assets. Well, I'm hers. I'm an undercover informant for the DEA."

His years of training were the only thing that kept him standing. He forced his knees to lock as his gaze darted between the card in his hand and the furious woman in front of him. His mind raced to catch up with her revelation. Thoughts slammed into him from all sides, but before he could give voice to any of them, Valerie was ready for a fight.

"You say anything to Paul... you call anyone and tell them what's going on, then you could blow my cover and put my life on the line. You might hate me right now, but I don't think you want me dead." Her voice hitched, but she swallowed, regaining control of herself.

He opened his mouth, but she wasn't finished.

"I was recruited four years ago after one of our trips to Colombia. That was the trip where we were blindfolded and taken close to one of the cartel's compounds. DEA and the Colombian counterpart took notice. Agent Sellers contacted me once I got back to the States. Everything was kept very secret, but she and her team wanted to know where we'd been taken and what we'd seen. They were uncertain of Paul simply because he is Colombian-born, but I knew they could trust him. It didn't matter... they decided to work with me alone. My real job *is* working with Paul. My job as his assistant, the research I help with, everything from the university, and my relationship with him and his wife... that is *not* fake. But I also have a relationship with the DEA and have been willing to do what I could to help. Beyond that, you are *not* on a need-to-know basis."

He'd never felt so stunned. A heavy sigh left his lips. "I didn't realize—"

"No shit. But you sure as hell came in here slinging accusations."

"I'm sorry, Valerie." His conscience weighed heavily. "But you have to admit that it looked—"

"To hell with what it looked like, Adam." She threw her hands into the air. "You know what? It doesn't even matter. We shared being in each other's space for two days and a couple of great kisses. Other than that, we are nothing."

"You know that's not true."

"I know I hoped we were going to be something." She scoffed. "I totally get that you haven't known me long enough to trust me. I totally understand that we haven't built anything beyond the superficial. But I can also tell you, I've got absolutely no fucking desire to spend any more time in your presence than I have to. So we'll go back to California tomorrow. You return to your life. I'll return to mine. And other than that? Nada!"

She was pissed, but he needed her to understand the situation from his point of view. He stepped closer, lifting his hands toward her. "Let me make this right—"

She backed up and shook her head. "Oh no, Adam. No way."

"Look, I really am fucking sorry about how I came in here. You're right. I was slinging accusations, and I shouldn't have done that." Deciding to come completely clean, he added, "I have a small camera on the hallway, just to make sure that an alarm goes off if the doors open unexpectedly. So I knew when you left. When I saw that you'd stepped onto the elevator, I had my people check the elevator security feed because I wanted you safe."

She rolled her eyes, and he stepped forward again.

"I'm telling you the truth. It was because I was worried. I didn't know what was happening, but I was afraid for you."

"Yeah, your words when you came in here certainly showed me how much you care. Jesus, stick it on a Hallmark card because I do *not* believe you."

"Valerie, now that I know this, it makes sense. But it makes me worry much more about you, knowing you're putting yourself in danger."

"Get out."

He jerked slightly, then tried again. "Let's talk about this. I want to help."

"Get. Out," she repeated, her body still trembling. "If I didn't have to see you again, that would be fine by me. Unfortunately, we have to be in each other's presence tomorrow until we get back to California. As unpleasant as that will be for both of us, I'm sure we can deal. But other than that, Adam, we have nothing to say to each other. Now, the fact that you've alerted the people you work with could've put me in jeopardy. So thank God it's over and done with, and no one is the wiser. I assure you, I'll report to Robin so that she's aware of the breach." Lifting her hand to point toward the door, she reiterated, "Get out of my room."

As much as he hated leaving, he knew he had no choice. Sighing heavily, he handed the small leather case back to her. She didn't reach for it, so he leaned over and placed it on the bed. Turning, he walked to the door, then stopped. Looking over his shoulder, he said, "You were the first woman I'd met who I wanted to spend more time with and get to know. What I did, I did because I was concerned. What I said here, I should never have said. For that, I am truly sorry, Valerie. You have no idea how much I regret that."

Her gaze never wavered, but he could see her body shake harder, probably with the combination of adrenaline, fear, and anger. He wanted nothing more than to pull her into his arms, hold her close, and promise that he would never let anything harm her—even himself.

But right now, he did the only thing he could do. He walked away.

11

A week later, Adam's feet pounded up the trail along the ridge, part of the mass of acres that Carson owned near the compound. Used for training, today Adam was not running in solitude. The race up the mountain was a herculean effort on Adam's part, but it was more from trying to outrun the demons in his head and not beat any of the other Keepers.

Reaching the top, he discovered he wasn't the first but wasn't the last. Within a few minutes, the others seemed to surround him as they sat in the shade, drinking water and resting before they began their descent.

"Are you going to tell us what the hell is going on?" Hop asked.

Adam looked over to see who Hop was speaking to, only mildly surprised to see everyone's gaze on him.

"You've been as pissed as a hornet whose nest got swatted down," Hop continued.

"There's no need to deny it," Natalie said. "We've all noticed but decided to see if you could work things out yourself."

Dolby, Rick, and Poole all laughed, shaking their heads. They'd certainly been poked fun at when tied up in knots about a woman. As much as Adam hated talking about himself, he figured the least he could do was share a little, considering they had all been aware of what happened during the last dance with Valerie. *Well, not aware of everything.*

"Hell, I don't suppose it makes any sense not to fill in the gaps of what happened in DC." He winced, hating to expose emotions. But the other Keepers always had his back, just like he had theirs. And it didn't seem right not to be honest with them, even if it flung him way out of his comfort zone.

"I enjoyed the time I spent with Dr. Mendez and Valerie Clemens." He swallowed as an image of her filled his mind, much like it had for a week. "Especially Valerie."

Abbie, Rick's wife, nodded. "I had a feeling it was something like that."

Leo looked at Natalie and said, "Okay, fine. I owe you."

Brows lowered, Adam stared until Natalie explained.

"Leo said he didn't think you'd fall for anyone on

a mission. But I told him it's something that happens to all Keepers."

"Not to me!" Jeb retorted. "You'll see, I'll be the one to hold out. I'll break the crazy streak you all have going on."

The others hid their smiles as they turned back to Adam. He sighed, downing the last of his water as if it could extinguish the smoldering regret in his gut. Sitting with his knees bent and his forearms resting on them, he looked at the others. "By the second night, we... well, um... we made plans to see each other when we returned to California."

"And then...?" Bennett asked, his voice laced with empathy and his eyes filled with understanding.

Adam laughed cynically, shaking his head in an unsuccessful attempt to dispel the memories. "You all know the rest. I watched the security footage from the elevator and the info on the man she met with." His eyes met Carson's, and a dull ache settled in his chest. "You said to stick to my assignment, and I did. Stayed away from Joseph Perez." His jaws hurt from gritting his teeth so hard. "But fucking hell, I lost control with Valerie and acted rashly."

"Adam, I can't imagine that," said Abbie. "You're always so cautious in your actions."

"Yeah, well, I shot that trait to shit." Swiping his hand over his face, he said, "I went into her room and accused her of everything I thought she was doing. Fuck, I might as well have hurled stones. And then told her that I couldn't believe that I'd planned on getting to know her more—"

"Ouch." Ian winced.

"You got that right," Dolby said, his face scrunched as though in pain. "Man, it's hard to come back from that."

Rolling his eyes, Adam threw his hand up in defeat. "Great. More uplifting news. Keep it coming."

"Sorry," Dolby muttered.

Adam waved it off. Shaking his head, he let out a long sigh. "No worries, man. It's all on me. Squarely on my fucking shoulders."

"So when she explained, what happened?" This came from Abbie, her voice tinged with the sweet hope that characterized her.

"I was shocked at first. Disoriented. Hell, it didn't seem real. Then as it sank in, I apologized. But she wasn't having it. She was more than pissed and kicked me out. The following morning, she was curt, barely speaking to me. Her interaction with Dr. Mendez was as always, but to me… she froze me out. Every time I tried to get her alone to apologize again, she managed to always be around someone. I finally figured I'd have a chance on the flight since I was sure Dr. Mendez would sleep."

"I take it that didn't work?" Carson asked.

Sighing heavily, he shook his head. "She put on earphones and refused to look at me for the duration of the flight. Once we were back, she immediately climbed into her car to take Dr. Mendez home. I kept trying to take her to the side and get her to talk to me. I've even sent a multitude of texts like some fucking teenager. Nothing. So that's that. I fucked up."

Adam spread his hands wide, his shoulders sagging as he exhaled. "What really sucks is that I not only can't talk to her, but it's the knowledge that the DEA is using her. An *informant*." He glanced toward Carson. "I checked on Agent Robin Sellers. Seems she's climbing up in the ranks. Shitty for her to use someone like Valerie to do her dirty work, though." He leaned his head back against the rough trunk of a tree.

"She's in danger as an informant," Leo said. "All the risk and no protection if something goes sideways."

Adam's eyes flashed. "I wondered why Valerie would have agreed to inform on the cartels to the DEA."

"Maybe she just has a strong moral compass," Abbie added, the hopeful specter still in her eyes.

"You're more right than you think, but it's still personal," Adam explained, barely holding in his emotions. "I didn't do a lot of digging into her. It didn't seem right. But what I easily learned was that her dad was a police officer. He was killed when she was in high school. It was a drug bust gone wrong."

"Shit..." The breathed curses were heard from most of the other Keepers.

"So this Agent Sellers is using Valerie's painful past to get information," Ian growled.

Carson stood on a flat boulder, looking over at his crew before his gaze settled on Adam. "Sometimes an agent has to cut an informant loose... especially if the right coercion is applied."

Adam stared at the unspoken question in Carson's eyes. Nodding slowly, he said, "Yeah. Agreed." The pressure on his chest eased just the barest amount, knowing he might not be able to change the past, but he could keep Valerie from being used more in the future.

Hauling himself to his feet, he met the gaze of his friends. "So... I've been a real shit this past week... I'm sorry."

"You don't owe us anything, man," Bennett said, shaking his head. "But you owe yourself something."

He cast his gaze around at the other Keepers, seeing them nod. "You're going to tell me to keep trying, but I won't harass her. She has a right to cut me out, and I have to accept that, no matter how much it shits me to do so."

Natalie stood and stretched. "Look, Adam, I'll be the first to agree that she can do or feel however she wants. And no way would I think it would be right for you to harass her. But who knows? Hell, not even I can stay pissed forever, right, babe?"

Leo chuckled as he stood and wrapped his arms around her, then looked at Adam. "No one can hold a grudge like my woman, and even she forgives me when I'm a jackass."

They all stood and began the run back down the mountain trail. This time, he didn't feel the hounds of hell were chasing him. His pace slowed as he let his mind wander along a mental path centered on Valerie. Soon, Poole came up beside him. The two ran in silence for several minutes.

He knew his friend would wait for him to give more. "She's a smart, beautiful, and caring woman. She genuinely likes Dr. Mendez and has a relationship with him and his wife that... well, on the day we flew back, Dr. Mendez admitted to me that he and his wife consider her to be the daughter they never had."

"And you fell."

His head swung around so hard he almost stumbled. Righting himself, he let Poole's words settle. "I wouldn't go that far, but I couldn't believe how quickly I felt that she was someone I really wanted to get to know better."

"Then I wish you luck, man. No one deserves that more than you." With that, Poole jogged ahead, leaving Adam to run back in solitude with only his tumultuous thoughts for company.

Adam leaned back in his chair after scraping the last of the apple pie from his plate. "Dinner was real good, Mom. Thanks."

"I agree, Martha," his dad said, leaning over to kiss her cheek. "Good as always, and your apple pie rivals my grandmother's cooking."

Adam smiled at his parents' obvious love. He carried his plate to the sink and began to wash. They fell into the old habit of him washing, his dad drying, and his mom putting away the leftovers.

His mom leaned close and whispered, "I'm wrapping the apple pie for you to take with you."

"I heard that," his dad complained.

"I'll fix another one for you," she promised. Turning back to Adam, she said, "We didn't ask about your trip to DC. I haven't been there in many years."

"It was fine. Just business."

"Oh, so you didn't get to enjoy anything?" Her voice held disappointment.

He knew she was referring to sightseeing, but all he could think about was the kiss with Valerie that he'd more than enjoyed. He'd continued to remember that kiss even though she'd never responded to any of his texts. *Hard to forget perfection.*

Realizing his parents continued to stare, waiting for a reply, he shook his head. "Nah. It was just work, and I didn't get to see any of the sights."

His dad turned to his mom and said, "That's where we should go for our next vacation. Take a trip to Washington, DC, and check out all the museums."

Their conversation centered on the idea of another vacation, and the last thing Adam wanted to do was replay his disastrous trip. Walking into the living room, he stepped over to the fireplace mantel and perused the familiar photographs proudly framed and displayed. He and his sister when they were kids. He in his Army uniform. The whole family at the beach many years ago. He stared at his sister's senior picture and sighed as his parents entered the room.

"Well, I need to head home. Charlie will wonder where his dinner is."

His mom laughed as she handed the pie plate to him. He kissed her cheek while accepting her warm hug. "Love you, darling."

"Love you, too, Mom."

After shaking hands with his dad, he waved goodbye and carried his apple pie goodness out to his SUV. It only took twenty minutes for him to get home, but he thought of Valerie the whole way. He had a feeling that he'd never think of the nation's capital in the same way again.

12

Valerie walked along the campus sidewalk, her mind churning with turmoil. Since returning from Washington, DC, a few weeks ago, her emotions had run the gamut from angry, sad, frustrated, fearful, livid, and heartbroken. She felt like a hormonal teenager churning through emotions faster than finding their next favorite song to listen to.

Finally, she stopped outside the old, familiar building housing her and Paul's office and stopped. Her heart felt so heavy she wondered how she could even walk up the stairs. *How had everything gone perfectly right so quickly and then exploded into dust?*

In the last couple of weeks, she'd tried to convince herself that she'd only been interested in a pair of broad shoulders, great body, thick black hair, and piercing blue eyes. But at night, alone in bed, she knew it was more than that. Somehow, in the few days she was with Adam, she felt her heart open to the possibility of something more. Something real.

She wished she could hold on to her righteous indignation. *After all, he accused me without having all the facts!*

But when she considered who he was, his background, and his job, she knew what he discovered would have thrown him. *If only we'd had more time to get to know each other. If only we'd had a chance to build a more solid relationship.* But wishful thinking didn't change anything.

For several days after they'd returned from California, Adam had texted her numerous times. He apologized. He sought her forgiveness. He wanted to have a chance to talk. But just like the night in the hotel, she'd refused. But not because she didn't care. There was no way to have him in her life right now. It was too difficult.

Agent Sellers had emphasized how much danger she would be in if anyone else found out she was passing information to the DEA. *"Don't think the cartels won't go after you, anyone you love, or even Dr. Mendez."*

So as frustrated as Valerie was about how she and Adam parted, her hands were tied. Sighing heavily, she thought of her dad. It'd been almost fourteen years since he'd been killed, but at times of stress, she'd still talk to him as though he was still with her. *"Oh, Daddy, I wish you were here to tell me what to do. When I started this, I thought you would've been so proud of me. But now? I have no idea what I'm doing."*

Her phone vibrated inside her purse. Pulling the phone out, she was surprised to see who was calling. "Yes?"

"You must have some very powerful friends in high places," Robin said, each word whiplash sharp. She'd always spoken to Valerie with a voice that perfectly blended professionalism and friendliness unless she needed to make a particular point. Right now, curt had taken over any former pleasantness.

"I don't know what you're talking about. What's going on?"

"I was called into my supervisor's office this morning. I was told that I was no longer, under any circumstances, to use you as an asset."

Valerie sucked in sharply as her body jerked. "I don't understand."

"I certainly don't understand, either! But there it is."

Valerie had no idea how to respond, so she remained quiet.

Robin sighed heavily, then added, "I know I explained the dangers to you when I first approached you. And, of course, in this business, there are always risks. Your father knew that."

Valerie winced. She'd hated the first time Robin had mentioned her father. She hadn't been so naive that she didn't realize Robin was using that heartache to make Valerie feel like she was avenging her dad by giving evidence she discovered about the cartels over to the agent. *Not that there was ever much evidence I had to turn over!*

But now, hearing Robin's words, they didn't carry the same punch as they had before. *Dad would never have wanted me to take risks.*

"Anyway," Robin continued, her voice taking on the tenor of someone now disinterested. "We won't have any more contact with each other." Another little sigh was heard over the phone, and then, in a gentler voice, Robin said, "For what it's worth, I'm sorry, Valerie. But I thank you for everything you've done and wish you well."

Before Valerie had a chance to respond, the call was disconnected. Her legs gave out, leached of energy, and she plopped down on a bench nearby. Her already chaotic mind was filled with the new information. Ease of freedom filled her as she readily acknowledged that she'd begun to hate the fear that plagued her every time she passed along information. And on the trip to Washington, DC, the level of risk had increased exponentially by having to come almost face-to-face with someone from the cartel.

Her brother would be livid if he knew what she was doing. And in her heart, she was certain her father would tell her to stop. And now, with someone else's intervention, that had happened. *But who? Who got to someone in the DEA and called a stop to me being an informant?* No one knew but Adam. She inhaled sharply again, almost choking on the gasp. He was the only person who could've possibly had the connections to reach above Robin to call a halt to her being used as an asset.

Her brain seemed to be a step behind as she slogged through the multitude of thoughts. With an upcoming trip to Colombia, she was now off the hook for trying to gain any information on the cartels. Her body felt almost weak with the reprieve. *And Adam is responsible.*

She had no idea if that realization made her delirious with relief or pissed at his continued high-handedness. But in the crazy mix of those two emotions, she realized another emotion stood out most of all. Grief from knowing he wasn't in her life and wishing he was.

Valerie had always loved her trips with Paul, no matter where they went, but right now, as they revisited Colombia, she loved the time with his family. Arriving in the country a day earlier than needed, they had enjoyed the hospitality of Paul's relatives on a small farm outside of the capital. When they visited his cousins, they were always greeted warmly and treated as honored guests. It was here, with the people eking out a living in difficult circumstances yet sharing everything they had, where she had felt their kinship in every warm embrace.

They'd sat around the table eating farm-fresh

food after one of Paul's nieces taught Valerie how to make empanadas, frijoles rojos, and coconut rice, and the conversations centered around family. Once more, it made her realize how much she missed those times when her father was alive and her home in California included all her family sitting around the table, much like this.

That night, sharing a room with one of Paul's nieces, she lay in a small bed with a thin mattress and relished the fresh breeze through the window. Allowing her mind to roam, she was here, free to do the job she loved and meet people she cared about without the worry and stress of what Robin would want her to do. And Adam had made that possible. She quietly reached for her phone and scrolled back through some of Adam's apology texts. They had stopped coming, and she'd discovered she missed them. Then the messages started again just before she left for Colombia.

She smiled, remembering the evening in the hotel room when they spent a long time getting to know each other. She remembered feeling so comfortable with him… thinking how easy it was to talk to him. Thinking of their kiss. *Until…*

She sighed, thinking of the ugly scene in her hotel room. *Is it possible to put that behind us?*

Her fingers hovered over the keys as she was struck with a sudden urge and decided she no longer wanted to avoid all communication. She typed, **In Colombia with Paul for work. With his family**

now. The message was simple, and she grimaced as she eyed the text. *That's dumb.* Her finger moved to delete, but before she chickened out, she hit send instead. Her body tightened, but then she let out a long breath. *It doesn't matter—*

The three dots appeared and blinked almost immediately in the chat window. Her chest tightened again, this time in anticipation. Then the dots disappeared. Then reappeared. That occurred three times, and she wondered if he really was typing a text, didn't know what to say, or if her mind was playing tricks on her.

Stay safe. Let me know how you are.

She almost laughed aloud. After the "please forgive me," "I'm sorry I was such an ass," and "I'd really like to see you again to say I'm sorry in person" texts he'd sent, this appeared very *safe.* He probably wondered if it was a joke. Deciding to see if he really was there, she typed, **Trip kicks into high gear tomorrow. Lectures and field visits.**

Three dots appeared again, and she pushed herself to a sitting position in bed, staring at her screen.

How are you traveling?

Chewing on her bottom lip, she continued the thread. **By helicopter, courtesy of the univ and by Jeep when in the agriculture fields.**

Do you have security with you?

Are you serious? On a shoestring budget? We

don't have RAND money to spend on big bodyguards.

I could come there. On my own. Free. Like a vacation for me.

A tiny giggle threatened to slip out, and she pressed her lips together to remain quiet so that she didn't wake up Paul's niece sleeping soundly in the other small bed.

A vacation of lectures you don't care about and trips to study crop fields. Hmm. Doesn't sound like a vacation.

The three dots appeared and disappeared a few times again, and she held her breath as she waited. This was worse than being a teenager. Finally, a text appeared, and her stomach flip-flopped.

Anywhere close to you would be a vacation.

Letting out a long, slow breath, her eyes remained glued to the luminous screen. *Wow.* His text reverberated throughout the room before settling deep inside. Her fingers quivered as they hovered over the keyboard as if her whole body sensed the gravity of her response.

Filled with the idea that what she was doing could be monumental… a pivotal moment in her life, she slowly typed. Each keystroke echoed inside her heart. **You asked for forgiveness. It's given.** The instant she pressed Send, she felt an invisible weight lift from her chest. He had been angry and acted precipitously, but the situation was bizarre. And their connection had been so new, having only just begun sharing about themselves.

To hold on to her anger would imprison her as much as him. In light of the number of times he'd reached out to her, no matter how he would respond, letting go of the negative felt like an act of grace toward both of them. She willed her gaze to move from the screen but was entrapped in the desire to see his response.

Those words mean a lot to me. I should never have made those assumptions. You were so brave.

It's over now. I was relieved of those *duties*. Funny... someone with pull put a stop to it.

If I'm the guilty one, will you stop talking to me again?

This time, a little snort escaped. **No. It's all good. But it is late, and I've got a busy day tomorrow.**

Thank you, Valerie. Really... thank you for your forgiveness and for talking to me. Sleep well and stay safe.

Good night. Now, sliding back down underneath the covers, sleep was hard to find, considering her mind dwelled on the gorgeous man who hadn't left her thoughts in the weeks since they'd met, even after she'd walked away and slammed the proverbial door. Now, he'd firmly taken an honored place at the front and center of her thoughts.

A few nights later, Adam sat in the dim light of his room, his eyes focused intently on his phone's glowing screen. **Will you meet me in Mexico at the end of your week?** Adam looked down at the message he'd typed and sucked in a breath. The words felt like a desperate gamble and a calculated risk all at once.

His thumb hovered over the Send button. He dragged his tongue over his bottom lip before he let out a long hissing breath and sent the message.

He and Valerie had spent the past several nights texting long into the night. After weeks of silence, when she'd finally sent her first message, his heart had leaped against his rib cage, and he feared what her words might be. When she had forgiven his rash behavior in DC, his heart had leaped again, but this time with relief soaring through his body.

They had continued to text, and he found her as easy to converse with as he had when they'd had dessert in her room before everything went to hell. He'd never engaged in digital conversations before, but with her, the manner wasn't tedious. They had swapped stories of what they were working on, and she included a few of her misadventures. Once again, he felt they were on the brink of something special and decided he didn't want to waste any more time.

He'd asked Carson about taking a couple of vacation days. Carson had just smirked and said, "Anytime. You know that."

And now, he waited to see what her response

would be. Would she think it was too soon? The three dots appeared on the screen, and he held his breath. *How the hell did I become a man who stared at the dancing dots as though my life depended on it?* A snort slipped out at the simple answer...*Since I met Valerie.*

Mexico?

He jerked at her almost immediate response, nearly dropping his phone. Typing as quickly as his fingers could manage while his heart now beat like a fuckin' teenage boy trying to ask a girl to homecoming, he hurried as though she might disappear.

I want to see you. Just a chance to spend time together. As soon as he hit Send, he realized he wasn't being clear. Before she had a chance to refuse, he quickly tapped out another text. **Separate rooms. No pressure. Just a vacation.**

For a long moment, there was no response—not even the three dots. Sweat formed on his brow. *Jesus, how do teenagers do this?* Finally, he let out a long sigh. *She's not going to answer.*

Suddenly, her text appeared. **I would have to change my flight plans. But yeah, sounds nice.**

Relief washed over him, although he would have felt more secure with a little more excitement from her. *It's okay... she said yes, and I sprang this on her with no preamble.* **Great. I'll fly down on your last workday and have rooms for us at the Vallarta resort.**

After a moment, she finally replied. **I just looked up the resort. Omg! It's right on the beach!**

Grinning, he breathed a sigh of relief at her renewed enthusiasm, even if it was over the beach and resort. **It'll be a chance to relax and get to know each other better.**

I'd like that. After this hectic trip, a chance to have a fruity drink on the beach with you sounds perfect.

With me... she said being there with me... An extraordinary sense of lightness swept over him. They continued to text more, sharing their day and making plans. By the time they stopped texting, Adam lay back in bed and felt the weight he'd carried on his chest for a couple of weeks finally lifted. Now, he just had to count down the next couple of days until he could see her again.

13

The National University of Colombia hosted Valerie and Paul's trip, and she'd worked with them to create the itinerary. As usual, she had packed a lot into their week at Paul's insistence.

They'd begun their weeklong professional stay by lecturing at the main campus of the university, one of Latin America's highest-ranking agriculture science programs. Then they'd spent the next six days traveling by helicopter, courtesy of the Colombian Secretary of Agriculture. At each stop, they'd presented a lecture at other campuses, including Medellín, Tunja, and Bucaramanga.

After the morning lectures, they would spend the afternoon traveling by Jeep to multiple agricultural areas to test plants and soil. She and Paul worked with a few other Colombian University students on small, privately owned farms and large government-owned fields. They analyzed fields growing coffee, tobacco, corn, sugarcane, cocoa beans, and vegetables. Now, she regretted trying to visit so many places in one week.

The helicopter pilot would point out the interesting sights as they flew low over the green hills, valleys, and villages. Occasionally, Valerie would peer down and wonder if the cartels owned the coca plants below. She snorted. Not surprisingly, none had been pointed out.

And each night, she would read Adam's texts in her hotel room with a smile. She hated to anticipate them in case they stopped coming, but so far, each night, he greeted her first, and then they chatted about their days. And now that they planned a weekend excursion to Mexico, she counted the hours until she could see him again.

Valerie cast a surreptitious glance at Paul, noticing the ashen hue of his skin and the sheen of perspiration glistening on his brow. *We're trying to do too much.* Barrancabermeja was their last university lecture stop, and as they completed the presentation, she was ready for an afternoon nap in the hotel and then packing for their departure tomorrow morning.

"Dr. Mendez and Ms. Clemens."

She looked up as a tall man wearing a dark suit and sporting a wide smile walked to the front to meet them.

"How wonderful to finally be able to meet you. I am Sebastian Cortes, the Assistant Secretary of Agriculture."

Shaking hands, Paul said, "It's nice to meet you, too. Please call me Paul."

"Valerie," she spoke up as she shook his hand.

Sebastian's dark eyes glimmered as he clapped his hands together. "My family estate is located about fifty kilometers west of here. My wife and I would love to have you visit us for lunch. My family has been in agriculture for centuries, and we have farms throughout the middle and northeast of Colombia. It would be my honor to host you for lunch and to have the opportunity to learn from you. I have a small private helicopter, and you could be my guests for the afternoon. I can have you returned here this evening."

Paul turned to Valerie, lifting his brow, acknowledging she was in charge of the itinerary. She wanted to insist they return to the hotel where they could rest until they left for Bogotá in the morning for their trip home—or rather, home for Paul and Mexico for her.

Whenever they traveled, regardless of their itinerary, Paul's penchant for impromptu side trips kept her flexible. Sighing, she knew he would love to see more of the agriculture. This type of deviation was exactly the kind of adventure that invigorated him. So she nodded. "This was our last lecture for the trip. We've already sent back the samples we collected, so as long as we're back at the hotel this evening, we'll be on schedule for our return flights."

Soon, they were ensconced in a small helicopter,

peering down on jungles, farmland, and small villages until a large white house came into view in the middle of lush green gardens with towering palms, vibrant flowers, and pruned shrubs. "No shortage of water here, is there?" she mused aloud.

Paul nodded, adjusting his glasses as he also looked downward. "The wealthy can water their lawns, and the poor don't have the resources to keep their crops alive."

She turned to look at him, alarmed at the pallor of his skin. "Are you ill?"

"Just a little tired." He removed his glasses and rubbed his eyes. "Perhaps it's age catching up, but I do feel a bit depleted."

Reaching over, she gently placed her hand on his arm. "You're *not* old, but I am worried about you."

He offered a faint smile, far from his usual vibrant energy. "I'm sure I'll feel better when we land, and I have a chance to eat and rest."

She had always been amazed at Paul's energy, resilience, passion for his career, and the stamina to continue getting into the field so that he could research. But this trip had become a whirlwind as he'd accepted more side trips than originally planned. She and Paul enjoyed the guest lecturing, but traveling was difficult. Adding in the various stops for rudimentary research had left both of them fatigued. "This is the last trip we make where we try to do so much!" she vowed, eliciting a chuckle from him.

She thought about Adam and wondered if he had

landed in Mexico yet. The idea of seeing him tomorrow for a weekend of lying in the sun, drinking fruity cocktails, and spending more time with him made her long for this part of their journey to end.

Suddenly, the helicopter began its descent, and she jerked around to look out the window. She couldn't shake the sense of apprehension that tickled the recesses of her mind.

They had barely landed with a light thump onto a concrete helicopter pad when a uniformed man appeared and opened the door. He offered his hand, and she nodded in gratitude as she climbed down from the helicopter. Turning, she reached back to assist Paul, but the man who had helped her offered his assistance.

Once they were both standing, they thanked the pilot and followed the man toward the large house in the middle of lush landscaping. The house was pale yellow, two stories, with a red-tiled roof. Built in Spanish style, they walked toward an open patio framed with palm trees. Nearing, they could see the patio included a swimming pool.

Never awed by signs of wealth, she nonetheless was struck by the estate's beauty. Glancing at Paul, she smiled as his gaze ignored the house and was focused on the flower gardens and native plants surrounding the patio.

"At the risk of sounding ungrateful," she whispered to him, "I really hope Mr. Cortes plans on allowing us to sit in the cool and rest."

Paul offered a tired nod. "I agree."

Entering the house through the heavy, intricately carved wooden doors, Valerie was met with the tasteful exhibit of wealth. The palatial entry foyer of tiles in shades of terra cotta and warm browns complemented the pale walls decorated with artwork showcased in heavy frames. A curving grand staircase of dark wood with a black wrought-iron railing swept her gaze toward the upper floor and the high vaulted ceilings.

Light flowed through tall, arched windows, falling onto the antique wooden tables holding vases filled with bouquets in bright yellows and oranges. Glancing to the side, she peered through a wide doorway into what appeared to be a formal living room, the dark furniture in the light-filled room providing a sense of stability as though the house had stood for centuries when it was probably newly built.

Her gaze swung back to the wide hall next to the stairs. A distinguished man wearing a dark suit walked toward them, his lips pressed tightly. "Good afternoon. I am Jorge, Mr. Cortes's manservant. If you'll follow me, I will show you where you can refresh. Mr. and Mrs. Cortes will host lunch shortly."

They were led down a wide hall and passed a library that, even at a glance, was so appealing she vowed to sneak another peek if possible. Jorge waved his hand toward an inviting sunroom filled with comfortable furniture, plants, and a panoramic view of the side of the estate with mountains in the distance.

"There is a restroom just across the hall. Please make yourselves comfortable in the salon."

Paul waved her toward the restroom first, and she slipped in, grateful to relieve her bladder and to find a basket filled with rolled washcloths. Dampening one with cool water, she washed her face. Cognizant of the time, she hurried out to where Paul waited in the salon.

She was drawn to the view through the floor-to-ceiling windows overlooking the lush garden. The evidence of wealth seemed incongruent to the government career Sebastian held, but family money could have easily accounted for the estate.

Paul soon returned to the room, drawing her attention to him. As though on cue, a servant walked in with a tray of ice water with a few slices of cucumber in each class. Once their thirsts were quenched, she sat on the sofa as he walked over to one of the expansive windows, staring out over the view. "It's lovely, isn't it?" she remarked.

"It's supposed to be."

She smiled at his expected answer. She and Paul much preferred the natural vegetation over precisely manicured lawns. Before she could comment further, heels tapping on the tiled floor drew her attention toward the doorway.

A beautiful woman entered, her warm smile welcoming. Her dark hair was pulled into a low bun at the back of her head, and when she turned toward Paul, Valerie could see a silver filigree comb holding the thick tresses back from her face. Black slacks and a pale blue silk blouse set off her tall, athletic body and flawless makeup. Around her wrists were multiple silver bracelets, making a gentle jingling sound as she moved her hands.

"Dr. Mendez," the woman exclaimed. "Welcome to our home. I am Carlotta Cortes. My husband was so pleased to tell me he had convinced you to join us."

"Thank you, and please call me Paul."

Turning, she reached out and clasped Valerie's hand. "And you must be Ms. Clemens."

"Valerie."

"Of course, Valerie. Come and make yourselves comfortable, and Sebastian will join us momentarily."

"It was very nice of your husband to offer the use of his helicopter to bring us here," Paul said. "We were able to see much of the farmland in the area."

"Sebastian and I were raised on farms but met at the University of Colombia." She waved her hands as she spoke and smiled. "Of course, as you can imagine, he was an agriculture major. My father wanted me to become a teacher, and I love children, so it was a good fit. I taught for several years until Sebastian and I had children."

"Your home is absolutely beautiful," Valerie acknowledged.

Carlotta smiled widely, beaming with appreciation. "Thank you! We love it here, too. We bought the estate about ten years ago as Sebastian's career took off, and it took a few years to get the house redone in our style and complete the gardens."

"I couldn't help but notice that all of your garden plants are indigenous to Colombia," Paul said.

Carlotta clapped her hands and nodded. "That was one thing Sebastian was adamant about. We would not introduce plant species that were not native to the land. We wanted the landscaping and gardens to be beautiful and used only local sources." She tilted her head to the side. "Perhaps, after lunch, you would like to walk around?"

Paul was a little slow to answer, and Valerie jerked her eyes toward him, noticing the return of perspiration beading on his forehead. "I would be honored to walk around your gardens," she agreed. "Our week has been rather hectic, and perhaps Paul would be allowed to rest."

"Certainly!" Carlotta's expression turned to one of concern. "Anything you need, please let me know."

Jorge stepped into the room and bowed slightly toward Carlotta. "Ma'am, Mr. Cortes has called and will arrive in a few minutes."

"Please inform Maria that we will have lunch as soon as he arrives."

"Ma'am," he said, bowing again before turning and walking out of the room.

Carlotta was the perfect hostess, and the conversation continued with ease. Valerie felt her attention ping-pong between Carlotta and Paul, and her concern for his health increased.

Her attention jerked back to the doorway as Sebastian walked into the room and smiled widely, appearing every bit as debonair as he had earlier.

"Paul and Valerie. So glad you were able to join us," he greeted before turning to kiss his wife on the cheek.

"I will inform Maria that you are home, and lunch will be served soon," Carlotta said. She inclined her head toward Paul and Valerie before walking out of the room with a grace that Valerie could only hope for but knew she'd never possess. Sebastian settled onto the sofa and said, "I hope you have been welcomed."

"Your wife and staff are very accommodating," Valerie assured.

Nodding, he turned to Paul. "I was only able to catch the last part of your lecture. I hope you wouldn't consider it impertinent of me to ask for more clarification after lunch?"

"Of course, we'd be happy to."

Carlotta returned. "If you are ready, lunch is served. Since you are our honored guests, but this is an intimate gathering, we thought perhaps lunch in the garden would be acceptable."

They followed the beautiful couple through an elegant dining room, past a table that could easily hold twenty people. Valerie was thrilled not to be sitting in the opulent room, and as they stepped outside, she gasped in delight at a small table set in a gazebo near the pool with lush trees and flowering shrubs around.

Servants brought out the dishes, and she found favorites among the offerings. Pork Milanese, rice, fried corn, red beans, and fried plantains were followed by torta de tres leches and small cups of dark coffee.

"All of the food we are enjoying came from our farm, including the pork raised by one of the neighboring farmers," Carlotta said, pride evident in her voice.

"It's all delicious," she and Paul agreed. Valerie hadn't realized how hungry she was and had to temper her ravenous tendencies. Glancing at Paul's plate, she noticed he ate well enough that their hosts wouldn't be insulted, but he hardly ate with his typical appreciation.

When they finished and the servants had returned to carry away the platters, Carlotta said, "I hope you will not find me lacking as a hostess, but my children will soon arrive home from school, and I always like to greet them. Paul, if you would like, I'll have Jorge show you to a guest room where you may make yourself at home and lie down to rest."

"Valerie, if you do not feel the need to rest now, I would be delighted to show you around our gardens," Sebastian offered. "And to hear more from your lecture if you would be so kind."

Jorge appeared on cue and ushered Paul from the

room. Valerie stared at his back, concern pushing out her interest in seeing the grounds. Paul turned and offered a small smile. Her chest eased, and she called out softly, "Rest. I'll check on you shortly." Worry filled her, but she turned and followed Sebastian out of the salon and onto the back patio, hoping she would not regret this added side trip in their itinerary.

14

As Sebastian escorted Valerie along the manicured paths that skirted the sun-drenched pool, her eyes were ensnared by the banana palms. Their fronds stretched above the azure tiles that framed the pool, casting shade over the clear water. The vision created beckoned her, and she longed to jump in to wash the travel weariness away. Dragging her attention back to Sebastian as they walked among flower gardens, she offered perfunctory appreciation as he pointed out the various plants, trying to hide her fatigue.

She followed him through a maze of botanical grandeur. They stepped through an arched gate in the concrete whitewashed wall surrounding the estate. Curiosity had sparked at the view of the farm fields before them. "Are you from this area?" Valerie asked.

"My family owned a small farm about twenty-five kilometers from here. When I was a young boy, larger farms bought and combined many smaller ones. My family was still able to work the land. My father had insisted that I remain in school beyond when many boys would drop out to work the farms. The new owner learned this and paid for me to attend the university. I was most fortunate. I continued my education and was able to obtain positions in the Department of Agriculture. Once I had achieved that position, I was able to purchase all this land and build my home."

She couldn't imagine that his government employment paid so well but ignored the niggling curiosity, determined to get through the afternoon and continue her journey—straight to Adam.

They had stopped on a hill and looked over endless valleys of picture-perfect farmland. "Your crops are doing very well."

"Many of the ideas from the research, such as what you and Paul have provided, are utilized here. Underground irrigation, for example. And we rotate crops sooner than we used to implement in past years."

"I noticed wind turbines," she said, staring into the distance where she could see a few in the valley as well as the one nearby.

"Yes!" His face lit with excitement. "We use wind energy to keep the water pumps going during times of drought. In fact, I now am part owner in a company that makes the turbines."

She nodded noncommittally, realizing he must

have made a great deal of money in his various endeavors to have an estate rivaling any she had seen. In light of this tidbit of information, her curiosity returned, and she wondered why he would continue his government position.

As they walked around, he continued, "We also use carbon farming, a suggestion that came directly from Paul's and your research. Cover crops and compost. Our smaller area farmers assist in these endeavors."

"I congratulate you on your applications of the various methods to increase production in the face of climate change." She looked in the distance as they made their way around the estate. "Is that a greenhouse?"

"Yes. I'm testing new ways to create stronger, more resilient plants."

Interest blossomed, and she turned to him. "May I go inside? I'd love to see what you've done."

"Perhaps on your next trip," he replied smoothly, directing her back toward the house. "I must check in with my wife and greet the children."

"Of course," she agreed, disappointment filling her. She was surprised that as much as he wanted to show off his farmland, he didn't jump on the opportunity to spotlight the greenhouse.

They made their way back through the wall gate. It was only about eight or nine feet tall and gave a sense of privacy but hindered the view of the surrounding valleys. Glancing at the house, she imagined they would have a beautiful view of the vista from the upper balconies with the mountains rising in the background.

"May I ask about the wall around the estate? Is that for protection?"

"With three young children, we find that it's necessary to allow them to play while making sure they don't wander." Sebastian then turned toward her and sighed. "Plus, there is no escaping the fact that Colombia is a country of…"

"Drug cartels and danger," she ventured when he seemed to flounder.

A hasty intake of air was heard, then he nodded slowly, his smile no longer in place. "Yes. Just so."

"And I can imagine a man in your position needs protection."

"You are very kind to put it so succinctly and without judgment."

She wasn't sure about the judgment part of his statement but nodded politely.

"There is a great deal of money offered to government officials and a great deal of coercion."

Knitting her brow, she turned to face him more fully. "I understand buying the police and putting members of the Drug Task Force on their payroll, but the Department of Agriculture?"

He chuckled and cast his gaze around the garden they stood in, surrounded by lush flowers and shrubs. "They have their hand in a great many departments, Valerie. I'm sure some of my co-workers have used their influence to change agriculture policy."

Now, the sharp intake of air came from her. "I see. Well, I commend you for your fortitude to remain steadfast in the face of that kind of pressure."

She glanced behind them, then added, "I really should go in and check on Paul. Would you have someone show me the way?"

"Of course." He waved his hand in front of her, and as they walked toward the house, he added, "I have enjoyed our visit, Valerie. I hope if you and Paul return to Colombia, you will grant me the honor of another visit."

Once more, she nodded noncommittedly, and as soon as they entered the house, a sweet-faced young woman met them. "This is Roseanne. She will escort you to a guest room where you may refresh yourself. I will let my pilot know that you will be ready to leave in about an hour and will see you off."

Thanking him, she followed Roseanne to the expansive front foyer, where they ascended the wide staircase to the second floor. She tried to shake the suspicion that had hold of her but couldn't imagine how Sebastian and his wife afforded the estate, considering the humble beginnings of each. "The Corteses have a lovely home."

"Oh, Mr. Cortes spares no expense when it comes to his estate. He's very particular and wants things the proper way."

"I understand he is from this area," Valerie said, blatantly fishing.

"His family owned a small farm nearby. Of course, he works for the Colombian government, and he's paid very well for his important job."

Valerie wasn't sure if Roseanne was loyal, naive, or lying. Or perhaps, a combination of all. Shaking her head to dislodge the thoughts, she sighed. *It's not my business. Just check on Paul and get ready to leave.*

Roseanne stopped outside a door and turned to Valerie. "This is the guest room where Dr. Mendez is resting. The room and en suite bathroom just across the hall are also available for you to use."

"Thank you." She turned and stepped into the room, her eyes landing on Paul as he lay on top of the covers of the large bed in the room. At first, not wanting to disturb him, she tiptoed over to the doors, slipping out onto the balcony. Just as she assumed, she could see the farmland stretching as far as the eye could see, with the mountains rising in the background. The sound of shouting could be heard, and she watched as a gate opened near the front of the estate and a black SUV drove through, followed by two Jeeps with armed men. For some inexplicable reason, she stepped back into the afternoon shadows.

Sighing heavily, she closed her eyes for a moment, allowing the gentle breeze to soothe her frustrations. She now wished she and Paul had not accepted the offer to visit. They were exhausted from their trip, and her imagination ran rampant. She vowed that the next time Paul wanted to cram so much into one week, she would insist on a longer trip or fewer places to visit each day.

"Valerie?"

She turned quickly to see Paul trying to sit up. She rushed over, alarmed by the grayish tint of his skin. "How are you feeling?"

"Okay..." He spoke with effort, and she wasn't convinced.

"I'm concerned, Paul. I think we need to leave immediately so you can see a doctor."

"I'm sure I'll be able to..." He grimaced and clutched his chest, falling back onto the bed.

Screaming for help, Valerie grabbed his shoulders to assist him, then loosened the buttons on his shirt. He continued to gasp for air as she struggled to help. The door burst open, and Jorge rushed inside, his eyes wide as he took in the scene before him.

Looking over her shoulder, Valerie cried out, "Help! Please help him!"

Soft, gauzy curtains blew gently in the evening breeze. Valerie stood in the large, opulent bedroom gazing out the window at the night sky, exhaustion pulling at her very core.

She was grateful that Sebastian had immediately called for one of his friends nearby, who was a physician, and his wife, a nurse. He also arranged for the helicopter to fly Paul, the physician, and his wife to Barrancabermeja, where he was admitted to the Magdalene Hospital. The small helicopter couldn't carry her at the same time, but Sebastian had assured her that it would return first thing in the morning, and she would be flown to join Paul.

Carlotta, the perfect hostess, had fussed over Valerie, making sure she had everything she needed for the evening, including sleepwear and toiletries, since her luggage was back at the hotel. But as she looked around the bedroom, she knew she would not get any sleep. The bed, covered in exquisite linens, beckoned, and she sighed.

She'd spent hours on the phone with the attending cardiologist at the hospital and Ellen while Sebastian spoke to the American ambassador. She desperately wanted to be at Paul's side and was frustrated to be stuck in the middle of the countryside, even if the surroundings were luxurious. Sebastian had explained that the roads were not safe at night but that she'd be there soon with the early morning helicopter flight.

She'd just talked to Ellen again to find out that Paul had a mild heart attack and was stable. *I'd hate to see a major heart attack if that was mild!* Ellen informed her that the American embassy was ready to medevac him out to Los Angeles the next day. Ellen was on her way there and would stay with her sister, who lived in LA.

Grateful Paul was receiving the care he needed,

she felt the weight of her predicament in every fiber of her being. She sank onto the plush settee adjacent to the panoramic windows overlooking the gardens but no longer appreciated the view. Sighing heavily, she thought about Adam, who was already at the resort, and knew she couldn't delay the phone call any longer. With a heavy heart, she sent a text.

We need to talk. Is this a good time?

Within a few seconds, her phone rang, and a rueful chuckle slipped out. "Hey," she answered softly.

"What's going on? Are you okay?"

She loved that the first thing he asked was if she was okay. "Not really. Things have gone crazy here, and I can't believe I won't be able to come to Mexico tomorrow." Her body tightened in expectation of him blowing up. And this time, she wouldn't blame him for being upset since he'd already spent money and time flying to the resort.

"Tell me what's happening, Valerie. What's wrong?"

Suddenly, the tears she'd held back all day sprang forth. Knowing she was scaring him, she finally managed to say, "Paul had a heart attack and is in the hospital."

"Where are you? I'll come there." His normally careful words now rushed out, giving evidence of his take-charge personality.

Closing her eyes, more tears slid down her cheeks at the concern she heard in his voice. She swallowed past the lump in her throat. "That's what's also crazy." She explained where she was and how she and Paul had come to be at the estate. "So Mr. Cortes said he couldn't get a helicopter here tonight, and the roads were too treacherous to travel in the dark. Which makes no sense because I'm pretty sure he has a driver who would know his way around. Anyway, he's having a private helicopter return early to take me to the hospital. From there, Paul and I will be flown by a medevac airplane to Los Angeles, where Paul's wife will meet us. I know I could probably just take a different flight, but—"

"No, Valerie. You need to be with Paul. I get it."

More tears flowed. "You're being so nice about all this when you're already in Mexico waiting on me."

"It won't be the first time that plans get changed. I'm sorry as hell that Paul's ill, but if this is why you can't come to me, then that's better than you deciding that you no longer want to spend time with me."

"No," she said softly. "I was really looking forward to it. I wanted to… well, I wanted just to see you. Have a chance to see if what we initially felt was real. And if not, then maybe just friends."

"If friends are all we'll be, I'll be glad for the friendship. But I know you're the only woman I've wanted to spend more time getting to know. So we'll plan for another vacation. Plus, you sound exhausted. As soon as you get to LA, call me, and I'll come there. I can see you and take you home, as well."

"I'd really like that, Adam."

"Good."

She heard the relief in his simple one-word reply and smiled for the first time since Paul became ill. "I'd better go. I know I can't sleep, but I should try to rest."

"I want you to call me tomorrow morning. I want to know what's happening."

After promising to do so, she disconnected the call. She tried to sleep in the luxurious bed, but the linens that probably cost more than her month's rent could not lure her to slumber. Several hours passed, and she finally tossed back the covers. The illuminated numbers on her phone gave the time. *2:00 a.m.* Sighing, she climbed from the bed, finally admitting that the elusive sleep was not going to come.

Carlotta had offered a variety of food for supper, but Valerie's stomach had been in knots, so she hadn't eaten. Now, the idea of a slice of buttered bread and a glass of milk seemed just like the midnight snack her body craved.

She climbed from bed and looked around for her clothes. She wouldn't dare walk around the estate in a silky gown and robe loaned by Carlotta. She dressed in the same clothes she had worn to the estate, but Carlotta had a servant wash, dry, and press them sometime during the evening. A rueful chortle slipped out as she looked down and noted her clothes were much less wrinkled than when she'd been giving a presentation at the universities.

Having heard no other voices or noises, she

appeared to be the only person in the guest wing. She saw no one as her footsteps whispered along the wooden staircase the servants used to move between their area, the kitchen, and the upstairs guest bedrooms. Once in the kitchen, she hesitated to rifle through someone else's cabinets for bread and decided only to have a glass of milk. A small light cast a soft glow over the room, and she easily found the refrigerator. Clean dishes were drying on a rack, so she snagged a small glass and poured the milk. It was refreshing, and she hoped it would ease her churning stomach.

She washed her glass and replaced it in the dish drainer. Turning, she started to tiptoe out of the room toward the back stairs when she heard voices coming from the hall, just outside the kitchen. She darted to the bottom of the stairs and pressed her back to the wall, completely hidden in the shadows.

"It's unfortunate that she's still here. You were foolish to bring them here in the first place."

Valerie's eyes widened, wondering if they were talking about her. The voice was deep, masculine, and tinged with a gravity that sent a chill down her spine.

"I thought you said she had never seen you."

That voice came from Sebastian, sending alarm throughout her body. The opulent estate no longer felt suspicious but dangerous. The two men's voices came from around the corner, near the kitchen. She leaned back as far as she could, feeling the hard stair handrail dig into her spine.

"She hasn't, but that doesn't mean that I want this complication. It's too bad she wasn't able to go in the helicopter with Dr. Mendez."

"Then stay out of sight. She'll leave right after breakfast."

A chuckle was heard. *"Just hope she doesn't make the connection between us. I would hate for her to know her research is being put to use in your greenhouse for producing plants that I'm sure she wouldn't approve of."*

"She was asking about it, but I put her off."

"I don't trust her. Perhaps an accident—"

"Shut up! Are you crazy? After Dr. Mendez's heart attack on my property, the last thing I need is for her to go missing. Leave it alone. She will be gone soon."

The voices grew closer, and she realized the two men had entered the kitchen. The refrigerator door opened, followed by the clink of glass. From the shadows, she could see the back of two men as they opened the tops of their beer bottles and tapped them together.

"Let's hope you're right. If not, an accident can always be arranged."

Her breath lodged in her throat when she heard those last words. Her pulse pounded furiously in her ears as she peeked from the shadows, her body taut with tension.

When the man Sebastian was talking to turned to the side, she blinked in shock, her heart plummeting to her stomach. *Joseph Perez!* Her body shivered, and her legs threatened to give out.

The moment the two men's footsteps retreated and their voices faded down the shadowy corridor, she darted up the servants stairs as quietly as possible. Racing into her guest room, she gently shut the door and secured the lock with a soft click.

As the weight of the realization fell heavily, the room now felt like a cage. Heart pounding, she closed her eyes and tried to calm her racing thoughts. Sebastian knew Joseph. Sebastian, the Assistant Secretary of Agriculture, knew Joseph, a suspected cartel member.

She had wondered where Sebastian's money came from and had even surmised that some of his lands were being used for crops more profitable than coffee and beans. But seeing the two of them together slammed home the truth.

She stood in the center of the room for a moment, twisting her hands together. Swallowing deeply, she sucked in her breath and let it out slowly, forcing calm to replace the chaos of her thoughts.

Think. Analyze. Plan.

She looked out the window and eyed the trellis. She could escape to the ground using it, climb a tree, and continue over the wall surrounding the estate.

But what then? The Cortes estate was in the middle of hundreds of acres of farmland. She would have trouble seeing in the dark. And it would be daylight before she'd ever reach a village or someone could help her.

And who would help me? Who could I trust? Chances were high that most of the people who lived in the small villages and farms in the area would be loyal to Sebastian and the cartels.

If I just wait and let Sebastian fly me to Barrancabermeja early in the morning, I can fly back with Paul when he's medevacked out of here.

She hated the idea of spending one more minute in the house but knew any suspicious behavior on her part could be fatal. Feeling out of her element, she darted across the room and grabbed her phone, placing another call to the only person she knew she could trust.

15

Adam had disconnected from his call with Valerie, a gnawing disappointment scoring deep inside. He commended her loyalty to Paul and would never want her to go against her conscience. But as he stood at the open window of the resort room with the breeze blowing off the gulf waters, he couldn't stop the deep-seated feeling of melancholy from being unable to see her tomorrow. He'd had such plans... walks on the beach, lying in the sun, playing in the surf, eating whenever they were hungry, and drinking the cocktails she'd wanted to experience. And if he could have another earth-shattering kiss with her like the one they'd shared, he would have been a happy man.

Unsure what to do, his ability to make hasty changes to plans flew out the same window he was staring at. Before he had time to wander down the path of more disappointment, his phone rang, and her name lit up the caller ID screen. He grinned, and hope filled him as he wondered if she would make it to Mexico after all. Hitting connect, he greeted, "Hey, did you already miss me?"

"Oh God, Adam!" she whispered with terror, punctuating each word.

His momentary buoyant mood plummeted. "What? What's happening?" he barked, then immediately softened his voice. "Valerie, are you alright?"

"No. I… I went downstairs and overheard a conversation between Sebastian and the man from DC."

"What man?"

"The man from the cartel. Joseph. So then I knew that Sebastian was involved with the cartel. They were talking about getting rid of me or having an accident. Sebastian didn't want to, but Joseph did. I stayed hidden and then came back up to my room."

"Fucking hell!" Adam cursed as his blood ran ice cold. His mind raced chaotically, trying to figure out how to make her safe, hating his helplessness. "Are you in a locked room? Are you safe right now?"

"Yes. I thought of trying to escape, but I can't see in the dark or trust anyone to help me."

He paced the room, his hand tearing through his hair. Desperation filled him, an emotion he hadn't felt in years. Stopping in his tracks, he whirled around and looked at his suitcase. Stalking over, he started throwing things inside. "I'll come to you. I'll leave right now. I'll get your coordinates and come to you—"

She cut him off. "No, Adam, that won't work. By the time you get here, I'll have left. I told Sebastian and his wife that I would be ready to fly out by six o'clock, so that's only a few hours from now."

Fuck! He hated not being able to get to her in time. His heart threatened to pound out of his chest, drowning out the gulf waves in the background. "Yes, but I don't want you to stay there anymore."

"I'll be safe here. Their children are in the house. In fact, his wife mentioned that the children would be up early to get ready for school."

Think... slow the fuck down and think! He blew out a breath as he moved into mission-planning mode. She was right about the presence of children in the home. Sebastian wouldn't want to risk the publicity of an invited American guest being killed in his home. "What about the helicopter?"

"I was with the pilot when we came here yesterday, and he was the same one who flew Paul and the physician to the hospital. There won't be a problem there. He'll take me directly to the hospital, and I could meet you there. In fact, I can tell him that someone will be there for me."

"Okay, give me the hospital information and all the information on where you are right now. Then make sure your phone is charged, and you're packed and ready. Get downstairs to where the other household servants and the family are very early. Go to the kitchen or dining room. Stay there until you leave. Don't go anywhere that will make you vulnerable. I'll arrange a flight to Barrancabermeja and will meet you at the hospital. I'll work with my people, and you can call any of them, too. I'll text the phone number to get ahold of any of my co-workers working on this with me."

"Okay," she whispered, her agreement instant. Her trust in him caused him to grimace, remembering how he didn't offer her the same.

Her voice was less shaky than when she'd first called, but he still wanted to put his fist through the wall in frustration. *Or right through a fucker's face!* "You're doing good, but do not take risks. Call or text me in the morning when you leave."

They disconnected, and he immediately called Carson. California was two hours behind, but he knew his boss wouldn't care that it was midnight. As soon as Carson picked up, he blurted out the situation.

"I'm heading into the compound. I'll call the others and get back to you. Stay cool, and don't do anything rash. The way to keep her safe is to plan. You know that."

He did, but it didn't make the situation any easier to accept. "Fine. I'll be right by the phone."

Carson lived near the compound, and usually, a couple of Keepers worked a night shift so that a team would be assembled quickly. It would only take about thirty minutes to get them all there. Yet it was the longest half hour he'd ever remembered experiencing.

His phone rang, and he grabbed it, torn between wanting it to be Valerie and afraid that it might be. Seeing it was LSIWC, he breathed a sigh of relief and put it on video. Quickly gaining the attention of the other Keepers, he said, "Appreciate you all coming in. I know Carson has caught you up on what I told him. I need everyone's help."

As always with the Keepers, he had one hundred percent of their attention and acceptance.

He sent the text from Valerie that gave the hospital information. Jeb and Ian immediately got online to see what they could discover.

Carson looked at Leo and ordered, "Get ahold of Landon."

Information only took a couple of minutes to flood into the compound. Natalie and Abbie immediately pulled up maps of Colombia, and Dolby confirmed her location.

"Paul Mendez is at Magdalene Hospital in Barrancabermeja. Cardiac unit. He was admitted yesterday," Jeb confirmed.

"Why wasn't Valerie with him?" Bennett asked.

Adam said, "He was helicoptered to the hospital and admitted after having been treated by a private physician. There wasn't enough room, probably, since the physician's wife, a nurse, flew with them. And as we know, he came from the estate of Sebastian Cortes, the Assistant Secretary of Agriculture."

Natalie assured, "I've already got the Barrancabermeja maps pulled up."

Adam added, "They gave a lecture at the University of Bucaramanga yesterday morning. She said they were asked to go to Sebastian Cortes's estate and were supposed to be back in the city last night. Valerie said she would be transported by helicopter to the hospital in a few hours."

"I've got a lock on the Cortes estate, as well," Abbie said. "It's in the middle of a hundred and twenty acres of farmland. The estate is surrounded by a security wall, and there is a helicopter pad within the wall, outside the main gardens."

"Can we get into their security?" Adam asked. "I want my eyes on Joseph—"

"Landon is on the line." Leo interrupted.

"I just did a quick check with my CIA contact in Colombia. He confirms that Paul Mendez was transported by helicopter to the hospital in Barrancabermeja after suffering what appeared to be a heart attack. He's stable, and the ambassador is securing transportation back to the States."

"And Joseph?" Adam growled.

"Joseph Perez. According to my contact, he's known to be part of the Medellín Cartel, which is starting to work with the Sinoloans. Fucking nightmare. While he has a position of importance, there is nothing but rumors. That's how he's able to travel to the US sometimes. Fucking goes to the Colombian Embassy in DC."

"The goddamn fucker is after Valerie!" Adam exploded. "And I can't fucking get to her!"

The others were quiet for a few seconds, and he instantly knew that losing his shit wasn't helping. "Sorry," he mumbled.

"No worries," Bennett said. "We're already outfitting a team. Hop will fly me and Poole down there."

Hop jumped in. "We can be down there in seven hours, with one stop. Teddy is already getting the equipment. Give us thirty minutes here to get ready, and we'll be in the air ten minutes after that."

Carson jumped in. "Adam, we've arranged a private plane for you to get to Barrancabermeja. He's at the airport now, and he'll be ready as soon as you can get there. Contact Valerie and tell her to stay at the hospital. Paul isn't scheduled to be medevacked out until midmorning. You'll be there before then. In fact, you and Valerie will arrive about the same time."

Normally, his mind easily calculated the multitude of mission parts, but he struggled to keep everything straight when all he could think about was Valerie. "Hop, what if you're midair on the way here when I get to Barrancabermeja?"

"No worries, we can stop and meet you somewhere. There's a chance they won't have room on the medevac airplane for too many extra people. If you stay or if both you and Valerie stay behind, we'll be there by late afternoon to pick you up."

"Okay, thanks." Adam closed his eyes and willed

his heart to stop racing. His mental list skills were shit at the moment. "Really, guys... thank you."

"Hell, man... you've done it for us. We're there for you."

Carson added, "This is an active mission, all Keepers on point. Get to the airport, Adam, and we'll work it from here. I'll have Abbie contact Valerie to get a pulse on how she's doing."

"That'll be good. She'll feel better talking to someone. I'll be in touch." Disconnecting, Adam grabbed his bag. He'd packed while talking, and with a last look around, he headed out of the resort. In less than an hour, he was in the air. Lungs aching. Jaw clenching. Muscles taut. Heart pounding. *Hang on, babe... I'm coming.*

16

Just as the sun began to cast a radiant glow of dawn over the mountains to the east, painting the sky in hues of soft pastels, Valerie barely gave the view more than a passing glance. She had been sitting, waiting to leave her room as soon as it was light. Descending the grand staircase, the lavish surroundings only filled her with unease. She hadn't slept after calling Adam, having talked with one of his co-workers named Abbie, who assured her a rescue was on its way. The rest of the night had passed uneventfully, although in her utter fatigue, the idea that she had imagined the scene in the kitchen struck home.

But she did recognize Joseph—there was no doubt. And all the pieces fit together. Sebastian's wealth. His ability to manipulate the agriculture laws and policies. All the while learning the best ways to keep the coca plants thriving when others flailed with the changing weather.

Following Adam's advice, when she arrived at the bottom of the staircase, she quietly walked to an ornate settee and placed her bag and purse on the seat next to her. She waited, willing her racing heart to calm.

Within a few minutes, Jorge walked by, his footsteps faltering as he saw her sitting in the foyer. "Ms. Clemens! I was unaware you had risen."

Suppressing the urge to divulge that she hadn't slept, she managed a feeble smile. "I know Mr. Cortes is going to have his pilot fly me to Barrancabermeja, where I will meet with Dr. Mendez. I wanted to be ready."

"I understand. I'll let Mr. Cortes know that you are waiting. Have you had breakfast?"

"No, but thank you. I really don't want to eat before getting onto the helicopter."

"I'll have the cook pack a small bag. Perhaps some buttered bread, cheese, some fruit, and water. That sounds like a poor offering, but it might work in case you get hungry."

"Thank you," she repeated, her lips quivering as she nodded. "That actually sounds like the perfect thing to take with me."

He held her gaze, his eyes seeming to assess her carefully. The gravity of the moment hung thick between them before he inclined his head in a small bow. He rounded the bottom of the staircase and disappeared to the second floor, leaving Valerie filled with silent dread.

A few minutes later, she looked up to see Sebastian coming down the staircase. She felt her body tremble on the inside and prayed the expression on her face remained neutral. But even with her concern over Paul, she couldn't dislodge from her mind the vision of seeing him with Joseph the previous evening, sending icy tingles down her spine.

"Jorge has just informed me that you hope to leave as soon as possible. I understand. He's having our cook prepare you some food and drink that should be acceptable, even if you feel slightly ill. Once you reach the hospital, you might be busy with Paul and not be able to get something to eat for a while."

"Yes, that would be lovely. I spoke to his wife, and I know he might be medevacked out today, and I would like to be with him. So I'd be grateful if your pilot can take me as soon as possible."

She forced her gaze to hold his during the entire time, but even though he smiled, she felt chills throughout her body.

"Certainly. I'll see to it right away. If you would like to wait in the salon, I'll come back and get you in a few minutes and take you to the helicopter pad."

Jorge had reappeared with a tote bag in his hands. "Follow me, please, Ms. Clemens."

She followed him into the same salon where she, Paul, and the Corteses had been the previous day. As she stared at the beautiful room, it was hard to imagine that it had just been yesterday when she had felt so comfortable in their presence. Now, all she wanted to do was escape.

"I'm sure you will find everything you need in there," Jorge said, handing the bag to her. "I wish you well on your travels, Ms. Clemens."

Thanking him for the food, she slipped the strap over her body, where it hung against her hip next to her purse.

Each minute crawled like hours until finally, Sebastian stepped into the room. "We're ready, Valerie."

She followed him outside, where Carlotta met them and offered a warm hug.

"I am so very sorry, Valerie. Sebastian and I want to wish you the very best on your travels today, and of course, we'll keep Paul in our prayers. I hope you'll return to visit us again on your next trip to Colombia."

With a noncommittal nod, she forced her lips to curve as she returned the hug. Offering her thanks for the hospitality, she hurried over to climb into the small helicopter, instantly seeing that it was not the same one she and Paul had flown in on. This one was smaller, only having one seat next to the pilot. And the uniformed pilot was not the same as yesterday.

Introduced as Raul, he smiled at her and inclined his head in greeting, but all she could focus on was his uniform and the weapon secured at his side. A sense of foreboding moved through her. Forcing a smile, she accepted the assistance into the seat and was soon buckled in with the headphones in place. Her purse and the lunch tote sat on her lap, clutched tightly in her fingers.

"You do not need to be nervous. I am an excellent pilot, and we will get to our destination shortly."

"Can you get me to the hospital in Barrancabermeja?"

"I'm not authorized to land near the hospital. But Mr. Cortes has friends who are in the industrial area near the river. I will land there, and he has arranged to have someone drive you to the hospital."

She looked out the side window as they lifted into the air and grimaced. She hated the answer he'd given, not trusting Sebastian. Nor Raul, for that matter. But now that she was in the air, she had no alternative but to go where he took her. Looking down one last time, she watched Sebastian and Carlotta walk back inside their house, leaving Jorge to stand vigil until she was out of sight.

Facing forward, she stared out the front windshield, refusing to look away again. She might be at Raul's mercy while they were in the air, but she doubted he would do anything until they landed. She needed to keep her wits about her if he was also a friend of Joseph's.

Exhaustion tugged mercilessly at her, and she blinked rapidly, afraid her tears might fall. She pulled out her phone, not trying to hide her actions. She typed a message to Adam, letting him know she had left. **In the air. Different helicopter. Different pilot.**

The reply came quickly. **Stay safe. See you soon.**

It wasn't much, but it seemed like Adam was reaching through the abyss and touching a part of her that simply didn't want to be alone.

"Just letting a friend know where to meet me," she said, hoping if Raul were in league with Joseph, he would know she wasn't completely without someone nearby. She shoved her phone back into her purse and stared out the front windshield, trying not to panic as her stomach flip-flopped when the pilot veered to the west. *God, I just need to get there in one piece.* And prayed that Sebastian really would have a car waiting for her.

Valerie continued to stare out the front bubble windshield of the helicopter, saying nothing. The pilot did not speak either. She kept an eye on the direction they were traveling, knowing the mountains had been to the east of the Cortes estate, and they needed to travel west. In the distance, beyond the fields and villages, she could finally make out the outline of the city.

Relief washed over her, but she still didn't feel that her ordeal was over. *But I'm close. As soon as we land, I can get to the hospital, and then I'll be safe.* As they approached Barrancabermeja, he circled around the city, and she could see the Magdalene River running by the edge of an industrial area.

Unable to hide her surprise as they descended onto an empty concrete parking lot, she blurted, "Why are we landing here?"

"It's an industrial park and refinery. Over there is where most of the oil in Colombia is refined."

"I don't understand why we're here."

"Mr. Cortes has friends with interests in the industrial area. He was able to arrange for my landing here."

"I realize you said you can't land near the hospital, but here? Outside of the city? There's no one around!"

"Mr. Cortes has arranged for transportation to the hospital for you."

The landing skids settled on the concrete, and the pilot nodded. "You will get out here, and your transportation will be here soon."

She didn't know much about helicopters but had certainly flown in enough to know that the blades stopped spinning before she had ever gotten in or exited. "Aren't you going to turn off the blades?"

"I'm going to leave immediately so your transportation can come."

She looked around, not seeing any people and certainly not seeing a nearby vehicle waiting to pick her up. Shaking her head slowly, she said, "But I don't—"

"Get out, Miss Clemens."

Her head whirled around, now seeing that he pointed the gun at her. Eyes wide, she forgot to breathe as she stared at the weapon.

"Get out. My instructions were clear, but I have been paid more to allow you to leave freely. I will have no problem forcing you if you do not get out on your own."

The air seemed to get sucked out of the helicopter as she gasped, dragging in ragged breaths. "You were hired to kill me?" she managed to ask, her words as choppy as her breathing.

He shook his head. "I was paid to keep you here until someone else came, but I had a counteroffer of more to let you go."

"But what… I don't… what will…"

"Ms. Clemens, I don't care what will happen to you. I just need you to get out if you want to have a chance."

Afraid to move, she barely managed to get her shaking hands to unsnap her seat harness and get ahold of the door handle. She did not want to be left in this empty parking lot, surrounded by warehouses, concrete buildings, smokestacks, and factories. But staring at the gun a few inches away from her, she couldn't think of an alternative plan.

As the door opened, the sound of the blades swirling created a thunderous cyclone above. She leaped down to the ground, her heartbeat pounding. She crouched low, her palms scraping against the gravel as she scuttled away from the helicopter as quickly as she could. Shivering in terror, she frantically scanned her surroundings, her gaze settling on the closest building. Crates were stacked outside near a door, offering a possibility of covering. Still scrambling in a low crawl, she raced as fast as she could and jumped behind the closest crate. Raul lifted the helicopter into the air, and with complete indifference, he steered away from her until he was out of sight. Suddenly, the silence surrounded her, and instead of offering peace, she felt disoriented by the void it created.

Blowing out a long breath, she looked around the desolate parking lot, trying to analyze the situation that made no sense to her. The lot was empty and surrounded by a chain-link fence. No vehicle was in sight, and with the fence gates closed, she wondered how someone would get to her.

And what if they do? Will there be someone to take me to the hospital as Sebastian promised or someone from Joseph who wants me dead?

But even considering that possibility didn't explain what would happen to her now. Deciding that waiting was the worst thing she could do, she pulled her phone out, opened the map app, and tried to make sense of where she was in the city.

Still hiding behind the crates, she turned around slowly until she discerned that the Magdalene River was behind the massive building on her left. The main part of town was to the east, which was on the other side of the parking lot and other buildings to her right. And she hated to feel like a sitting duck. *If I could get to the river, I might have a better chance of finding someone who could give me a ride to the hospital.*

Looking down at her phone, she tried to call Adam, but it went to voicemail, most likely due to him being airborne. Next, she dialed the number he'd given her, glad when the woman identified herself.

"Valerie, this is Abbie."

"Oh, thank God. I can't get ahold of Adam."

"Valerie, I see your location. You're in an industrial park... near an oil refinery?"

"That's where the pilot dropped me off. He pulled a gun on me—"

"Dammit! Okay, Valerie, I've got you on speaker."

Trying to calm her staccato heartbeat, she gave his co-workers what information she had. "If the pilot wanted to kill me, he could have. But he just left me in the middle of nowhere. I'm hiding behind some crates because I don't know if someone is after me or if they've forgotten about me and just want me to get to the hospital and leave. I don't know."

"Is anyone around?" Abbie asked.

"No... it's weird. I looked at the map on my phone, and this industrial area is huge. But the parking lot is empty, and I don't see anyone around."

"You're not at the oil refineries. It appears you're near empty warehouses."

"I'm not sure. There's some noise coming from inside, but I don't see any vehicles around."

"Don't snoop," Abbie warned. "You never know what or who might be around."

"Okay, but Sebastian lied. There's no one here to take me to the hospital. I pulled up my location on the map, and I'm going to make my way toward the river without being seen. Once I get there, there are trees, and I think I can make my way to a housing area where someone can drive me to the hospital."

"Hang on. We're in communication with Adam—"

"I tried to call but couldn't get through. Has he landed?"

"We have ways to communicate besides the satellites for your cell phone. Carson is talking to him now. He's just landed at the airport, but it will be a forty-minute drive to where you are."

"I need to get away from here. There's a fence all around, and it appears to be locked. There's no way he can get to me if I stay."

"Get to the river if you can do so without being seen, and then hide. We'll send Adam to you."

"Yeah…" Her stomach lurched, and she wrapped her free arm tightly around her middle. Blowing out a breath, she shook her head as she looked around. "Okay. Hide. I need to get to the other side of this warehouse."

She disconnected and had just started to pocket her phone when it vibrated. Seeing Adam's number, she gasped. "Adam!"

"Fucking hell, Valerie. Carson just filled me in. I'm on the ground here in Barrancabermeja and getting transportation to get me to you. It'll take about forty minutes or so before I can get to where you are. Find a place to hide. If you have to move, we can track you. Stay in contact."

Her chest depressed, but she was uncertain if she

was relieved or distraught. But just knowing he was close made her feel lighter. "Okay."

"I'm leaving now. I promise... promise I'm coming for you. Nothing will keep me from getting to you, okay?"

Just by hearing his voice, she found drawing air into her lungs easier. "Okay," she whispered again.

Disconnecting, she knew he would keep his promise. He was coming. Now... all she had to do was stay safe until he arrived.

With renewed determination, she jogged from one stack of crates to another. When she came to the end of the building, she peeked around the corner, glad to see no one walking around. She would have thought there was no active production occurring in the building, but she could see a truck sitting near the side in the distance. Listening more intently, she realized the truck was idling, and someone was inside. *Shit!* Deciding to stay put until Adam arrived, she hunkered down, dragging her purse and tote into her lap. She cursed under her breath, fury warring with the fear that seemed to have taken permanent residence in her gut.

She looked back one last time. Still unable to see a vehicle that would have shown up to take her to the hospital, she no longer considered that Sebastian was really going to help her. *He's in on this... whatever Joseph's plan is.*

17

Adam stared down at the countryside as the private plane began its descent into Barrancabermeja. Colombia was lush and green, interspersed with villages and a few cities they had flown over.

He was on his radio with LSIWC as the wheels touched down, discovering that Valerie had been in contact with them. He thanked the pilot, knowing he would be paid well, and grabbed his bags. The pilot had taxied to a private hangar, and there, just as expected, was a vehicle and driver waiting for him.

Carson's voice came across the radio as he was ready to climb inside the small, nondescript sedan. "Valerie is not at the hospital. We've given new instructions to the driver to take you there."

"Where is she?"

"Sebastian Cortes's helicopter pilot dropped her off at gunpoint in an industrial park area along the Magdalene River, northwest of the city."

"Goddammit! Is she okay?"

Just when he thought he would have her safely in his arms in a few minutes, he was now filled with fury at the thought of someone holding a gun on her.

"We have a lock on her location, and she's safe for now. She's hiding, waiting for you."

"How long will it take me to get there?"

"It looks like you can be there in a little less than an hour."

Turning toward the driver, he barked, "Get me to the address you were given at the industrial park on the northwest side of town. If you get me there as fast as you can, I'll double your pay."

The driver's eyes widened, and he nodded his head in jerks, the creases emanating from his eyes deepening as he smiled. "Yes, yes!"

"I'm getting ready to call her," he said. "Anything I should know about ahead of time?"

"She's fine. Shaken up but unharmed. She didn't want to get out of the helicopter, but the pilot pulled out a gun and said his instructions were for her to leave or he'd forcibly remove her. She did as he asked, but the promised car and driver weren't there for her, and no one showed up. She felt unsafe after he left and decided to hide."

"What the fuck is his game?"

"I don't know, man. But our fear is that, while Sebastian was trying to keep her alive and move her along, Joseph might have stopped those plans after she left the estate."

"He never knew she saw him in the States."

"Maybe he just didn't like being so close to her. He sees her as a loose end."

"Why the fucking industrial park?"

"Again, it seems like that's where Sebastian has a warehouse, building, or something. She said it looks empty."

"All right, thanks. I'm going to call her."

The driver took off with such speed that it caught Adam off guard, and his back was pressed against the seat. Feeling the need to make sure the man understood, he said, "Double your pay if we get there fast, no accidents, and no getting pulled over by the fucking police."

"No problem, man. You ever watch *Fast and Furious*? I've been living to do this shit for a long time."

Adam might have found the man's speed dedication amusing some other time. Right now, all he cared about was getting to Valerie.

As the driver hurled the car down the road, he avoided downtown by taking the backroads. After only about thirty minutes, Adam could look out the window and observe huge buildings with smokestacks and what looked like miles and miles of factories. He found out from Natalie that Valerie was still north of the oil refineries. He gave the driver more directions, watching as they moved onto a road that appeared to parallel the factories on one side and the river on the other.

The sick feeling that had been in his gut ever since he got the call from Valerie in the middle of the night had not receded, and it wouldn't until he saw her. Calling her, he breathed in relief as she answered immediately.

"Are you close?" Her words rushed together.

"Almost there. I've got your coordinates and will be there shortly."

"Are you driving?"

"No. Got someone who knows the shortcuts."

"I don't see how you're going to be able to get to me, Adam. A tall fence surrounds me. I was going to climb over, but a big truck was parked around the corner. I don't want to be seen."

The driver was slowing, and Adam jerked around to see what was happening.

"They blocked off the area up ahead that you want to get to. Cars are backed up, and it seems someone up there is checking before letting anyone through."

"Fuck!" He thought for a second, then tapped his ear radio. "The driver can't get me to where she is. Somebody's got this warehouse blocked off from down the road. I'll have to get out and go on foot. That means a driver isn't going to be able to take us anywhere else, so I'll ditch this and will have to have Hop and the others arrange to meet us."

Switching over to his phone, he said, "Valerie, I won't be able to bring the car in. Someone's got a roadblock up here. I'm getting out and coming on foot. Let me check with my people, and I'll get back with you. Stay where you are."

Once more proving her trust in him, she whispered, "Okay."

He turned to the driver. "Turn around here. I don't want to gain any attention. Get me over to the edge of that building, then I'll jump out, and you can keep going." He pulled out a wad of cash from his wallet and handed it to the man. "This is the extra beyond what you've been paid and to keep your mouth shut."

"Thank you, mister. And no problem... I won't tell anyone."

The man did exactly as he asked, turning calmly in the road to head in the other direction, then moved behind some trees, where Adam alighted quickly. He'd already shuffled his belongings around, taking necessary items and shoving them into a heavy backpack. Leaving the excess toiletries and clothes that he'd taken to use in Mexico, he said, "What's left in the bag you can have."

Closing the door, he watched the driver continue down the road. Shifting the pack onto his back, he jogged past a few buildings, crouching low and out of sight.

Natalie radioed, "I've got you on satellite monitoring. Continue in the direction you're moving until you pass the next building. There's a parking lot on the far side, and some cars are there. You can go around the backside, and there are trees between the building and the river. Get past that building, continue through at least half a mile of empty, overgrown lots, and then you'll face the fenced-in parking lot where Valerie was left. She's on the far side."

Once he moved past the building Natalie indicated, he came to an expanse of land with overgrown grass and shrubs with trees around the edge. Glad that his driver had been able to get him as close as he had without detection, he stayed low as he moved through the tall grass, noticing that he was approaching the northern end of the refinery and industrial park. Ahead, there appeared to be a warehouse with no people or cars around.

Tapping his radio, he asked, "Who the fuck owns this? Cortes?"

"It appears that a holding company owns the building, and it looks like there may be one shell company after another," Jeb reported. "Chris has been following the trail since I first heard of this, and it looks like it may lead back to Cortes."

"If he had Valerie brought here with the intention of getting rid of her, that may be why the blockade is in the area. If someone was supposed to come after her and can't find her, they're looking."

"Adam, get ready for company. Satellite shows a small tanker truck coming from the river port north of the area. Abbie has let Valerie know she needs to stay hidden because the truck is now coming through the gate and going to the warehouse."

Fucking hell, can this get any more complicated? He

continued on until he was almost to the building. Calling Valerie, he said, "I'm almost here. Are you still within the fenced parking lot area?"

"Yes. I'm hidden behind some crates on the north side of the building. But Adam, I heard some noise, and when I peeked out, I saw a truck roll by. They came through the gate. I guess the driver had a key."

"I know about them. Chances are the warehouse isn't empty. It's being used for something and only supposed to appear empty."

Her voice cracked. "How close are you?"

"Give me a few minutes, and I'll give you a hug."

Navigating the labyrinth maze of weathered crates and discarded pallets, he moved like a shadow. Treading softly, he was careful not to scare her as he came near. Calling again, she picked up immediately. "I'm just around the corner, almost within sight. I wanted to give you a heads-up so I don't startle you."

"Okay, good," she replied, her voice trembling.

Slipping around the final obstacle, he met her gaze, and at that moment, his chest constricted. An electrifying thread crackled in the air between them. She leaped to her feet with a sob erupting from her lips. Rushing forward, he steadied himself as her body slammed into his. Both dropped to their knees as he wrapped his arms around her and pulled her tightly to his chest. She filled the spaces within him he hadn't known were empty.

A protective bubble covered them momentarily as he murmured soothing words, keeping out the chaos swirling around. They remained on their knees, wrapped in each other, while their heartbeats echoed in unison. Struck with the realization that his arms were around someone precious, he held her tighter.

In the middle of a mission, amid danger, all the emptiness in his life that he never even knew existed was filled.

18

A guttural sob tore free from Valerie's lips as Adam darted around the corner and rushed toward her. A spear of relief shot through her in a way she'd never felt before. Her chest constricted as her heart expanded, causing a bittersweet pain that only eased when his body met hers, and she was engulfed in his embrace.

She had only been alone for an hour. The sensation of his arms enveloping her made her feel as though she had been alone ever since the night they kissed and then argued weeks earlier. Being with him was like coming home. Safe. Secure. Where she belonged.

Her fingers clutched his shoulders as she pressed her face against his chest, burrowing in deeply. "I can't believe you're here. I can't believe you came for me."

"I couldn't *not* come for you, Valerie."

She jolted slightly, his words leeching out the warmth. Sniffling as she leaned back, she nodded. "Of course, that's right. Your company must have been asked to help with Dr. Mendez—"

His hands lifted to cup her face, and the warmth of his palms against her cheeks caused her eyes to close, desperate to yield everything to him, even if she was part of an assignment.

But he wasn't finished. "If you think for one moment, Valerie, that I'm not here just for you, you're wrong. Because, somehow, with just one kiss, my heart was already calling for yours. So this has nothing to do with work and everything to do with you and me."

She blinked her eyes open wide, unheeding the tears that slid against his fingers as his hand still held her face. She'd never heard anything so beautiful in all her life, and he was staring straight into her eyes, giving her everything. Her breath hitched. "Y… yeah?"

He closed the distance and whispered, "Yeah." His breath puffed against her face just before he placed a soft kiss on her lips. A barely-there touch that awakened the heat in her cold body.

"But, Valerie, we gotta get out of here."

Suddenly jerking, she blew out her breath. "Do you know where we should go? I know you said to head toward the river, but that truck came up, and I got too scared to move."

"Who was driving?"

"Um... I just saw one man. He got out to unlock the padlock on the fence gate, and then once he drove through, he locked it again. He went inside, and I haven't seen or heard anything since."

Adam stared at the side of the truck. "Stay here."

Before she could protest, he darted to where the truck was parked, ran to the far side, and returned. He fired off a text, then grabbed her hand. "Let's go."

"What? What's there?"

He had grabbed her hand and tugged, pulling her to her feet. "We're going over the fence. We need to go quietly and race to that grove of trees over there."

Nodding her assent, she trailed him, racing to the chain-link fence behind the truck. She was struck with the realization that the truck placement hid their movements from the prying eyes of anyone inside the building. He reached over and pulled her purse and tote bag from around her neck, then effortlessly tossed them to the other side, where they landed with a thud on the hard-packed ground.

"Go," he commanded, his palms spanning her waist. His grip was tender but firm as he easily lifted her.

She fumbled as she placed her hands and feet into the openings of the fence. She climbed to the top with some agility but no elegance and faltered as she attempted to swing her leg over. Glad the fence was only six feet tall, she finally succeeded. As she descended on the other side, exhaustion and adrenaline waged a war inside, making her muscles shake.

Opting for expedience, she propelled herself backward, barely managing to land on her feet.

Meanwhile, Adam tossed his pack over and then, with much more athletic prowess than she'd displayed, easily scaled to the top and swung over to the other side. Valerie snatched her purse and tote while he grabbed his pack. Taking her hand, they ran through the tall grass of the next lot to a growth of trees.

Crouching low to the ground, Adam scanned the area. Mimicking him, she peered through the foliage, although she was clueless as to what she was looking for. Mercifully, she didn't hear anyone shouting or see anyone moving around.

She battled back the desire to pepper him with questions, not wanting to distract him or impede their progress. He looked at his watch, and she observed it wasn't just a watch but more of a miniature computer screen. He began to speak, but she didn't understand what he was saying. She also realized he had a radio earpiece.

"Yeah, that's what I thought. Guess that tells us what the fucker is doing," he muttered.

Her stomach unleashed a growl as he spoke to his team, betraying her hunger. She now wished she'd eaten something last night. Pressing her hand to her waist, she willed her stomach to settle and kept her gaze on Adam.

He sat back on his haunches, his dark cargo pants

stretched taut over his thighs. His black T-shirt showcased his chiseled muscles. His black hair was slightly mussed as though he'd dragged his fingers through it in frustration. She tightened her hands around the straps of her bag to battle the urge to reach over and smooth his ruffled hair. They might have shared a life-altering kiss, but she'd yet to have her fingers in his hair.

Finally, his gaze moved to her as he finished his call, and she forced all of her thoughts back to what he needed her to do.

"We're going to head to the river. If we can make it unseen, we'll go down the road as far as we can and find a place to hide until my team arrives to get us out."

"They're flying in?"

"Yeah, but they're not here yet, and they'll land wherever we need them to." He reached over and placed his hand on hers, still gripping her purse, and gave a little squeeze.

Exhaling deeply, she offered a smile, realizing that after all the fake smiles she doled out at the estate, her smile came from her heart when with Adam. "Okay. You lead, and I'll follow."

The tension in his face eased ever so slightly, and his lips barely curved to offer just a hint of a grin. "I don't know a man alive who wouldn't love to hear those words from a woman."

She rolled her eyes and stifled a chuckle, playfully slapping his arm. Somehow, in the middle of this fucked-up nightmare, they managed to find a moment of levity.

Still crouching, he took her hand in his, and they slogged through the waist-tall grass that covered an empty lot the size of a large city block. When she'd looked at the map, it appeared that the oil refineries and industrial park factories were to the south, and the helicopter had let her out at the northern end.

"Is this good or bad that we're where we are?"

He glanced over his shoulder and looked at her. "What do you mean?"

"It just seems like we're moving away from civilization. And I thought maybe if we were closer to the refineries where there would be a bunch of employees, that would be better."

"That might normally make sense, but we don't know who the good guys are versus the bad guys. I don't know what was happening in that warehouse near where you were dropped off, but I know enough to know that we didn't want to be anywhere near that place. And sure, maybe most of the people who work for the factories or refineries are good guys, but all it takes is for one of them who's not to put in a call to Sebastian or Joseph. Right now, we're a lot safer getting away from here."

They reached another grove of trees and stopped for a moment. It was late morning and not at the fullest heat of the day, yet sweat ran down her back. Amazingly, Adam didn't appear to be sweating as heavily. She remembered what was in her tote. "I've got some water. One of the servants gave me this before I left."

At Adam's nod, she unzipped it and peered inside, surprised at the bounty. "Wow, there's water and cheese sandwiches, what looks like granola bars, some nuts, and fruit." Sticking her hand to the bottom, she blinked in surprise as she pulled out several packets. "I don't know what these are."

Adam took them from her, and his eyes widened. "This is energy gel, the kind of stuff that distance runners use." He lifted his gaze to her and asked, "Who prepared this for you?"

"The servant told the cook to pack a bag for me in case I get hungry before I could get anything at the hospital."

"Well, someone wanted to make sure you had nutrition in case you weren't taken straight to the hospital."

Before she had a chance to ponder that thought more, he said, "Let's each have some water, and then we need to get down to the river. We'll be able to stay more hidden underneath all the trees that grow along the bank."

She took a swig, then handed the bottle to him, watching his throat work as he swallowed. He screwed the top back on and handed it to her, breaking her unabashed ogling. She followed as he turned and started walking at a fast clip in the direction they'd been heading. She wondered if extreme, intense situations caused the mind to slip into fantasies, especially if the man who rescued her was gorgeous and kissed like a dream.

They had another large, city-block-size lot filled with waist-high grass to get through before they made it to the river's edge. Staying behind him and keeping low, she hoped she was moving as quickly as he needed. Once they were ensconced among the trees, they found a small road that followed parallel to the river, and in the distance could see a few small buildings and houses.

"Do you think anybody will be looking at us from here?"

"I don't know," he admitted. "We don't know if the pilot meant that Joseph was sending someone to kill you or if Sebastian truly had someone to take you to the hospital. But once you're reported as missing, then someone will probably be sent to find you. I had to come the last bit on foot because of a roadblock. It could easily have been someone looking for you. And I sure as fuck don't want to hang around too long to find out."

She nodded, dropping her chin to her chest for a moment, unable to wrap her head around the situation. Suddenly, she remembered something Adam had said. "What did you see when you went to the truck and then talked to the people you worked with?"

"The back of the truck had a container, and the printing on the outside was in Chinese."

She held his gaze as she shook her head. "I don't understand."

"I looked further and could see the paperwork he had left on the seat. He was carrying a load of chemicals from China. Piperidine. It's one of the chemicals used to make synthetic fentanyl."

Gut punched, she dropped her mouth open as her eyes widened. "And that was where they had the helicopter leave me?" Each word grew a little higher and stronger, and he lifted a finger to place it on her lips.

"I'm pissed about that too, Valerie, but we'll deal with that later. Right now, we just need to get as far away from here as we can to a place where I can have my people pick us up."

Sucking in a fortifying breath, she stood straighter and nodded. She cast her gaze all around as they started down the edge of the road, staying mostly in the shadow of the trees and bushes. The Magdalene River was wide, and she could barely see to the other side. Large cargo vessels were traveling in the middle, along with a multitude of other smaller boats. It was a busy major waterway, cutting a swath through the middle of Colombia—and now, she realized that it could be a major transportation avenue for drugs.

It was almost noon, and more people were walking around and going about their daily business. She and Adam must have blended in because no one seemed to pay any attention to them. She gazed longingly at a few smaller shops and a restaurant, wishing they could stop and wait until Adam's co-workers made it to them. Sitting in the shade seemed preferable to walking in the sun, but Adam kept going. *And I trust him.*

The sound of a shot ricocheted over the area, and she screamed, clapping her hands over her head as she ducked.

Grabbing her by the shoulders, Adam called out, "Valerie! Valerie! It's okay!"

Her gaze jumped to him as he pulled her close, then shifted her to his side. "Keep walking. It wasn't a gun. It was a backfire."

An old motorcycle with a driver and two teenagers hanging on the back laughed as they rode past.

"Damn," she muttered, feeling foolish. "I'm sorry."

"No reason to be. You're exhausted and jumpy. Hopefully, we can get out of here soon."

Minutes later, the deep rumble of the motorcycle's engine reverberated louder. Craning her neck to see down the road, she watched it approach without the two boys riding along. The lone driver headed straight toward her and Adam.

Before she could figure out what was happening, another shot rang out, and this time, shards of bark from the tree beside her splintered over her. She barely had time to react before Adam's forceful shove sent her sprawling onto the ground.

"Stay!"

His barking command was quickly fulfilled as she ducked her head, and he disappeared from her sight.

Hearing his footsteps retreat, she raised her head just enough to glimpse what was happening. Adam deftly dodged the oncoming motorcycle and swung his backpack forward in one fluid motion, unseating the driver with brutal efficiency. The bike skidded sideways, the metal scraping along the road, eliciting a scream from the driver. Adam didn't waste a second as he hauled the young man up, jerked his helmet off, and landed a solid punch to his face. The unconscious driver crumpled to the ground. He grabbed the weapon from the road, checked it, then slid it into his waistband.

She couldn't believe people weren't running to the scene, but scanning their surroundings, she realized a convenient curve in the lane hid them.

"Come on!" Adam yelled.

Leaping to her feet, she sprinted forward, her heart hammering in her chest. Adam righted the toppled motorcycle with ease, giving it a cursory inspection. He grabbed the discarded helmet from the ground and secured it quickly on her head, snapping it under her chin before she could process what was happening.

He put the man's gun in his backpack and slid his arms through the straps with the pack on his front. Mounting the bike with ease, he revved the engine. "Get on." The urgency in his voice took precedence over her questions.

Dropping her unspoken protestations that he wasn't wearing a helmet, she also kept quiet that she'd never ridden on a motorcycle. She'd seen enough TV and movies to know to sling her leg over and press her torso to his back. Holding him closely, she squeezed her eyes shut as he revved the motor.

They rocketed forward, leaving her stomach lurching, and she prayed they wouldn't wreck. After a moment, she felt as though she could breathe and started to relax. They passed the next area occupied by some houses and stores before finally getting to where the lane traveled through a jungle path alongside the wide river.

She had no idea what was coming next, but with her arms wrapped tightly around Adam's waist, she trusted him completely. It wasn't just a physical connection but an emotional lifeline—one she didn't want to lose.

19

Adam loved the sensation of Valerie molded against his back. He'd never lost focus on a mission, always able to compartmentalize his emotions, but she presented a magnetic pull that made logic fly away. Her arms tightened around his waist, and he was once again grounded, wanting the time to see what future they could build. The feeling he'd had in Washington of wanting to get to know her more had only grown.

Growling at the forces against them, he needed all his focus to keep them safe. Reality set in as he noticed the gas gauge needle hovering precariously close to empty. As old as the motorcycle was, the gauge's accuracy was questionable. The engine sputtered occasionally, and he knew they would need to change tactics very soon.

He weighed their options as he navigated the treacherous roads through the jungle with the river still in sight beside them. Tapping his radio earpiece, he hoped to hear over the puttering motorcycle.

"I can see you're moving faster than a walk," Natalie said.

"Someone took a shot at us. Punk-ass young guy, but I've got no doubt he was looking for us. I took him out and took his motorcycle. Valerie is with me, and I need to know if it's safer to try to get gas in this thing, get off the road and hide, or get on the water."

"You've just passed Barranquito."

"Yeah, nothing much there. But if I keep going, we'll have to get gas and get away from the river where the road goes inland. And I feel like a sitting duck on this road. Got the jungle around, but nowhere to hide if someone comes in a more powerful vehicle."

"Okay, you'll come to a small industrial park in about three miles… not anything like what you came from. This only has a couple of small buildings. But there is a dock with boats."

"Got it. Any ETA on Hop?"

"He's over southern Mexico and will land there to refuel. Once he's back in the air, I'll let him know where you are."

Barking out his thanks, he disconnected.

As much as he wanted to keep Valerie out of his ever-changing decisions, she deserved to know what was happening, and he didn't want her to be surprised. "We'll ditch the motorcycle soon and get in a boat. We can make better time on the river and will have more ability to stay off anyone's radar."

She simply nodded, and he felt her trust down to his bones, a fucking gift he wasn't about to take for granted. Words he heard from the other Keepers ran through his mind—*it takes a special woman to be worthy of a Keeper.* Hell, he knew Valerie was special and proved it each minute. He just hoped he was worthy of her.

A few minutes later, he slowed as they came to the edge of the water, where he spied a dock a little farther up the river. There were a few small barges, as well as several smaller boats with single engines. He parked underneath the nearby trees, making sure to stay out of sight of the few men visible around the buildings off the road. Grateful no one was on the dock, he said, "Hop off. We'll leave the motorcycle as payment for the boat we're stealing."

She swung her leg over the back and climbed off, keeping hold of his shoulders. He quickly followed, taking hold of her arm until her legs were steady. Ducking so he could peer into her eyes, he searched her face. "You okay?"

Her head nodded in jerks, but her gaze was steady. "Yeah, I'm good." Her tongue darted out to drag over her lips. "What's next?"

"Let's get into a boat. Then we can pick our pace, pull over when needed, and hide where my men can find us once they get here."

"Got it," she said without hesitation.

He leaned forward and kissed her forehead, allowing his lips to linger briefly. Then he reached down to wrap his fingers around hers as they started for the dock. Once they were out of the shadow of the trees, he crouched, and she followed his lead. Dropping her hand, he motioned for her to stay as he moved out onto the dock first. Quickly ascertaining which boat would be the best, he chose a smaller one with a single motor. Checking the fuel, he was stunned that it was almost full.

Somebody would find the motorcyclist he knocked out, and he wanted to be far away before whoever hired the guy to shoot them realized they'd gotten away. Hopefully, they'd still be looking on the roads for a man and a woman on the motorcycle.

Looking over his shoulder to where he'd left Valerie, he signaled for her to come to him, and she immediately hurried over. He tossed his pack into the bottom of the boat, then turned and offered his hand, assisting her into the vessel.

"Sit there, in the middle." He gestured for her to sit on the small bench, the wood weathered and worn. He stepped in and settled behind her, next to the motor. Firing up the boat, he glanced toward the shore and sighed in relief. It appeared no one had come out of the building just on the other side of the lane. Having already untied the rope, he turned the steering shaft and guided them away from the dock, grateful for their unnoticed escape.

He'd chosen wisely because the engine was fairly

new, was in good shape, and would easily get them where they needed to go. With a practiced eye, he simultaneously assessed the river's currents and relished the view before him—both the natural beauty of their surroundings and the exquisite profile of the woman sharing the boat with him.

She reached into her purse and pulled out a hairband. Her fingers threaded through the unruly tresses flying about her face and pulled her hair back, securing it with the band. She turned slightly to the side as she scanned the river, and while her face was etched with fatigue, her gaze was filled with intelligence and curiosity. Drawn to her, he forced his gaze back to their surroundings.

He radioed their situation to the team, and Natalie confirmed that she had them on her satellite. "Keep following us, and let me know as soon as Hop calls in."

Valerie had indicated that she had not eaten this morning, and while he could function on little sleep or food, Adam knew she needed to keep up her strength. "How about some more water?"

With a nod, she leaned over to her tote and retrieved the half-filled bottle they'd shared earlier. When she handed it to him, he inclined his head toward her. "You first, sweetheart."

She unscrewed the top, took a sip, and closed her eyes for a few seconds as a look of pleasure moved over her face. Turning slightly, facing him more fully, she handed the bottle to him. "It's interesting how, in times of crisis, such simple pleasures become so profound," she said. "I was just thinking this water tasted almost sweet."

He nodded, then slaking his thirst, he urged, "You need to keep up your strength. Go ahead and eat something if you think you can."

Grateful for the motor's efficiency, he didn't have to shout so she could hear him. That was another bonus to having her sit near him instead of at the front of the boat. *That, and the fact that I just love having her as close to me as possible.* He could lie to himself and say it was only for her protection, and while that was true, it wasn't the only reason. He'd grown used to having her near in such a short time.

She dug inside the tote again, this time retrieving two sandwiches made with thick slices of homemade bread and generous portions of soft cheese. Splitting the meal between them, they ate ravenously. After he consumed his last bite, he looked up to see she'd done the same, and her cheeks were puffed out as she chewed.

She blushed and grinned, then swallowed. "I know I look like a chipmunk squirreling away nuts for the winter, but after I took the first bite, I realized how hungry I was. Plus, that sandwich was really good!"

"Yeah, it was." He chuckled, glad she'd eaten.

Their gazes held, and at that shared moment, despite their hasty escape and facing the unknown ahead, he felt a sweetness that belied the situation's gravity. Her innocence in the midst of corruption. Calm in the midst of chaos. It was a feeling unlike any he'd ever known.

"Do you want more? There's fruit, nuts—"

Shaking his head, he hoped for a different time and place when they could share a picnic without worry. "No. I'm good for now. We probably ought to save some in case it takes a while for us to get picked up."

They passed a variety of vessels on the river. Small boats and canoes with only one or two men standing in them, tossing fishing nets near the river's edge. They motored past larger fishing boats, small barges, and even small yachts. They maneuvered to the edge, giving plenty of room for the cargo ships. He continually scanned the river but didn't discern anyone paying attention to them. Nonetheless, he stayed close to the embankment, wanting a quick escape by foot if necessary.

After a while, Valerie looked over and blushed. "I've been in the field enough times that I usually find somewhere to take care of my needs, but I'm not used to traveling by boat. And… I'm getting desperate." She chuckled. "If I was a guy, I could whip it out and pee over the side of the boat. As it is, I'm not real keen on dropping my drawers and hanging my ass over the side."

Adam barked out laughter, shaking his head. He could only imagine how she'd gotten used to relieving herself in a variety of outdoor situations.

Glad she wasn't shy about nature's calling, he nodded. Looking at the area ahead, he offered a chin lift. "There's a decent embankment over there. I can pull to the side, and we can take turns going behind the trees."

"Thank God!"

He guided them to the embankment and killed the engine, and they gently bumped against a fallen log. He climbed out first with the rope and secured the boat to a tree. They were partially hidden from anyone else on the river. Offering his hand, he assisted her out of the boat and up the dirt embankment. He walked around, checking the area before pointing toward a small grove of trees. "You'll be fine back there. I'll keep watch but turn my back. Take your time."

"Thank you," she said again as she hurried in the direction he'd pointed. In a couple of minutes, she returned with a satisfied expression. Grinning up at him, she said, "You'll have to forgive my lack of decorum. I've been on so many trips on farms, fields, and forests that I've learned to take care of business wherever I could gain a bit of privacy."

Laughing, he nodded. "Same here." He headed over to disappear behind some bushes and then hurried back to where she stood on the embankment.

She peered up at him and shrugged. "I wasn't sure if I should get in the boat without you."

"We're probably as safe in the boat as anywhere.

Let's get settled, and I'll get the latest from my team."

Once they were back seated in the boat, he radioed in to LSIWC. "No problems on the river, and according to my GPS, we're close to Puerto Wilches."

Jeb confirmed, "According to Natalie's satellite images, as long as you're safe, you could stay where you are for a little bit. Hop plans to land at a small airstrip and acquire land transportation to get as close to the river as possible. But you will still have to go a few miles through the jungle to get to him. Carson has been in contact with an agent from the Colombian Drug Task Force that he trusts. Hop may have to land somewhere to meet with Captain Rafe Molina to arrange transportation by Jeep to get to you."

Scanning the area, he said, "We're almost at the hottest part of the day, and we stopped at the side of the river to take a quick break. We've got shade, fresh water, and some food. As long as no one on the river is coming after us, and no one can get to us by land right now, we're safe here."

"Sounds good. Stay where you are, and we'll contact you as soon as we know the next steps."

Disconnecting, he looked at Valerie, seeing the interest on her face. Relaying what was happening, he wondered what her response would be. Even though he'd only known her a short time, he wasn't surprised when she simply nodded.

"Okay, I guess that makes sense. There's no reason for us to go farther up the river and then have to turn around and come back just to meet them." Heaving a sigh, she lifted her hands over her head and stretched.

He noticed the dark circles underneath her eyes and the way her shoulders slumped slightly after she finished stretching. "Did you get any sleep at all last night?"

She shook her head, stifling a yawn. "No, none. Not even a tiny, little catnap. What about you?"

"I confess that I stayed up late, anxious for you to arrive in Mexico so we could start our vacation together. I think I had just closed my eyes when you called."

Her eyes filled with empathy. "Oh, that sucks. You were already at a resort ready for sun, surf, and fun." She smiled as she cast her gaze around the area, with the lush jungle on one side and the river on the other. "Well, this isn't exactly a beach, and I don't have the fruity drink with a little umbrella sticking out, but at least we're together."

Unable to stifle his grin, he nodded. "In that case, do we consider this to be the official beginning of our vacation?"

Her laughter was warm as she held up her hands and began ticking off their escapades on her fingers. "Well, let's see. Drug cartels after us. Somebody shooting at us. I had a gun pointed at my face this morning. And we're on the run for our lives." Laughing again, she nodded. "Sure! Why not? This is as good a time as any to start our vacation."

Chuckling aloud, he was amazed at how well she dealt with the crazy-ass situation. It wasn't that she didn't care—how she'd greeted him when he arrived let him know she was grateful he'd come. But now that they were together, she just kept rolling with the punches. *Yep, she's special.*

He slid to the floor of the boat and shifted around, finding a comfortable position. He patted the wooden floor next to him, and she joined him. They sat facing each other, leaning back against the bench seats. The boat was small and narrow, so their legs touched from hip to ankle. "You comfortable?"

She smiled as she reclined and let one hand rest on the side of the boat. "Yeah. It doesn't take much for me. In light of your experiences in the military, I don't want to overexaggerate my adaptability. But as long as I feel safe, I can get comfortable almost anywhere."

He looked down at her hand resting in her lap, so close to his thigh. He didn't even have to lean to place his hand on hers. His heart squeezed as she flipped her hand over and linked her fingers with his, warmth moving from their connection to his chest.

They were quiet for a moment, and the sounds of the water flowing, the birds in the trees, and the occasional fisherman calling out to one another filled the air.

He relished the easy camaraderie with her, and considering he never held hands with women, the simple act of holding her hand felt like the start of something. He looked down at their connection, then sighed, the emotional weight bearing down on the blissful interlude. The last thing he wanted to do was to upset her, but he didn't want to start a relationship with a secret.

"Something is on your mind, Adam."

He lifted his gaze and stared at her beautiful face. Sighing heavily, he nodded. "I want to get to know you, Valerie. I want you to feel like you can talk to me. I'm interested in everything about you and really want a clean slate for us. Or maybe a clean slate isn't the right phrase because I don't want to forget the time we spent getting to know each other in Washington. And I have to tell you, that kiss we shared rocked me more than any other kiss I've ever had."

A slow smile curved her lips, and her fingers squeezed ever so lightly against his. "I feel the same way, Adam. I haven't forgotten about that kiss, even when I lost my shit and got angry." She looked down for a moment, pressed her lips together, then took a deep breath. "I should explain. There are just things about me that you should know. Looking back, I realize that part of my history is why I became so angry with your accusation. But it was a bad time, and we both acted rashly. I'd like to think we can put that behind us and start anew."

"I'd like to, but I don't want to start with a secret."

Her head jerked slightly. "A secret?"

"Yeah." He pushed his hesitancy behind him and plunged forward. "When I first got the assignment to accompany Paul and you to DC, I read up on him and a little bit on you. Not much, but enough to understand your careers, why you were going to DC, and what we might face once there. But it was after we fought, and I knew I'd overreacted. I just wanted to do something to feel closer to you." He winced. "Christ, I sound like a dick when I say that."

"I don't understand," she said, her brow furrowed.

"I looked up more about you, which I know will make you angry. But, honest to God, Valerie, I just wanted to know more about you."

She stared for a moment, then dragged her tongue over her bottom lip. "You know about my dad." The words were spoken softly, but he felt each word like a punch to the gut.

He nodded, then was quick to add, "I only know that he was a policeman who was..." He sighed. "He was killed in the line of duty during a drug bust. That's it. I swear, as soon as I saw the headline, I stopped reading because it felt like an invasion. I want you to trust me." Gripping her hand tighter, he said, "Please tell me you can trust me."

She held his gaze, and a long moment of silence ensued, causing his heart to pound. Finally, she nodded. "I trust you, Adam. I trust you with my life."

He let out a long breath and felt the weight ease off his chest. "And, Valerie, I really hope you'll tell me about your dad sometime."

She looked down at their hands, gently rubbing her thumb over his knuckles. After a moment, she lifted her gaze, her soft smile gentle. "Thank you for your honesty. Truthfully, what you did isn't much different from scouring someone's social media. That's kind of the new dating norm now, I guess." A light chuckle slipped out. "You know, I said I trust you with my life, but that also means I trust you with my past."

In the silence settling over them, their hands clutched tighter. She chewed on her bottom lip for a moment, then added, "Um… anyway, I don't mind talking about my family."

Gratitude speared through him. "I'd love to hear about them."

Her expression softened. "I'd like to say my family was perfect, but no family is. My parents were in love, and I have an older brother who could sometimes make me crazy and sometimes make me feel protected. My brother thought at one time about going into law enforcement like Dad but decided to go into the military right after high school. Dad was proud of him. It didn't matter to him what we did as long as we were happy."

She held his gaze and sighed, her smile slipping away. "One evening when I was in high school, my dad was working late, and Mom was trying to decide whether she should just hold his dinner or fix him something different when he got in. I remember I was in the kitchen at the table doing homework while she fixed dinner. Funny… I can still remember that it was meatloaf and potatoes.

Weird, isn't it? How do certain things stay in our minds?"

"They say that smells especially remind us of memories."

She nodded, her fingers twitching on his hand. "Yes, I've heard that, too." Leaning forward slightly, she continued. "Then there was a knock on the door."

She drew in a shaky breath, and Adam was awed at her strength in telling her story.

"It was my dad's partner and the station's chaplain. As they stepped into the house, I glanced out the window and saw my dad's captain and two more police officers arrive." Her gaze lifted and peered straight into him. "I knew. Mom did, too. They told us what had happened. They assured us that it had been quick, and he hadn't suffered. They said all the right things, and as my mom's legs gave out, his partner stepped forward and just held her as she sobbed. The chaplain approached me, probably expecting to do the same thing, but I could only stare. I just stared."

He rubbed his hand over her cold fingers, hoping to infuse warmth into them. He wanted to offer sympathy but knew she'd heard it all before. And in truth, platitudes never helped.

She licked her lips, then continued. "Of course, I fell apart later. Daddy had a full police-command funeral. My brother came home, and we were surrounded by family, friends, and Daddy's entire force. Eventually, my brother returned to his unit, and Mom and I just existed for a while. It was like time stood still, and the world stopped revolving, and we were just stuck in this void."

"I am so sorry, sweetheart." The endearment fell easily off his lips but felt so right. She gave no indication that it bothered her and, instead, just squeezed his hand a little tighter, offering a tiny smile.

"I was lucky to have had him in my life for as long as I did. He was a good man. He was a good policeman. And he was a fabulous dad. He used to tell me, 'Life is what you make it, Sweet Pea.'" A rueful chuckle slipped out. "Sweet Pea. That was his nickname for me. And those words didn't mean as much to me when I was younger. But now I try to make my life something with meaning."

"You miss him every day."

Her eyes widened ever so slightly. Nodding slowly, she agreed. "Yes, I miss him every day." They were silent for a moment, then she held his gaze. "You seem to understand my loss in a personal way."

"Yeah, I do."

"Will you share? I mean, you don't have to. This isn't a tit-for-tat story time. But I'd like to know more about what makes you... well, *you.*"

He hesitated, uncertainty filling him. Only a few friends and Carson knew his story. And then, they only knew the basics. He'd never talked about his pain and loss, but staring into her hazel eyes, he realized he would bare his soul willingly to her, and she'd handle it with care.

20

Valerie held his gaze and her breath, desperately wanting him to share his story. When she'd bared her pain, talking about her beloved dad, she didn't see in his eyes what was so often presented by others.

Some people shy away when they're discomfited. Others offer a pat on the shoulder and a "Gee, your dad died in the line of duty. What a great honor for a policeman." *Really? I don't think my dad took it as an honor since he was deceased, and the family he left behind would've rather have had him with us.* She never said those words, though. She'd just nod and move on, not wanting to continue the conversation.

But in Adam's eyes, she saw understanding. And she realized he had his own story to tell and wanted him to want to share it with her. She waited and silently begged... *please.*

He looked down at their linked fingers and rubbed his thumb over hers. Then he lifted his head so that his expressive blue eyes stared intently into hers. "Like you, I had a great family. My parents loved each other and loved me and my younger sister. We were a typical middle-class family. I was three years older than my sister." He snorted and shook his head. "We were all really into sports. I played baseball, ran cross-country, and learned martial arts. My sister did gymnastics and martial arts, too. Our parents raced around trying to make it to every event, every game.

"After high school, I attended community college for two years and joined the Army. My sister graduated from high school and went to college about the same time I headed off to boot camp. In her second year, she suffered a pretty serious accident while doing gymnastics. She was in a lot of pain, and besides seeing all the sports physicians and physical therapists, she also saw a pain specialist. They were monitoring her for the pain drugs, but..."

Valerie managed to keep her breathing steady, but her heart had already started to pound.

Adam sighed. "They tried to wean her off the painkillers, but getting her hands on pills in college was easy. Eventually, she got hooked up with someone who offered her morphine. She got so bad that when my parents found out, they took her out of college and put her in rehab. On my next leave, I came home to check on her. She was clean and out of rehab but so embarrassed. We talked her through it along with her counselor. I told her there was no shame in trying not to feel pain, but we just needed to go about it the right way. I only had a week off after Ranger school but felt confident because she stayed out a whole semester of college. We'd video chat whenever I could, and I got letters from Mom and Dad saying she was doing well."

As Adam's story unfolded, Valerie's heart ached. Their fingers were still linked, but she leaned over so her freehand could also clasp his. She knew the tale would end in heartache and wanted to comfort him.

He looked down at their hands again. "Back in college, she was with the people who remembered her using. They're such fuckin' predators. They can smell someone's need and fear." Heaving a sigh, he shook the air as it was released. "It wasn't long before she was using again. Only this time, the addiction pulled her under. She ended up hooked on fentanyl and just got dragged in too deep. She overdosed and was already... already dead by the time her roommate found her. There was nothing that anyone could do."

She gasped as though all the air had evaporated from the universe, and tears filled her eyes. "Oh, Adam, I'm so sorry. So very sorry. Oh, honey, my heart aches so badly for you. You and your parents... and your poor, sweet sister."

His breath rushed from his lungs as his eyes roamed Valerie's face. Her emotions were evident, showing nothing but compassion. "No one's ever said they were sorry for her. I mean, of course, me and my parents… but no one else mentions her."

"Honey, she had an addiction. And it was tragic how it got started. I know that's not the life she would've wanted. And I'm so sorry that her life was cut short, and she, you, and your parents had to endure that pain." She hesitated, then asked, "What was her name?"

"Anna."

Wanting to erase the space between them, she scooted forward and leaned slightly to the side, pulling her hands from his to wrap them around his neck and press closely to him. His arms quickly snaked around her body, and for several minutes, neither spoke as they held each other tightly.

Strangely connected by not only their paths crossing now but also a shared cause of grief. The story of his sister and her father were different but linked, nonetheless.

Finally, she leaned back just enough to be able to peer into his eyes again, realizing she could drown in their blue depths. He lifted his arm, and she shifted around so they faced the same direction, her head tucked against his chest and his arm wrapped around her shoulders. They sat in silence for several long moments, connected, as she listened to his heartbeat. And found her heart beating in time with his.

Reaching over the bench, she grabbed the tote and then pulled out more food and water bottles. She stared into the bag for a moment, then asked, "It's really strange that the cook put so much in here, isn't it? Do you think she knew what was going to happen to me? I mean, certainly not all of this. But that I wouldn't be taken straight to the hospital?"

Valerie's stomach had growled loudly, causing them to chuckle and sit up, deciding that it was time to eat and drink more.

"I have no idea. There's no way of knowing who in Sebastian's household knew his business. Maybe she just wanted to make sure you were taken care of."

They shared another sandwich and a bunch of grapes before opening another water bottle.

She turned to face him. "Can I ask you a question?"

He nodded, his expression serious. "You can ask anything you want."

"I just wondered what's happening. I know you've got some of your co-workers flying in, and they'll meet us somewhere. But I wanted to know if more is happening."

He winced. "I'm really sorry. I never meant to keep you out of anything, and of course, you're curious. My friends left California not long after I called them, and that was right after you talked to me. They should be landing about now. I was told they would meet with a Colombia Drug Task Force captain, who will help them acquire vehicles to get to us. Once we have our coordinates, we'll know what we need to do to get close to them."

"They're meeting with the Colombian Drug Task Force?"

He nodded. "They're giving him all the information you and I relayed. Everything about Joseph. Everything about Sebastian. And what was found at that warehouse."

She blew out a breath, surprised at what was happening behind the scenes. "I feel rather stupid that I never thought about the Colombians having the equivalent of our DEA."

He stared at her for a long moment. "Can I ask you a question?"

Grinning, she repeated his words. "You can ask anything you want."

"How did you get involved with the DEA? I mean, I understood the *why* once I learned about your dad. But I guess I'm curious as to how it all came about."

"Paul and I had come back from the trip to Colombia… the one where we were kidnapped for a day. We were at a conference, giving a lecture about global warming affecting the crops in poorer countries, and since he was from Colombia, we had gathered data to present. We were also getting ready for another trip to South America. After the lecture, I was approached by Agent Sellers. Robin said that she wanted to talk to me privately. We went to lunch, and she said she was following some suspected cartel members who came in and out of our country using the embassy. She knew of at least one who had attended a lecture in the States and had been reportedly at one of our presentations when we were in Colombia. She wanted to know if I would be interested in letting her know if I was contacted."

"And I'll bet she mentioned your dad, didn't she?"

She blinked, jerking slightly. "Yes, but how do you know that?"

"Pretty typical of undercover operations. Find someone who might get information and then find out more about them. I assure you, Agent Sellers learned all about you before she ever approached."

Jerking slightly, she huffed. "So I was targeted?"

"Yeah, I'm sure you were."

She pressed her lips together and then sighed. "If I had known, it really wouldn't have mattered. She was right. I was anxious to avenge my dad's death just by working with her."

"I agree, but it shits me to think that she was putting you in danger."

"You didn't even know me then."

"Doesn't matter," he insisted. "When you care for someone, you care about all of them, including their past pain."

Gasping slightly, she gripped his fingers tighter. They sat, just staring for a moment, eyes devouring each other. He was right. She wanted to absorb any pain he'd ever experienced. Finally, clearing her throat, she continued.

"On another trip to Colombia, I was contacted by

phone call after a lecture. It said that someone wanted more information about cocaine production in light of global warming. If I agreed to get information to them based on our research, they would pay well."

"And you agreed."

"Absolutely. I gave Robin the information, and the contact only occurred about three times over the next couple of years. I was instructed where to leave the information on a thumb drive, and money was left for me. Each time, I informed Robin and turned the money over to her. And before you think she was just taking it on the side, she had me go to the Los Angeles DEA office, and it was turned over very officially. She said they were amassing their evidence for a case." Sighing heavily, she added, "I trusted her. Or at least, I didn't *not* trust her. I never felt like I was in danger. My job with the DEA was to let them know when and where the drops would be made, and they would gather whatever evidence they needed. And then we had the one at DC, where I foolishly ended up seeing the two men in the lobby."

His face filled with regret. "I'm still sorry about—"

"No, Adam. It's over. We both lost our cool in an extreme situation and didn't have enough togetherness to overcome what was happening."

He sighed, then nodded. "And the man in the lecture… the one who sat next to you and then talked to you?"

Laughing, she said, "I told you the truth. He just

asked me out, and I didn't want to go, so I turned him down."

They were quiet for a moment, then she lifted her hand and rubbed her forehead. "When Robin first approached me, part of me was thrilled. Being able to report on a cartel member to the DEA made me feel that I was avenging my father's death." She shook her head and scoffed. "What a stupid idea. Even when I was pulled off because of your influence, I wasn't disappointed about not working with them anymore. That night that you and I argued, I was angry but knew I'd placed myself in danger. My getting hurt would devastate my mother and brother. And Daddy would be so upset if he knew I was putting myself at risk."

He reached over and tucked a wayward strand of hair behind her ear. "After that night, when I realized I'd acted precipitously and felt like such an asshole, I was torn up inside, thinking about the risk you were taking. I was pissed at Agent Sellers because she knew the risks when she got into her career, and I felt like she was using you to further her own career without you fully understanding those risks. So I admit, I used some influence to pull you off being an informant."

"In reality, I should thank you. At the time, I just allowed it to fuel my anger, but now, I know my dad would want me to live my life." She looked at Adam and saw a man of strength, courage, and a strong sense of duty. Tilting her head slightly, she dipped her chin. "My dad was such a good man. Kind, caring, a good soul, and a wonderful policeman. He would go out of his way to help someone in need. I hope this doesn't embarrass you, but I have to say that my dad would've really liked you."

"It doesn't embarrass me at all, Valerie. I'm honored. From all you've told me, you need to know he would've been very proud of you."

She pressed a kiss to his lips, tentative and uncertain. She meant to offer the kiss as confirmation of their closeness and their shared comfort. But just as she started to lean back, her lips opened ever so slightly. Adam lifted a hand and cupped the back of her head, his fingers diving through her ponytail and angling her mouth so his tongue could slide in.

It was just as good as she remembered. The velvet touch as their tongues tangled. His masculine scent filled and surrounded her. Her breasts felt heavy as her nipples tightened, and the delicious jolt moved straight to her sex.

Giving herself over fully, she didn't mind handing control to him, and he sure as hell knew what to do with it. This man knew exactly what he was doing. The kiss stretched into long minutes of deep exploration and shared electricity.

She barely felt his hands move to her waist until he shifted her body to straddle him. The kiss continued while her needy core was pressed against his swollen erection. Layers of clothes were between them, but she began to drag herself over him, needing friction.

He slipped his hand under her shirt and palmed her breast, tweaking her nipples. Their mouths never separated, and she dry-humped him, becoming more desperate with each movement.

Mumbling against his lips, she said, "Oh God, if we don't stop, I'm going to embarrass myself."

He chuckled, the sound rumbling up from his chest and swallowed by her. It was almost as erotic as his kiss. *Almost.*

His hands separated, and while one stayed on her breasts, the other one dropped so that his fingers pressed where their bodies met. Between rubbing her core against his cock and him fingering the bundle of nerves, she cried out against his lips as her fingers dug into his shoulders. Wave after wave of bliss moved over her until she finally dropped her forehead, tucking her face against his neck. His hands slid around to her back, gently rubbing, as she caught her breath.

"Wow. I probably should be embarrassed that happened so quickly, but that felt too good for me to care."

He chuckled again, and her chest moved with his motion. Now, she had a heightened awareness of his swollen cock, and realized she'd just given him a major case of blue balls. Lifting her head, she looked around and discerned there was no way she'd feel comfortable trying to have sex in a small boat on the edge of a river. But she wasn't opposed to getting creative.

With a twinkle in her eye, she slid off his lap and knelt between his legs. It wasn't the most comfortable position, but she was willing to forgo a little comfort to give back to him what he'd given to her.

With her hands on his belt, she quickly unbuckled it and was unzipping when he grabbed her wrists.

"No, sweetheart, you do not have to do this."

"I know," she said, leaning in to kiss him softly. "But I really want to… unless *you* don't want me to."

His eyes widened, and he scoffed. "There isn't a man alive who wouldn't want to see your lips around his cock. And since I don't share, I'm glad that it'll be my cock that has that pleasure."

She laughed, then went back to work on his zipper. It took a bit of finagling, but she finally managed to free his cock. Staring at his erection, she mumbled, "Wow. You're… um… impressive." Lifting her gaze to his face, she admitted, "I really hope I get to find out what we can do if we finally come together. You know… if we were on a real vacation and not being chased by killers and drug cartels."

"Oh, Valerie, it's not *if* we finally come together. It's *when* we come together."

Grinning, she leaned down and took him in her mouth. Easing her lips over him, she licked and sucked, fisted the base, and alternated between fast and slow movements. It had been a long time, and she was hardly a blow job specialist, but she was determined to give it her best effort. And he was enjoying her efforts from the sounds he was making and the way his fingers cupped her head without forcing.

Finally, he groaned, "You've got to stop, babe. I'm gonna come."

Loving his feel and taste, she kept going, determined to see it through. He groaned again, and she felt the muscles of his thighs stiffen just before he came. She continued to suck until she had every last drop.

"Holy, fucking hell," he gasped. His head flopped back against the bench seat as though every ounce of strength had been stolen from him.

She slowly lifted her head and carefully tucked him back into his pants, mindful to zip without catching his dick.

He sat up and pulled her close, kissing her soundly again. "I never meant for that to happen, Valerie. I would never want to take advantage of you being out here with me. But that was fucking amazing."

"No one took advantage of me," she assured. "I didn't do anything that I didn't want to do. And believe me, I loved every minute!"

With a deep sigh, she shifted slightly so they sat close again, but she was no longer straddling him. She didn't know when they might meet his friends and hoped he wouldn't have to sport a hard-on when they did.

21

"Where do we meet you?" Adam hated to end his time talking with Valerie, but the longer they stayed on the river, the more likely someone would notice. He wanted her out of the country and safe.

"We're landing at Puerto Mosquito," Hop said. "It's a small airstrip, and Captain Rafe Molina, the DTF contact we've met here, has made sure it's cleared for us. We need you to go about twenty kilometers north on the river, and then Dolby and Poole will meet you with transportation. They'll bring you back here, where Valerie can give them all the information she knows."

Valerie grabbed his arm and shook it, her eyes wide. "Ask about Paul."

He nodded, wrapping his free arm around her shoulders. "And what have you got on Paul Mendez?"

"According to Jeb, he was medevacked out several hours ago. He's on his way to Los Angeles, where his wife will meet him at a hospital. The latest information showed he was stable and alert. Carson talked to his wife, who said Paul was worried about Valerie. We haven't told them anything other than she's being brought back privately."

He relayed that information to Valerie, who nodded empathetically as the relief was evident when her face relaxed.

"I don't want him to worry about me, so that's good. Please, thank your people for me."

He smiled. "Valerie says thank you. Same from me."

"She can thank us when she sees us, and that should be soon."

Getting off the radio, he ran his gaze over her, once again noticing the dark circles under her eyes, the fatigue in her shoulders, and the strain in her grip on his arm. He wanted nothing more than to get her settled somewhere safe, with food in her belly and a soft bed to sleep on. Preferably with him. Besides the tension and tiredness radiating from her, she had a glow. She was alive and living life on her terms. And being in her presence and sharing more of that life with her was rapidly becoming the most important thing to him.

"What did they say?" she asked.

"Well, are you ready to get rescued?"

Her lips started to curve before a giggle slipped out. "The moment you came for me. The moment my gaze landed on you coming around that corner…

that's the moment I was rescued. Don't think I'm not grateful for what the others are doing for us because I am. But to me, *you'll* always be the one who rescued me."

He leaned forward and kissed her, hating that he didn't have more time to take it deeper and show her how much she meant to him. "Damn, Valerie. You deserve so much more than what I've shown you so far. But I promise I'll give you everything once we're out of here and at a safe and comfortable place."

"If you just give me you, that'll be more than enough."

"Oh, plan on it." With another hard, quick kiss, he leaned back and started the motor, steering the boat out into the river's main stream. Tapping on his radio, he connected to Natalie. "Let me know when I'm close."

"You got it," she replied. "It'll be good to have you home, and I can't wait to meet Valerie."

He smiled as he steered them north, keeping his eye on the river while also watching Valerie. She looked from one side of the river to the other, staring at the jungles and farms to the east and the other boats on the river. "What are you thinking?"

"Just thinking about how everything in my life brought me to this moment."

His chin jerked down slightly as he was startled by her response. "Wow, that's a whole lot deeper than I thought." Laughter slipped from her lips, and he loved the sound. "Sorry, I didn't mean to call a halt to your mental wanderings."

She shook her head. "It's all right. I guess it was kind of heavy."

"Tell me more."

Her shoulders hefted. "I love the work I do, but I'm smart enough to realize that, in many ways, Paul became my surrogate father figure. So Dad's death literally led me to Paul's door. My dad's death and my work for Paul led me to Agent Sellers. That led me to meet you and, ultimately, the need to be rescued when it all blew up."

"There's a lot to unpack there, sweetheart. Sometimes life just happens."

She slowly shook her head. "No, I don't believe that. I mean, yes, we do make our own decisions, but the past can shape us." She sighed. "Maybe I just don't want to think that my dad died for nothing."

Understanding flooded throughout him. How many times had he wanted Anna's death to not be in vain? "You're right."

With one hand still on the motor handle, he reached out with the other and squeezed her hand. "I'm just glad we found each other."

Her lips curved until a wide smile spread over her face. Then her smile wobbled ever so slightly. "Do you think it's crazy? Us, I mean."

"I don't think there's anything crazy about us." As the words left his mouth, he realized how true they were. "Sweetheart, it doesn't matter how two people meet. It doesn't matter what happened in their lives to create a place where their paths crossed. All that matters is that they found each other."

"Oh God, Adam, that's beautiful."

He looked around, ensuring he kept them moving north at a slow but steady speed, then turned back to her.

"You and me? Maybe to some people, it wouldn't make sense. Maybe for them, it would be nuts to start talking about a *you and me.* But when I met you, I wanted to get to know you. And the more I learned, the more I wanted to be around you. If we'd had a chance to spend more time together, I wouldn't have jumped to such rash conclusions. But I know you now, and I'm sorry I didn't trust you then."

He couldn't imagine her smile being any more beautiful than how she looked at him right now. And he wanted to kiss her. "Come here, babe—"

Suddenly, Natalie interrupted his thoughts as she radioed. "You'll come to another fork in the river in one kilometer. Keep to the right, and you'll see a bridge passing over. You'll dock at the base of the bridge on the east and meet the Jeep."

Once again, the conversation he wanted to continue with Valerie was halted, and he longed for the time when they could talk together with no distractions. Now, he needed to focus on their surroundings the way he should have been all along.

There were many places where small islands were in the middle of the river, but he easily found where they needed to go using his watch's screen and Natalie's directions.

"See that small bridge up there? That's where we'll meet my people."

"I know this sounds strange, but I swear I'm nervous."

He chuckled and patted her shoulder, letting his fingers rest there. "Don't be. We're gonna be out of here soon, and you can put all of this behind you."

She twisted around and shook her head. "I only want to put the bad things behind me. There were a lot of good things on this trip, and I'm looking at the most important one right now."

"Damn, woman. Hold those thoughts until we can be alone."

He let go of her so he could guide the small boat to the embankment, where he spied two Jeeps with Dolby and Poole and several well-armed men. Adam heard the gasp from Valerie and assured, "It's okay. Those are two of the Keepers and the Drug Task Force."

Dolby jogged to the edge of the embankment, where he leaned over and grabbed hold of the front of the boat as they drifted to the edge of the river. "Good to see you, man!"

"You, too!"

"You must be Ms. Clemens. My name is Dolby. Let me give you a hand, ma'am."

Dolby held his hand out and guided Valerie to the

end of the boat, where he lifted her gently and set her feet on the ground.

"Thank you so much for coming for us, and please, call me Valerie."

Adam had a strange desire to slap Dolby's hands away even though he knew that was ridiculous. Dolby was infatuated with his beautiful wife. Nonetheless, Adam hastened out of the boat to take Valerie's hand to guide her up the steep embankment. At the top, Poole's hands shot out to assist her and take Adam's pack from him.

Once on firm ground, he, Dolby, and Poole offered back slaps and shared thanks. Then with his hand gently on Valerie's back, he guided her over to the Jeeps.

His gaze cast over the four heavily armed Colombian men who were not wearing any law-enforcement insignia. One man exuded leadership and stepped forward.

"Miss Clemens. I'm Captain Rafe Molina. I'm glad to see you well. I'm sorry that Colombia did not offer you the hospitality you've come to expect."

"Thank you, Captain. I assure you that my feelings about your beautiful country are unchanged, although my understanding of what you must deal with in your job has greatly increased."

"You're very generous, and I know our agriculture department and universities owe you and Dr. Mendez a debt of gratitude."

Stepping forward, Adam said, "I know you have

some questions for her, but right now, she's exhausted and would benefit from being out of the sun. Is there a place at the airfield where we can take a break before the interview?"

"Absolutely, and my apologies. I should've thought of that first. It is only about a twenty-five-minute drive to the airfield. I assume you would like to travel with your friends, and we will be right behind you. Once there, Ms. Clemens, you may certainly be indoors. As soon as I get your statement, you'll be free to go, and my men will have a raid to conduct."

Adam felt the captain's gaze boring into him, underscoring the urgency of speaking with Valerie, but for now, he didn't care. They could wait. All other priorities took a back seat to get her comfortable with access to running water, a restroom, and some food. Then and only then would he relent to her being interviewed.

Ignoring the knowing glances and barely concealed grins exchanged between Dolby and Poole, he assisted Valerie into the back seat of one Jeep, then settled in next to her. Her fingers clutched her purse and the tote, almost as if they were lifelines. He wrapped his arm around her shoulders, his protective instincts swelling within. Dolby climbed behind the wheel and with Poole in the passenger seat, they pulled onto the narrow road leading away from the river.

Conversation was difficult over the roaring

engine, but as he kept his arm securely around her, she eventually relaxed, slumping against him.

As they neared the airfield, the Jeep slowed, and Poole twisted in his seat, eyes locking on Adam. "Don't be thrown by Rafe. He's gruff, but he's fully vetted. He's not dumb enough to think he can take down all the cartels, but he's determined to be a thorn in their side for as long as possible."

Adam nodded, admiring the man's tenacity in the ongoing drug wars in Colombia. "Got no problem with him as long as he treats Valerie with respect."

Poole's lips quirked upward, but before he had a chance to say anything, the Jeep stopped outside a small building. The airfield was small, but seeing the airplane Hop had waiting for them was a sight Adam was grateful for. He alighted first, then turned and held on to Valerie as she stepped down to the ground. Once inside the small hangar, he spied Hop and hurried over. The two hugged as they slapped their backs. "Damn, man, can't thank you enough for getting to us." Turning, he reached for Valerie. "This is Hop, and this is Valerie. Hop is going to fly us out of here."

"It's good to meet you, Valerie," Hop greeted, offering a hearty smile.

"Same here." She laughed. "And I wholeheartedly agree with the flying out part."

Adam spied a couple of doors near the back, but cognizant of the room filling with Rafe's men, he leaned toward Hop and, in a lowered voice, asked, "Bathroom?"

"Right over there." Hop pointed in the direction of the closest door.

He lifted his chin in thanks, and then, with his arm around her shoulders, he escorted Valerie over, whispering, "Take your time."

She shot a grateful nod at him, then hurried inside and closed the door. Unwilling to leave the area, he walked only a few feet away to talk to the other Keepers. A few minutes later, the door opened, and she stepped back into the main area of the hangar. She'd splashed water on her face and had run a brush through her hair.

"Okay?"

Her face shone with gratitude. "Yeah, thanks. The cold water felt good. I think I left you some."

Chuckling, he squeezed her shoulder. Throwing a pointed glance at the other Keepers, he headed into the restroom. He knew they'd protect her, even from Rafe wanting to question her without him around. Hurrying to finish, he walked out and didn't miss the smile she sent his way. Moving to a table with only three chairs in the middle of the hangar, he, Valerie, and Rafe sat. The three other armed men stood behind their captain.

Adam knew it was an intimidation tactic and grinned as Dolby, Poole, and Hop stood behind Adam and Valerie, their legs apart and their arms crossed over their chests.

But he should've known that Valerie was cool under pressure. She answered Rafe's questions and precisely reiterated what had transpired with Sebastian and Joseph. Finally, Adam described the truck he'd seen outside the warehouse.

Rafe stood and, with a curt nod, acknowledged them both. "Thank you, Ms. Clemens. I applaud your bravery and ingenuity. I wish you a safe flight back home and must warn you about a return trip to our country. We have someone on the inside who has been feeding us information. We were alerted of your disappearance about the same time that Lighthouse Security contacted us. And the information given to us is that Joseph Perez knew of your escape and, in all probability, ordered someone to try to kill you. His reach is limited, which is probably why only one attempt on your life was made by the man on the motorcycle. If you'd stayed longer, I have no doubt that he would have sent more people to hunt you."

"What was supposed to happen? When the helicopter pilot left me outside the warehouse?"

"I don't know of a definitive plan, but the person I have on the inside indicated that you were to be met there by someone who would ensure you were never seen again. They managed to delay that from happening, giving you time to escape."

She gasped, and Adam tightened his grip on her hand.

"But," Rafe said, "I am pleased to announce that I have a raid on a warehouse to perform." With that, he shook their hands, then turned briskly and headed out to a waiting helicopter with his men.

Valerie slumped back in her chair and heaved a sigh of relief. "How soon can we leave?"

The men chuckled, and Hop said, "Fueled up and ready to go. The next stop is Mexico for refueling, then home to California."

Adam nodded, then looked down at Valerie, hoping he knew the answer to the question he wanted to ask. Gaining courage, he blurted, "What do you say if we get off in Mexico? We could take some time just for us."

Her head swung around so fast that her ponytail slapped against his cheek. His smile faltered as he observed her wide-eyed, mouth-agape expression. Just as he was ready to backtrack, thinking he must have misunderstood her need to return to California immediately.

"Really? Are you serious? Oh, please tell me that you're not kidding right now!" Her eyes were bright, and he loved that she didn't hide her interest. She squealed and threw her arms around his neck.

Relief shot through him as he hugged her in return. "We are owed a vacation, remember?"

"Oh, I remember, but I just didn't know when we might be able to plan something."

"I was afraid after everything that happened, you might just want to go back home."

She shook her head and leaned back to hold his gaze as they both ignored the other Keepers nearby.

"I'll call Ellen to check on Paul as soon as we get to Mexico. But there's nothing I can do for him right now as long as he's in the hospital. We had already planned a break when we got back from Colombia, anyway, so there's nothing at the university I need to do. I'll call one of the other assistants and make sure that they handle our soil and plant samples carefully, but I'm all yours for Mexico, the beach, a palm tree hut, and a fruity drink with an umbrella sticking out of it."

Chuckling, he said, "I think your standards have gotten higher. Before all of this, you just wanted a fruity drink. Now you want one with the umbrella sticking out of it."

"After what I've been through? I definitely deserve the umbrella in the drink. In fact, pineapple chunks and cherries should be attached to the umbrella stem in my fruity drink!"

The other Keepers laughed, shaking their heads. "Valerie, I like you," Hop said. "I can't wait until you meet my wife, Lori."

"I was just thinking the same thing," Dolby agreed. "We want to make sure we all get together when you two return to California. My wife is Marcia, and I'll make sure she gives you a call."

Poole clapped Adam on the back as he walked by. "You know my Tricia will be glad not to be the newest one in the group."

As the other men walked over to the plane, she

lifted on her toes and whispered into Adam's ear. “What was that all about?”

“Let’s just say you’ve already gotten the Keeper seal of approval. I know that sounds crazy because you and I are just starting out, but believe me, those are some of the best men I know, and praise from them is high praise indeed. And, of course, I might be biased, but I agree with them.” He kissed her lightly. “Let’s get out of here, sweetheart.”

After another bathroom break, he escorted her to board the plane. Adam held her hand during takeoff and watched as she peered out the window. After a few minutes, she turned toward him and yawned.

“Come here,” he encouraged, holding his arm up.

She leaned closer. While she rested her head on his shoulder, he laid his cheek against the top of her head. He couldn’t imagine a better feeling than having her close.

22

When Valerie and Adam landed in Mexico, she'd offered heartfelt hugs to Hop, Dolby, and Poole. Then she and Adam said goodbye, caught a taxi to the resort he'd only left the day before, and hit the stores to purchase a few clothes, swimsuits, and toiletries.

Adam asked for two rooms at the reception desk, but Valerie quickly stepped closer and whispered, "One room." The look on his face was priceless. To drive home her point, she lifted on her toes so that her mouth was close to his ear. "It'll be a waste of money to have two rooms 'cause I don't plan on sleeping alone now that I've got you all to myself."

A wide grin curved his lips, and he returned to the receptionist counter. "Make that one room. King bed. With upgrades."

Her eyes widened. "Upgrades? What sort of upgrades?"

She soon discovered it included a Jacuzzi tub large enough for two, sparkling champagne mimosas served with a gourmet breakfast each day, and discounts for their meals and drinks. But what she was most excited about was their own private cabana on the beach that she couldn't wait to experience.

Exhilarated but exhausted, the first thing they'd done once inside the air-conditioned room was lock the door and flop onto the bed. She was desperate for a shower, but sleep called louder than the desire to be clean. Even the fact that a gorgeous Adam was lying next to her didn't tempt her to stay awake. In fact, she swore she heard a snore from him just before she fell asleep. Mad, passionate sex would have to wait.

Awaking hours later, it was nighttime, but as soon as they showered, they found the resort still abuzz with life and the restaurants open. Famished, she devoured a full meal, groaning in delight with every bite.

They'd held hands while strolling along the floral trail leading back to their resort room. It was as though they'd known each other for much longer than reality. As she looked up at him in the moonlight, her heart began to race, just knowing he'd chosen her.

They made it back to the room and fell into bed, both finding sleep almost instantaneously. When she woke the following morning, the room was empty, but a flower and a note lay on the other side of the bed. Smiling, she rolled over, sniffed the fragrant tropical bloom, and read the note.

As soon as you wake, go to Cabana 16. Wear your swimsuit. Breakfast and I await. Adam

She had shoved back the covers, raced into the bathroom, and jumped into the shower. Glad she had the foresight to buy a razor, she shaved, then washed and conditioned her hair and quickly toweled off. Slathering on sunscreen, she slipped on the bikini she'd just purchased and pulled on a sundress over the top. Grabbing her purse, she filled it with her sunglasses, sunscreen, and the floppy hat. Jamming her feet into flip-flops, she locked the door and hurried along the floral-lined path to the beach. Staring at the gorgeous gulf, she jogged down the line of cabanas, searching for the designated one.

She breathed deeply, catching the delicious salt-air breeze off the Gulf of Mexico and the floral scents wafting from the beautiful floral landscaping nearby. This was no ordinary vacation… she was in paradise.

She couldn't remember the last time she'd taken a real vacation. Trudging through forests, toiling in cultivated fields, running tests on plants, soil, and water, and sleeping in discount hotels due to budget constraints did not count as a vacation.

Anxiously searching for her cabana, she was ready to be a goddess of leisure. There, Adam lounged, turning his sunglass-covered eyes toward her. He shoved the glasses onto his head and jumped to his feet. "Hey, sweetheart," he greeted, wrapping his arms around her. "In case you're wondering, leaving you in bed this morning was hard as hell. I wanted you to rest, but if I had stayed in bed with you longer, neither of us would have rested."

His words sent a tingling down her spine, a tantalizing preview of what the rest of their vacation might hold. Her heart pounded in anticipation. She started to open her mouth, but he placed a finger over her lips.

"We have plenty of time to learn about each other. But right now, I just wanna take care of you," he said.

Adam had said many special things, but wanting to take care of her right now was one of the best.

She sat on one side of the double lounger, and he waved to one of the servers hovering nearby. Three servers arrived with their hands full of large platters a few minutes later. Setting them on the small table in the cabana, they smiled as they whipped off the covers, showing two hearty breakfast plates, a separate plate of pastries, and a large bowl of fruit. Another server brought a tray with a coffee pot, cups, and two mimosas. She laughed when she saw an umbrella sticking out of one of them.

They spent the morning eating, lounging in the sun, snoozing in the shade, walking on the beach, and playing in the crystal-blue water. They napped on the thick-cushioned chaise lounge under the open-sided, palm-branch-topped cabana with gauzy curtains. Two sides had the curtains tied back to allow a perfect view of the water and the cool breeze to caress their skin as it danced over their bodies. The other two sides had the drapes down to provide privacy.

And every moment, they grew closer. If he wasn't reaching out and touching her, her hand would find him. Rolling over to her side, she traced her finger over the tattoo on his shoulder. "The lighthouse is beautiful. I assume it ties in with your employer?"

He smiled, and for a moment, she forgot what she'd asked.

"We all have this tattoo. There's a tracer underneath the skin, under the lantern. It's a way for us to be able to locate each other if we lose contact during a mission."

Her mouth fell open. "Wow. That's really kind of James Bondish, isn't it?"

He laughed and rolled toward her, pulling her into his arms. "Wanna head back to the room?"

"Oh, yeah," she murmured.

After gathering their belongings, they wandered back to the room hand in hand, and the tingle of excitement grew as she anticipated their first true evening together when they weren't being chased or recuperating from their ordeals.

Entering the room, he checked it first, and then she followed. She heard the lock click behind her and turned after tossing her tote, hat, and sunglasses onto the nearest chair. "Do you know what I wanna do?"

His blue eyes darkened, but he remained silent.

"I want to take a shower."

He didn't show disappointment but simply smiled and nodded.

She grinned, arching one brow. "But I don't want to shower by myself."

At that, his eyes widened as he sucked in a quick breath. "You want company?"

"Definitely." She nodded, staring up at him with blatant desire.

"Got anybody in mind you'd like for company?"

She stepped forward and dragged a finger down over his chest before lifting on her toes and kissing the underside of his jaw. "Most assuredly."

"And should I hazard a guess as to who you want to share your shower with?"

Their words had been joking, their tones light. But now, she gripped his biceps and stared up into his beautiful face. "I only want you."

"Oh, sweetheart, you've got me."

He bent, and with one arm at her back and the other under her knees, he scooped her up, and she wrapped her arms around his neck as he carried her into the bathroom. Their cabin had a Jacuzzi tub and a shower that was easily big enough for her and Adam to get creative.

He flipped on the water, and as the steam began to rise around them, he stripped her slowly. Pulling her sundress over her head, he leaned down and kissed her as his fingers unhooked her bikini top. He whipped his T-shirt over his head as it fell to the tiled floor. Now, both naked from the waist up, her eyes devoured his muscles as his gaze and hands roamed over her breasts.

"You are so beautiful. I noticed it the first time I saw you, but I was determined not to pay attention to that."

Her brow furrowed as she shook her head and looked up at him. "What do you mean you weren't going to pay attention to that?"

"You were someone I was supposed to protect."

Understanding dawned. "Oh, I see. I was part of the job, and you had too much integrity to act upon the attraction."

"Yes, but it actually goes deeper than that."

"Really? I'm intrigued."

"It has almost become a joke among Keepers. It seems that everyone has ended up with a partner they met while on a mission."

"Hmm, doesn't that make it a little awkward when they go back on another mission?'

"Not when they've met the right person. It's not that they fall for someone every time. Instead, they fall for the right person at the right time. Think about Hop, Dolby, and Poole. They're now married to the women they fell in love with." His eyes widened as soon as he spoke, and he shook his head quickly. "I didn't mean to scare you. I mean, didn't want to imply that we're going to get married... oh shit, I'm fucking this up."

She laughed, seeing the normally calm Adam become flustered. "Don't worry, I'm not expecting a ring. But I really would like to get lucky in the shower."

"Hell, yeah," he agreed as they both shucked the rest of their clothes.

Now, with his full body on display, and his erect cock jutting forward, she inhaled deeply, staring. "Jesus, you are even more beautiful naked than I could've imagined. And believe me, I have imagined a lot."

He checked the temperature of the water before guiding her under the spray. She groaned as the hot water pounded her muscles. He turned her so her back was to him, and she waited, not knowing what he planned. She was almost startled when his hands began lathering shampoo into her hair. Once again, she groaned in pure pleasure.

After he washed her hair, she turned around and picked up the body wash. As she ran her soapy hands over his chest, torso, and back, it was his time to growl, and she loved hearing the deep sound rumble from his chest.

She'd never had sex in a shower, and other than a few romance novels she read, she had no idea how the mechanics of such an act would work. The idea that a man would hold her with her back pressed against the shower wall might sound amazing in a book, but she wasn't convinced it would be very comfortable.

On one side of the shower was a tiled bench, and she smiled as he led her to it and helped her to stand on it. She was at the perfect height for his lips to encircle a nipple and pull it deeply into his mouth. She felt completely safe with his body pressing against hers, one hand holding her waist while the other palmed a breast, and his teeth and tongue working the other. He moved back and forth between her nipples, and she felt the tingle of electricity moving along her nerves between her breast and her core. Her hands gripped his shoulders, and then he began to move lower, kissing the water droplets off her belly and down her mound.

He squatted in front of her, placing his face now directly at her sex. Instead of being embarrassed, she opened her legs as wide as she could, and then, as he encouraged her by nudging one thigh, she lifted one foot and placed her knee over his shoulder. His hands still held her firmly, and she no longer even thought about falling as soon as he licked her folds and sucked on the bundle of nerves.

Her body quivered as she felt the coil tighten inside. Desperate for release, she moved her hips, and he shifted one hand around to insert a long finger into her channel. Moving it in just the right way, he found the spot she'd been anxious for him to touch. The water from the rain showerhead pelted down on her breasts, and with his finger tweaking inside her core, he gently scraped his teeth along the taut bud. She felt the coil suddenly spring loose, and her body shattered from deep inside. She rode wave after wave of pleasure until finally she could open her eyes and stare down at the man who leaned back and smiled, licking his lips before gently kissing her belly and then each breast as he slowly stood. She was no longer sure her legs would hold her, but he already anticipated her weakness.

He picked her up carefully and set her feet on the plush bathmat before flipping off the water. Grabbing two plush towels, he dried her gently and then his own body as she patted her wet hair. She lifted on her toes, and he met her, their lips sealing.

Still naked, she led him into the room toward the bed. Surprised when he stopped, she turned to look up at him. Her chin thrust out slightly as her head tilted. "What's wrong? Um… don't you… uh… you know…"

He scoffed, then cupped her face in his hands. "Yeah, I want to—more than my next breath. But you need to know, Valerie, that we can stop right here. You don't owe me anything. We can crawl into bed and just hold each other, and I'd be a happy man."

She moved closer and smiled. "I'd be a happy woman just being in your arms, too. But I have to add that I'd really like it if we burned up the sheets the way I know we could."

Eyes wide, he sucked in a quick breath, then whooped as his hands dropped to her waist and lifted her. Tossing her gently, she bounced on the bed and laughed. She barely had time to catch her breath before he landed on top of her, his weight held off by his forearms planted on either side of her shoulders.

Holding his gaze, she smiled and whispered, "I've wanted to do this since... well, let's just say that I noticed instantly how gorgeous you were when we first met. Like you, I forced down my attraction, knowing it would make the professional setting difficult. But when we kissed that night, I felt something shift inside me. That feeling hasn't changed."

He slowly lowered his face, and their eyes stayed locked on each other. Finally, his lips sealed over hers, and his tongue swept through her mouth. The velvet touch sent electricity moving through every nerve of her body, and desperate need deep inside had her wiggling her hips slightly, wanting his impressive cock to take care of every need.

And her hands roamed over his shoulders and back before reaching down to grasp his muscular ass, squeezing as she lifted her hips. And after their fun in the shower, she was primed and ready. She spread as wide as she could, his hips filling between her thighs, and his cock head pressed tightly against her.

His tongue continued to swirl inside her mouth in a teasing dance against her tongue. Finally, when she thought she'd go mad with longing and was ready to beg him, he slid one hand down to slip through her folds, and she knew he'd find her drenched.

He suddenly stopped, and she blinked up at him. He pushed off her, then stood at the side of the bed, looking down, twisting around as though searching.

Stunned, she leaned up, propping herself up on

her elbows. "What's wrong? What are you looking for?"

"I'm so sorry—fuck! I'm trying to find the bag from the drugstore. I bought condoms and can't figure out where the hell I put them!"

"Oh shit!" She sat up, her gaze jerking around the room as well. She spied the white bag near his backpack beside the small table and pointed. "There. Over there."

He stalked to the table and bent to snatch the paper sack off the floor, giving her a spectacular view of his ass.

"I'm so fucking sorry, Valerie. I feel like an idiot," he groaned as he ripped open the box and jerked out a foil packet.

"Don't apologize on my account. I haven't had enough time to stare at your naked ass. I think that's just become one of my favorite things to do."

Walking back over, he looked down at her, still smiling. "Well, let's see if I can give you a few more favorite things to do with me." He grinned as he rolled the condom on his impressive erection.

Crawling back over her, he moved his forearm under her thigh, opening her even wider as the tip of his cock nudged her entrance. He finally lifted his lips off hers and held her stare. "You can say no, sweetheart. You can always say no."

"But I don't want to say no. All I want is to feel all of you in every way possible. Please, Adam, don't make me wait another second."

A beautiful smile curved his lips, and she was sure she'd never seen anything more beautiful in her life. He eased his cock in, inch by inch, allowing her to stretch until she was filled and he was buried to the hilt. So moved by the beauty of their connection, she couldn't speak but hoped that he could read everything in her expression.

He searched her face, then smiled again. Beginning to ease back and forth, he slowly increased his pace as she clutched his shoulders, wrapped her legs around his waist, and urged him on with her heels against his ass. They started slow, but soon, the pace once again had every nerve firing.

The coil deep inside tightened until, finally, she shattered and once again rode out each wave of pleasure.

23

Adam couldn't drag his gaze away from Valerie's face. She was always beautiful. Wide, hazel eyes. A few pale freckles dusted over her cheeks. A mouth that he longed to kiss and was slightly swollen right now. She was beautiful when talking about her work or the people she cared for. She was beautiful when dressed for dinner or with messy hair from the breeze while sitting on a boat in the middle of a river.

But right now, having just come, her face was flushed, her eyes were hooded, and her body now lay limp with her arms splayed out to the side. And he'd never seen anything more beautiful in his life.

He slowed his thrusts, dragging his cock along her channel, holding back on his pleasure to give her a chance to recuperate from hers.

Her eyes blinked several times before opening fully, and her wet, plump lips widened into a smile that shot straight to his heart. Moving as though her muscles were completely relaxed, she raised her arms so that her hands could clutch his shoulders again.

"Oh... Adam."

She didn't have to say anything else. His ego didn't need declarations of his sexual prowess. Women who felt the need to fill the air space with empty platitudes always annoyed him. Instead, she was perfect. Lying there, she fully enjoyed the aftermath of her orgasm, so no other words were needed.

Now, he could see the interest flaring in her eyes once again, the hazel growing dark as she lifted her hips and pressed against his pelvis.

Lowering himself, he kissed her lightly, then began thrusting faster, harder, and deeper. The little moans from her that escaped with each movement filled his ears, urging him on.

Her sex was now slick but tight, the friction with each drive had his heart pounding as his blood pumped along every vein. Finally, he felt the burning in his groin and cried out as he thrust and held the position as his own orgasm hit. Then slowly, thrusting until every drop was wrung from his body, he gasped, his lungs aching as he tried to draw in air.

He barely managed to open his eyes and, through the haze, was thankful he had. Because now, staring up at him while holding on tightly to his arms was the most beautiful sight he'd ever seen in his life.

With his chest still heaving as he fought to

breathe and his heart pounding, he was cognizant of not crushing her. Gently sliding out, he knew this time with Valerie had shot to his favorite memory of all time. Kissing her lightly, he mumbled, "Be right back."

He hated to leave her side and the warmth of the bed, but he needed to deal with the condom. He'd hoped there'd be a time soon when they wouldn't even have to bother with one. As he washed his hands, it struck him that he never had that thought with any other woman. He'd never considered going bareback.

But with Valerie, he wanted more. More of her body. More of her time. And if he was honest, all of her heart.

When he walked back into the room, his breath caught in his throat as he looked at the bed. She was lying on her side, with her elbow crooked and her head resting against her hand. Naked. Comfortably lounging. And utterly gorgeous. But it wasn't just her body that captured his attention and his heart. It was the gentle, soft expression on her face. Her smile widened, and she patted the bed next to her.

He acquiesced quickly, pulling the covers over them as she snuggled close to him. Wrapping his arms around her, he tangled their legs, and their hearts beat as one. He knew he'd found what the other Keepers had. And fell asleep with a smile on his face.

Adam pulled up outside of Valerie's two-story townhouse. As he looked through the windshield, his gaze roamed over the outside, particularly noting the safe neighborhood. "Nice."

They had flown back to California after two more days of utter bliss in Mexico. Lounging on the beach. Eating delicious food. Playing in the surf. Taking long walks along the beach. And nights of passion.

Now, he'd driven her to her place, glad that it was only a two-hour drive from where he lived but also hating that it was a two-hour drive. He was ready to see her car parked in his garage but figured that notion might scare her off.

She smiled at him. "It's only a rental, but after years of having small apartments or sharing a house with other students, I love having more space. The garage leads straight into a small laundry room and then the kitchen. I enjoy hosting my mom when she visits and have a place that feels like a home." Turning to look at him, she asked, "Would you like to come in?"

Considering he didn't want their time together to end, he nodded. "Absolutely."

Once inside, she gave him a quick tour of the living room, kitchen, and dining area. Upstairs, the two smaller bedrooms, and then hers. She looked over her shoulder and smiled when she stepped into her bedroom.

He grinned as well, and then they both burst into laughter. He enveloped her in a hug, kissing her deeply. "Looks like we both like the idea of spending time in here," he said as her eyes twinkled.

"Yeah. I kind of wish I hadn't promised Ellen that I'd come over to check on them."

He sighed and nodded. "Me, too. But I know they want to see you." He kissed her again. "I'm not leaving until I know when I can see you again."

She bit her bottom lip, a playful, coy expression filling her face. "Well, I *do* have to check my social calendar. It gets *so* filled, and I might not—"

"You'd better write me in your social calendar," he insisted with a grin. "In fact, you can fill me in on all your available spots and get rid of anyone else."

They stood with arms around each other, and she slowly nodded. "I'd like that." Cocking her head to the side, she asked, "And what about your social calendar?"

"You're already the only one on it."

"Yeah?" she whispered, her sweet breath puffing across his lips.

"Yeah." With that assurance, he kissed her again, then slowly moved her toward the bed. "Maybe we should test out your bed before I go."

She gently pushed him back and then, with a gleam in her eye, whipped her T-shirt over her head. "That's a good idea. Since I hope you're here often, we need to be sure it's the right *fit*."

Chuckling, he pulled his shirt off, as well. "Well, it's all about the *right fit,* isn't it?"

Falling onto her bed while still laughing, he couldn't imagine having to go back to his lonely house. And for right now, he was glad he didn't have to.

Adam sat in the main LSIWC compound room. Looking at the computer screen with Jeb, he was going over a rare kink in one of his programs.

"I fucking can't figure out what is fucking wrong with this fucking program!" Jeb growled.

Adam's brows shot to his hairline to hear Jeb lose his cool. Adam had always considered himself the more silent, stoic Keeper compared to the others, but no one was as quietly focused as Jeb. And to hear him so frustrated was almost amusing if Adam didn't also share Jeb's irritation.

Carson walked over. "What's happening? Have we been hacked?"

"No," Jeb rushed, shaking his head. "Just… I don't know. Something's not right, and I can't figure it out. But don't worry, I will."

"I never doubted it," Carson said, clapping Jeb on the shoulder. "Take a break and go pound on the heavy bag if you need to."

"Nah, I'll be fine. Sorry," Jeb mumbled.

"No worries, man. We'll get it straight."

Leo looked up from his computer screen. "Look at this." He switched his view to the large screen on the wall.

The newscaster was discussing a large drug bust in Colombia involving the Assistant Secretary of Agriculture.

"Sebastian Cortes was arrested after a raid on a warehouse in Barrancabermeja produced evidence of illegal fentanyl processing. A separate raid on his personal estate discovered acres of coca plants growing in fields on the property. He claims he knew nothing of the warehouse, which should have been empty, according to him. He also denies knowledge of the cocaine-producing plants even though some were found in the greenhouse on his property. The Colombian Drug Task Force is looking into his accomplices and finances for more evidence of wrongdoing."

"So Rafe Molina got him. Good. I'll let Valerie know." Adam was glad to be able to pass along the news to her.

"When are you going to bring her in to meet everyone?" Carson asked, spearing Adam with a pointed look.

"Jeannie wants to meet her, right?"

Nodding, Carson said, "My wife takes her responsibilities very seriously."

"Responsibilities?" Leo asked while laughing.

"Yep... wife, mother, nurse, and head of the

check-out-who-the-Keeper-has fallen-for committee."

The others laughed as well. Nodding, Adam said, "I'd like to bring her up here this weekend. She's been working extra hard as Paul decides what to do in light of his health."

"Is he retiring?" Abbie asked.

"Sort of. He's talked to Valerie a lot over the past week and has decided that he won't travel as much and certainly won't travel out of the country. I think the trauma of having even a mild heart attack somewhere not near his wife or medical care really scared him. So he'll continue to teach a couple of classes with Valerie as his assistant, and they will continue their studies, only in a much more limited context."

"How does she feel about that?" Poole asked.

He rubbed his chin and shrugged. "It's a little hard for me to tell. I haven't seen her since last weekend, and even though we video chat each evening, I know she's under a strain trying to figure everything out. Her pay will be greatly reduced with Paul's decrease in his research."

Before anyone had a chance to comment, Rachel hurried in. "Landon's on call for you."

Leo immediately transferred his screen from the news to Landon. Everyone's gaze focused on him.

"What have you got for us?" Carson asked.

"I wanted to let you know that it's hit the news that Sebastian Cortes has been arrested." Carson was already nodding, but Landon wasn't finished. "And I need to let you know that Joseph Perez has disappeared. The Colombian police don't have him in custody, and I've talked to Rafe Molina, and he thinks Joseph has left the country."

Adam's heart beat faster, but he couldn't believe Joseph would come to the United States. "There's no way he can get into the country, can he?"

Carson's face showed his anger. "You know as well as I do that money can buy almost anything, including a fake passport, fake ID, whatever he might need. He won't waltz into the embassy but could manage to get into the country."

"Why the hell would he come here?" Dolby asked, shaking his head. "Wouldn't he be safer with his cartel friends? Mexico? Venezuela?"

Landon grimaced. "I'd say the cartel isn't very happy with him or Sebastian right now. They may all be on the cartels' shit list, but I wanted to let you know."

"What about Valerie?" Adam asked. He leaned forward in the seat, his heart pounding faster. If he was hoping for assurances from Landon, they weren't forthcoming.

"I don't know. I don't have any information that points to him knowing anything other than she probably saw him at Sebastian's house. He would've been in on the plans to drop her off at the warehouse, and when she escaped, he would have assumed she turned over evidence."

Adam shot up from his chair, his finger deftly

dialing Valerie's number. It rang, but nothing. *Come on, sweetheart, pick up.* With his phone clapped to his ear, he strode, his gut clenching while calling over his shoulder, "No answer."

"I'll fly. We can take the bird," Hop called out, urgency in his movements as he leaped to his feet.

"I'm coming," Jeb threw out with resolve, also launching from his chair. Simultaneously, the others moved into action.

Everyone volunteered to go, their combined voices shouting out, but Carson gave the command. "Bennett. You're the best shot we've got. Everyone else, work it from here." Turning toward Adam, he grabbed his shoulders and held his stare. "Stay calm and stay focused. That's one of your gifts. Don't lose that now, not when she might need you."

Adam offered a perfunctory nod, but his insides felt like the churning waves pounding the rocks below the lighthouse.

By the time they bolted into the equipment room, Teddy had their needed equipment already on the table in the middle of the room. Gearing up with military precision, Adam focused on the task, jolting when Teddy grabbed his shoulders.

"You know what to do, so tighten your emotions and get it done, son."

Letting out a breath, he offered another perfunctory nod but knew they were right. "I've got this."

Teddy clapped him on the back. "Always knew you did."

Running out the door, he, Jeb, and Hop climbed into Bennett's new SUV and headed to the helipad where Hop's bird waited, ready to fly.

Twenty minutes later, as they lifted into the air, Adam's gut had twisted into a fiery knot. His war-drum heartbeat pounded every time he tried to call her, and there was still no answer.

24

Valerie blew out a long breath with a heavy sigh. Nothing was going right today. One complication after another dragged her under the weight of upcoming decisions. If it wasn't for the glimmering promise of a weekend at Adam's house, she wasn't sure she'd be able to maintain a hold on her fraying sanity.

Ever since her return to California, she'd visited Paul each day. He'd wanted to talk about work matters, and while she'd been skittish of the stress it might cause him, Ellen had assured her that Paul found solace in talking things through with her.

There had been no surprise bombshells in their discussions. She had expected him to retire someday, and his health had accelerated the timeline. Given his condition, flying off to far-flung destinations without ready access to medical facilities was no longer something he should consider.

Paul wasn't ready to retire fully, and Valerie was committed to helping him transition. But it meant navigating uncertainties around her own job. With fewer responsibilities at the university, her pay would be reduced. She could continue leading some of the research trips but wasn't sure who would fund them without Paul. She could apply for another university position somewhere and work with someone else, but that was unpalatable. *But might be necessary.*

The last thing she wanted to do was add more stress to Paul, so she'd assured him that she was fine and everything would work out. On her way home, she stopped by the grocery store and, walking up and down the aisles, considered that she needed to economize even more than normal since she had no idea what her salary would be. She scrutinized price tags and searched for discounts more vigorously than in the past. Now, walking into her townhouse, she sighed heavily. The idea that she might need to take on a roommate loomed.

"Ugh!" The very notion of a roommate disrupted her vision of the life she had achieved. Now that she was in her thirties, she craved her independence and her home. While stowing her groceries, she continued to imagine how her life would change—sharing a pantry and refrigerator, noise when she had to study, or someone wanting her to be quiet when she watched TV. The thought of having to listen to them when they brought someone over wasn't palatable. That last thought gave her pause, and she leaned forward, resting her head against the cabinet door. Having someone else living with her would interfere with spontaneity when Adam was with her. "No," she moaned out loud. "Not unless there is no other choice!"

With those words ringing in her head, she looked around for her phone, wanting to call Adam and tell him about her day. Not seeing it on the counter, she stood with her hands on her hips and turned around in a circle, trying to remember when she had it last.

"Oh shit!" She remembered that as she'd pulled into Paul's driveway, her purse toppled over, and much of the contents spilled onto the passenger seat floor. Going back into the garage, she scrounged in her car, unearthing not only her phone but two pens, a lipstick, and a crumpled flyer from one of the local pizza delivery shops. Gathering everything, she walked back into her house and dumped her findings on the kitchen counter. Her phone screen was lit with missed calls and texts. Looking at the last one Adam sent, she read, **I am on my way to you!** Grinning, she started to scroll through the others when a knock sounded on her front door.

Walking into the living room, she peeked through the security hole and spied a man on the stoop with his head turned away as he looked behind him. Thinking it was her neighbor, she unlatched the door and threw it open. "Hey, Randy—"

The man turned around, and she jerked slightly as she stared in shock. *Jorge?*

In one swift motion, his hand shot out and flung the door open, propelling her backward before slamming it shut and locking it. He no longer appeared as the calm manservant in Sebastian's household. Gone was the formal suit, and in its place, he wore dark jeans and a dark shirt, showing he was much more fit than she'd imagined. Fear intermingled with confusion, and the air around them grew cold.

"What are you doing here?" she shouted, then turned on her heel to race down the hall. Her progress was halted when he grabbed her arm and jerked her around. "What are you doing?" she cried out again, trying to dislodge her arm away from his strong grip.

"Be quiet!" His gaze hastily scanned the area, then he returned to her. "Are you alone?"

"No!"

He didn't buy her lie. "Yes, you are. I don't have time to explain, but we need to get you out of here!"

She blinked, unable to process his meaning, but years of her mom and brother's warnings, as well as all the safety precautions of traveling around the world, self-preservation kicked in. "No!"

"You are in danger. We need to get you out of here."

"What do you mean I'm in danger? From you?"

"I am here to protect you," he argued. "I worked as an informant for the Colombian Drug Task Force. I was a plant in Sebastian Cortes's household. He'd been under surveillance for over a year with me gathering information. We were closing in on him, but I was worried we might not get what we needed. Thanks to you, we managed to get the evidence necessary for his arrest."

"Me?" she gasped as her chest hurt from lack of oxygen. "I don't understand."

"Sebastian didn't want to have a part in killing you, but I knew Joseph was arranging it. I interceded with the helicopter pilot to ensure he left you before anyone arrived. He was never going to shoot you, but by threatening you, he made sure you were forewarned."

Anger filled her, and she shook her head. "Why didn't he just tell me? I didn't know what the hell was going on or what to do. That was a ridiculous way to try to let someone know they're in danger."

"I couldn't give him too much information in case he was captured."

For the first time, she saw an emotion pass over his face. Regret. A heavy sigh left her lips as her mind continued to churn over what was happening.

"All that matters now is that Sebastian is behind bars, and Joseph is in the wind. I have contacts that got me into the country because I needed to warn you. You're not safe here."

"Safe?" Cold settled throughout her body, and she stared. "Safe from... Joseph?"

"I assumed you either saw or heard him at Sebastian's estate. You can be sure that he's made that assumption, too."

"I need to call Adam!" She dislodged his arm as she raced to the kitchen, where her phone was still on the counter. Grabbing it, she dialed, and he had just picked up when she rushed to say, "Sebastian's manservant is here! He came to tell me that Joseph is after me!"

"What the– is he there with you now?"

"Yes, and I don't know what to do. He says he wants me to get out of here so I can be safe. He said Joseph is coming!"

"You do *not* go with anyone. I don't know who's in your house or what he's doing, but– Dammit! We just landed close by, and I'm on my way to you."

Suddenly, a staccato of firecrackers nearby filled the air, causing her heart to lurch into her throat. Immediately, the harsh crackle of shattering glass sounded. She screamed as Jorge lunged forward, tackling her to the floor. Her phone skittered across the kitchen, sliding far beyond her reach.

Pinned facedown with Jorge's weight on her back, she was terrified to move. She worked to suck in oxygen as the pressure of Jorge's body on hers stifled her breath.

He shifted his position, and the agonizing pain in her rib cage caused her to cry out until her eyes locked onto the gun in his hand. The sight of the weapon paralyzed her, too scared to make a sound.

This was the second time she'd been in the presence of a gun, and while his weapon wasn't pointed at her, terror once again struck her. Caught in a nightmare, she felt a silent tear slip down her cheek.

Jorge lifted his weight off her, but the ease of pressure did little to relieve the pain in her ribs or the fear coursing through her body. Unsure she should move, she twisted to stare up at him. He placed his finger to his lips and shook his head as he crouched beside her.

Another volley of bullets began flying again, shattering through the kitchen's sliding glass door, spraying shards of glass in all directions. She screamed again, and her arms instinctively darted upward to shield her head. With her body shaking, she tried to push upward, the need to flee overtaking all other thoughts.

Jorge collapsed on top of her again, knocking her to the side. She curled into a fetal position, crying in agony at the pain radiating throughout her torso. With sudden bravery and strength that could have only come from adrenaline, she tried to push him off, but he didn't move on his own this time. She managed to roll him to his back, then gasped at the grim sight of the blood covering his shirt. Ignoring her pain, she managed to get her legs free and scrambled to kneel over him. "Oh God. Oh God. Jorge!"

"Well, well, Ms. Clemens. We finally meet face-to-face."

At the sound, her gaze darted upward to find Joseph standing in her kitchen, his gun now trained directly on her. His dark eyes held no compassion. Instead, his gaze sent chills through her veins. Still kneeling over Jorge's body, she barely breathed as her body shivered in despair.

She remembered Adam had said he was on his way, but she had no idea if he would reach her in time. The pain made her reckless as she stared. "What do you want? What do you want from me?"

His sneer morphed into a cruel smile. Shaking his head while his gaze never left hers, he taunted, "Something you cannot give me."

"I can't imagine what your plan is." She continued to stare up at him, trying not to look at the gun in his hand, but was unsuccessful. She grimaced as the pain increased, causing her voice to quiver. "I've got nothing for you. I can't help you in any way."

"You completely misunderstand why I'm here, Ms. Clemens. You're right… *you* have nothing I need, but killing Jorge will go a long way in righting the wrong he did. Sebastian took him in, gave him a home, and was betrayed by this swine."

She dropped her gaze to Jorge, her gaze snagging on the blood. So much blood. Her hand still rested on his chest when she felt a slight, almost imperceptible movement. Stifling the gasp that almost slipped out, she shifted in her kneeling to keep Joseph's gaze on her and not on the still-alive man on the floor.

"You can't get away." She wanted to buy time,

hoping Adam would come. Slowly standing, she stifled her cries as each faltering movement sent agonizing pain ripping through her insides. Glancing at the phone on the floor, she realized she had never disconnected the call. *Please, God, let him hear that Joseph is here.*

"Maybe not, but—"

He stopped as the sound of footsteps came from the front of her house and her back deck. She watched in horror as Joseph whirled around, firing through the now-shattered open doorway.

Another shot rang out, followed by more shouting from the front and back. She heard a policeman call out somewhere in the melee, ordering Joseph to drop his weapon.

Gripping the counter to hold her body upright, she was unsure what to do or if she should even move. Joseph whirled around and rushed toward her. She barely had time to throw her hands up to ward him off when he grabbed her and pressed the gun to her head.

She warned, "Don't come in!" but Joseph tightened his arm around her middle. She cried out as dark spots swam in her vision.

In the stillness, she heard movement coming from the front hall and the shadow of a body on her back deck.

"I've got her," Joseph called out. "If you want her alive, you'll let me get out of here."

The crunch of a footstep on broken glass had her

swing her gaze around, and she saw Adam with his weapon, pointed toward Joseph, stepping through what used to be a sliding glass door and into the kitchen. Another man, similarly dressed, walked through directly behind Adam. Staring, it struck her that the man was not as tall but broader and just as nice looking as the other Keepers she'd met. Staring, she blinked several times as her vision blurred, wondering if it was a Keeper employment prerequisite to be fit *and* attractive. Shifting her gaze to Adam, she wanted to reach out to him and let him know he was the most gorgeous man she'd ever seen.

"Valerie? Sweetheart?" The words fell softly from Adam's lips, but she found it increasingly hard to focus. Thoughts were as blurry as her vision.

"I want safe passage out of here, or she dies," Joseph growled.

Armed men with guns came from the hall, SWAT clearly written on their vests. Two other men stepped through the back door, FBI on one and DEA on the other.

"My kitchen is getting crowded," she mumbled.

"Valerie, I want you to keep your eyes on me," Adam said in an eerily soft voice.

"Jorge was shot," she mumbled.

"Keep your eyes on me, sweetheart," he repeated.

She lifted her gaze from Jorge up to his, and her heart melted when she stared into his eyes. "The first time I saw you... your eyes were the color of the

Centaurea cyanus flower." Speaking seemed to take all her energy. "You're so pretty." No longer able to hold her eyes open, she slumped. The sound of a gunshot blasting in her ears and the shouts from all around faded into quiet.

25

The moment Adam heard the terror in Valerie's voice cutting into him through the phone, his pulse skyrocketed in a way it never had on any mission.

With her on speaker, Jeb had heard and was instantly on the radio to the compound. "Find out from contacts in Colombia who the hell Jorge is! Manservant of Sebastian Cortes. He's in Valerie's house, claiming Joseph is coming for her."

Barely hearing Jeb, Adam focused on Valerie's voice, wanting to be the calm she needed, but he could not stop his heart from racing when she said Jorge wanted to get her out of her house. That was the last thing Adam wanted to happen since he had no fucking idea who Jorge was.

Hop had gained permission from the local FBI to land at a local police station's helicopter pad, where they were met by someone from the DEA and local law enforcement. But when she'd called, they were still a few agonizing minutes away from her house, when the sounds of gunfire could be heard, and then Valerie's high-pitched shriek was like a bullet to his heart.

They were in a DEA vehicle, and he roared, "Gunfire! Get us there now!"

He called out her name several times, but her voice was distant even though he could still hear sounds through the phone. *Had someone taken it from her?* His gut wrenched at the idea that Joseph had gotten to her and, maybe, the unknown Jorge was working with Joseph.

When her muted voice could finally be heard, relief surged through him that she was still alive. The voices were barely audible, but he ascertained that Joseph had breached her house.

Relating what he could to the DEA agents in the front seat, they screeched to a stop outside her townhouse. Two local police cars and a SWAT team had just arrived, probably called by the neighbors who gathered at the end of the street.

With clipped explanations, the teams separated. One headed toward the front door, others surrounding the side where her garage entrance lay, while he, Jeb, and Bennett's boot steps pounded to the back. His heart lurched at the sight of the sliding door from the deck obliterated from the outside with shattered glass within the kitchen. Avoiding the porch steps that would put him in view of the man in the kitchen, he scaled the side and quietly slipped over the railing. Jeb was right behind him, and he trusted Bennett would position himself outside.

Once there, he held his breath at the sight of a motionless body sprawled on the floor, and after a second of panic, he ascertained it wasn't Valerie. He could barely make out the shadow of someone standing in the room, but they were behind a small wall. He remembered the shape of her kitchen, and a column of cabinets was at the end of the counter. She was hidden from his sight.

The SWAT team members who entered from the front walked silently down the hall toward the kitchen with their weapons raised. He signaled for them to stop.

Joseph called out, his voice echoing with deadly warning. He was willing to kill Valerie unless he was able to escape. Wanting to lay eyes on her and see the man who dared to threaten her, Adam stepped through the door, his gun trained on the man he could now see. Dark hair. Dark, soulless eyes. His arm was tight around Valerie's stomach, and she cried out. The sound of her pain cemented the resolve in Adam's mind. With Jeb right behind him and other law enforcement entering the small space, he held his breath, keeping his eyes on Valerie and Joseph.

She was covered in blood, and he had no idea if it belonged to her, the man on the floor, or Joseph. But even if one drop was from her body, he wanted revenge. Aware that Bennett was at the window with his kill shot lined up reassured him.

Needing her attention, he called to her softly. She looked up toward him but was barely coherent, her eyes hazy with pain. She mumbled about her kitchen being crowded, and he knew she was barely hanging on. Calling softly again, he wanted her eyes on him. She mumbled again, and he repeated what he needed.

She stared at the man on the floor, then, after Adam's last request, she lifted her head, and her lips curved. "You're so pretty," she mumbled. She was barely hanging on, and this ordeal needed to end. If law enforcement wanted to bargain with Joseph, that was on them. All he wanted was Valerie.

With weapons from the other law enforcement aimed at Joseph, Adam kept his eye on the trigger finger of the weapon held to Valerie's head. He wasn't at an angle where he could get a clear shot but knew Bennett had everything under control.

Staring at Valerie, he willed her to pull strength from him, but her eyes flickered closed, her face went white, and she slumped.

Joseph wasn't expecting her deadweight and lost his grip on her. A shot rang out through the window over the sink, knocking Joseph backward against the refrigerator, his body slumping as Valerie fell to the floor.

Adam was at her side in a heartbeat. "Valerie! Valerie! Sweetheart!" Rolling her gently over, he ignored the cacophony from law enforcement all around. Joseph's blood spatter was on her face, but the amount of blood soaking her shirt caused his heart to sink.

Her eyes blinked open, and then immediately, she winced and cried out again.

"Where are you hurt?" He tried to remain calm, but his trembling hands and the strident tone in his voice gave away his emotions.

"Not... mine," she moaned. "Jorge. Tried... save me... got shot."

"Where do you hurt?" he repeated more softly.

"Ribs," she whispered, her face contorting in pain as she swallowed with difficulty. "He... tackled me... when Joseph... shooting. I... cracked something."

"Adam," Jeb said, placing his hand on Adam's shoulder. "Look."

Adam's gaze jumped to where Jeb pointed, now seeing fresh blood oozing on her shirt. Ripping the material, he gasped. "Fuck, babe. You've been shot."

He started to call out for help but heard Jeb shout for a medic. He feared the grazing injury might have nicked a rib or her lung.

The small kitchen became a hive of activity as paramedics swarmed in. Adam refused to let go of her hand, only relenting when Bennett grabbed his shoulders and whispered in his ear. Allowing the paramedics to stabilize her, they loaded her onto a stretcher and started down the hall toward the front door.

Jorge and Joseph were also loaded onto stretchers, both men handcuffed.

Valerie's head rolled to the side, glancing over as her stretcher was being carried to an ambulance, her hand clasped in Adam's. "Jorge tried to save me," she said, still wincing with each word. "He was with their drug task force."

"Babe, honey, DEA will sort that out. I don't want you to worry about anything."

With that, she closed her eyes but held on tightly to his hand, which was good because he wasn't about to let go. He crawled into the ambulance with her, and as the door closed, he looked out to see Bennett and Jeb offering chin lifts. He knew they would meet him at the hospital.

Hours later, he sat rooted on the side of Valerie's hospital bed, daring a nurse to ask him to move. He hadn't let go of her hand other than for them to take her to imaging.

When the doctor came in to confirm that the bullet had traveled through her side, grazing her rib but missing anything vital, and she also had two other cracked ribs, probably from Jorge falling on top of her, Adam wanted to find where Joseph was being treated in the hospital and beat the shit out of him. But staying with her as she was stitched and her ribs were wrapped was more important at the moment.

She squeezed his hand. "I'm gonna be fine," she said, her words slightly slurring.

"Yes, but it could have been much more—"

She squeezed his hand again, saying, "It wasn't." Sighing, she added, "My kitchen is a wreck. My door is broken, and glass is everywhere. There's blood on my floor. And I think there are bullet holes in my walls. Maybe one in my refrigerator, too."

"Don't worry about anything. I'm taking you back to my place when you're discharged."

"But I don't have any clothes, or my toothbrush, or my—"

"It's being taken care of."

"But—"

He leaned closer and kissed her lightly, barely brushing his lips over hers. A knock on the door had them both turn to see who entered. He grinned, seeing Jeannie, Stella, and Lori. Turning back to Valerie, he said, "Let me introduce you to some of my friends. This is Jeannie, Carson's wife. Stella is married to Chris. And this is Lori, Hop's wife. Ladies, this is Valerie."

The women hustled forward and gathered around the bed, smiling down at her. Jeannie said, "We're taking care of everything, Valerie. Hop flew back to pick us up and bring us here so we can arrange things."

"Thank goodness the police let us inside your house," Stella said. "We packed up clothes and toiletries and made sure to get your purse, phone, and laptop. If there's anything else you can think of, we'll get it before we head up to Adam's place to drop it off."

"Oh..." Valerie said, her eyes wide as she stared from one to the other.

"Jeannie's a nurse, and I'm a doctor," Lori said. "We'll make sure to check in with you once you're settled."

Valerie nodded, smiling. "I... well, I don't know what to say. But thank you is a good start."

The women smiled in return before saying goodbye. Jeannie looked at Adam and said, "We brought her car to the hospital parking lot, so you'll have transportation back to your place as soon as they discharge her. If you need anything, just call any of us."

"Sounds like you all have everything taken care of. Thank you." He hugged each one and said goodbye before they walked out, waving at Valerie before they left.

"Wow, your co-workers and their wives are really amazing," she said.

Sitting back on the edge of her bed, he held her hand and allowed his gaze to roam over her face, reminding himself that she was alive. "I was scared, babe. I never get scared like that, but seeing you and all that blood took years off my life."

"I tried to warn you, Adam. I didn't want you to rush in and get shot."

"You shouldn't have put yourself in more danger. I had a weapon and training. And good men at my back."

"And I had you," she whispered.

He cupped her face and kissed her again. "I'm taking you back to my house. I don't know how long you'll want to stay, but at least until you're well and your house has been made right."

"Ugh. My landlord will probably kick me out after all that."

"If he does, it'll be fine with me."

She held his gaze and said, "My life is kind of a mess right now, Adam. My job is uncertain. My housing situation is uncertain. And our new relationship has been a whirlwind of crisis since we met."

"Never thought life had to be easy. It just needs to be spent with people you care about. And, sweetheart"—he cupped her cheeks—"I care about you. I want us to take this relationship as far as it can go, and if I'm right, that'll be forever."

He kissed her again, and she melted into his arms. Just where he wanted her to be.

26

Valerie was tired of Adam hovering. It had been a week since she'd been shot, and he'd barely left her side. It wasn't that she didn't enjoy his company or love being in his house. She certainly wasn't sure if she'd feel comfortable returning to hers, especially since her landlord had complained about the cost of having a biohazard team come through to clean the blood from the kitchen. Add that expense to the cost of having the sliding glass door replaced and the bullet holes repaired, he wasn't keen on her returning. And with her employment salary up in the air, she wasn't sure she'd be able to afford another rental house.

Adam had insisted that she not worry about anything, but he was crazy if he thought she would stop worrying just because he assured her everything would be fine.

Her mother had come for a visit a few days ago and fell in love with Adam, making it known that she was thrilled her daughter had someone like him in her life. Her brother had threatened to ask for emergency leave to come to take care of whatever needed to be done, preferably kick some cartel ass. She promised him everything was under control, but it wasn't until after he checked on LSIWC and had a phone conversation with Adam that he finally agreed that she was in good hands.

Today, he'd finally gone to work, and she was lying on the sofa with Charlie curled up next to her. She looked out the window. The mountains were in the background, and he'd promised to show her the running trails when she was better.

The sound of vehicles coming down his drive met her ears, and she smiled as they parked. Numerous women climbed out with their hands full, heading to the door. Jeannie had called to see if she was up for company, and she eagerly accepted. She recognized Jeannie, Stella, and Lori leading the brigade.

She stood and slowly walked to the door, opening it just as they arrived on the porch. Her smile was so wide it almost hurt as she greeted the others.

The names ran together at first, but as they set the food on the counter, she made sure to speak to them all. She was excited to meet Abbie and Natalie, thanking them for their assistance while she was in Colombia. Then she met Marcia and Tricia thanking them for Dolby's and Poole's help getting her and

Adam out of Colombia. Diana was the next woman she met. The beautiful woman was a chemist, and Valerie was excited to meet another scientist among the group. Vicki was the last to come in. She was a nurse, and Valerie learned that she was new to the group, too. The last one in was an older woman with a warm smile and heartfelt hug.

"I'm Rachel, the administrative assistant for LSIWC. It's my pleasure to meet you."

She felt her eyes watering but blinked several times to keep the tears at bay.

"Adam was worried about leaving you alone today, and I assured him that we would check on you and keep you company," Abbie said, gathering the paper plates for everyone to use.

"I know you and Natalie work for the Keepers, so I feel bad that you're missing work to come here," Valerie said.

Abbie and Natalie laughed. "Oh, don't worry. We have a very understanding boss."

The other women laughed, and Jeannie looked over to explain. "My husband realizes the importance of hiring the best and treating them like family. He and the founder of Lighthouse Securities developed a model, and I wholeheartedly applaud it."

"How are you feeling?" Stella asked, leaning over to rub Charlie's fur.

"Better every day, although you wouldn't know it with the way Adam hovers."

"You'll get used to it," Marcia said, filling a plate. "They are all born protectors."

Natalie nodded. "It's not a job for us. It's not even a career. It's a way of life. You can't learn how to become a Keeper or a Keeper's significant other for that matter. A Keeper simply… is."

Diana laughed. "And when they find their significant other, the urge to protect becomes even stronger."

They ate their fill, and the conversation rolled easily from one topic to another. As Valerie watched them, she was struck by how diverse they were in careers and in personality, yet they were all joined together, very much like the other Keepers she'd met.

"You know," Rachel said. "There's a saying that it takes a very special woman to be the right person for a Keeper."

Valerie felt all eyes on her and couldn't help the nervous butterflies fluttering in her stomach.

"It's also been our experience that Keepers tend to find someone they met on a mission," Abbie continued.

"So," Jeannie announced, "welcome to Lighthouse Securities, Valerie. We're glad you're one of us."

She felt the tears she'd tried to hide slip down her cheeks. She blushed with embarrassment. "I'm so sorry. You probably think I'm very foolish."

"Not at all," they rushed to assure. "You've been through a traumatic time."

"It wasn't that," she said. "It was what you said about being welcome. When I was trying to pass information to the DEA, I thought that would make me closer to my father." She knew her background was no secret, and the other women would understand what she was talking about. "But instead, looking back, I think he would've just been worried out of his mind."

The other women nodded empathetically, but she wasn't finished.

"But when you just welcomed me to this… this…"

"LSI family," Jeannie said, supplying the right words.

Nodding, Valerie agreed. "Yes. When you welcomed me into the LSI family, I suddenly realized that being around people like you would be exactly what my father would want for me."

More hugs ensued, and then the desserts came out. And much to her delight, bread pudding was one of them. Conversations continued until the food trays were decimated, and it was time for everyone to leave.

Hugging each one, she now easily remembered their names and their partners. She promised to lie down and rest and waved goodbye at the door.

She'd had a wonderful time but was exhausted. Looking at the couch, she grinned. "Come on, Charlie. Let's go take a nap."

Later, she woke as she was being kissed. Eyes

popping open, she grinned at the sight of Adam sitting on the side of the bed, smiling down at her.

"Hey, Sleeping Beauty. I heard you had a good day."

"I absolutely had a fabulous day!" She stretched and only felt a small pinch in her side where, previously, she'd felt more pain. "And how I feel means that we can start enjoying ourselves." Her smile slipped as she added, "And it means that I need to start figuring out what I'm going to do with my life."

"You might not be happy with what I did, but I talked to your landlord and the insurance company."

Eyes wide, she gasped. "What did they say?"

"All the damages are being paid for, and he will be able to have the restoration taken care of. He was happy, but I told him you wouldn't return."

She blinked, her chin jerking back as her mouth dropped open. "You… you told him what?"

"Look, sweetheart. I'm not trying to take over your life, I swear. But it will take a few weeks for him to get bids for the work to satisfy the insurance company and finish the work. You need a place to stay during that time, and I'd be honored if you'd stay here."

Her lips curved as her mouth closed. "Honored?"

He nodded, bending closer. "Absolutely honored. And that gives you a safe place to stay as you figure out your life."

She lifted an eyebrow. "Just safe?"

"Well," he said, suddenly appearing nervous. "Safe. And with me."

She closed the distance and nuzzled his nose. "I can't think of anywhere else I'd want to be as I figure out my life. There are advantages to being here after all." Kissing him, she pulled him down next to her.

27

TWO MONTHS LATER

Sweat dripped off Valerie's face as she jogged over the glorious terrain of the trails near their house. *Their house.* She couldn't believe how quickly she'd come to think of Adam's place as hers, too. But once he'd brought her there to heal after getting shot, neither of them had been inclined for her to find another place. She often asked him, and each time, he just grinned and said, "Nope. Stay." Two words that strangely meant the world to her.

"You okay?" he asked, running next to her.

"Yeah, but I'm glad the house is close. I still don't have my full stamina back." She looked at him. "How the hell can you look so gorgeous even when you're all sweaty? I look like a mess."

"Why do you think I've always gotten behind you when we come to a narrow place in the path?" he quipped in return.

Her brow crinkled. "I don't know. Just being polite?"

"Nope. I like staring at your ass. Best ass I've ever seen."

She snorted, and they both laughed, barely making it to the back porch. As they were stretching, Charlie was just inside the door, already meowing for breakfast.

Falling into their routine, she showered quickly while Adam fed Charlie. Then she got ready while he showered. Downstairs, they fixed breakfast and stood at the front door for a long, hard kiss goodbye. He drove to the compound, and she walked into the home office Adam had set up for her.

Nowadays, she only goes to the university two days a week to assist Paul with the two classes he taught. They were only morning classes, and then they spent the afternoon reviewing their research. He was semi-retired and enjoyed the other days of the week with Ellen. She still occasionally had dinner at their house, now bringing Adam with her.

On the days that she wasn't at the university, she worked from home. She was now employed by RAND and only had to go into their California office once a month, working remotely the rest of the time. And with their salary, she made more money than she was before when she worked full-time at the university.

Charlie curled up in a sunspot near the window,

and she opened her laptop. She smiled as she looked at the photographs Adam had framed and placed on her desk. One taken by Stella with the sunset behind them overlooking the Pacific Ocean at an LSIWC party. One of her in the field with Paul, boots in the mud and up to their knees in crops. And one of her family when she was a young girl with Timothy next to her and their parents' proud smiles as they stood behind them.

"You'd like him, Dad."

Smiling as her computer screen lit with the remote meeting about to start, she grinned at the personal message box also lighting up as Jeannie and Rachel were contacting everyone about an LSI party for the weekend.

"Oh yeah, Dad. Life is what I made it."

Adam sat with Jeb, who was still working on the continued bug in one of his programs. For almost three months, Jeb had spent part of every day working to locate where the problem was coming from. He had it isolated to western Canada, but the precise location still eluded him.

"Don't worry, man. You're the best."

"I've even got Josh and Pippa from LSI Maine helping me. They're stumped, too."

Clapping Jeb on the shoulder, Adam said, "I'm heading home, and you should too."

"Yeah, well, you've got someone to go home to. Me? I'll just hang around here a little longer."

Grinning, he waved goodbye to the others and headed to his vehicle, unwilling to wait another minute to hurry home.

As soon as he pulled into the driveway, he felt the stress of the day fly away. His house was no longer empty, with only Charlie to keep him company. Now, it was a home. Valerie had hated to bring her things in, fearing her style might not work for him. He'd laughed and assured her that he had no *style.* Hell, furniture was just something he sat on, lay on, or put the TV on.

After going through what they each had, they had brought some of Valerie's furniture, and she combined them into a space that was calm, warm, and uniquely theirs. But just knowing she was there with him was all he needed.

He made it to the back deck when Valerie came flying toward him, a wide smile on her face.

"Hey, sweetheart," he greeted, lifting her into his arms so that her toes dangled just above the wooden planks.

"I've got the greatest news!" She captured his jaws with her hands and pulled him in for a kiss.

Not one to pass up an opportunity, he continued the kiss as he walked forward, setting her on the deck railing and then moving straight between her thighs. Bodies flush, he kept her steady with one hand around her back and slid the other along her cheek, his fingers tangling in her silky hair. His lips commanded hers in a claiming kiss. Just like every time they kissed, it was all he could do to keep from carrying her to the bedroom, stripping her, and then worshipping her beautiful body.

But the kernel of rationality still in his brain reminded him that she had news. Finally, dragging his lips from hers while still holding her close, he said, "I like that greeting, sweetheart. I know you had news, and I'll try to rein myself in so you can tell me."

The gold in her hazel eyes twinkled. "Don't worry, we can get back to ravaging each other after I give you my news."

Chuckling, he nodded. "Okay, lay it on me."

"I got a call from Mom today. She said Timothy has leave and will be here in two weeks!"

Her blooming excitement was contagious. "I can't wait to meet him in person."

"So I guess this is as good a time as any to ask you an important question."

A little crinkle settled between her brows, and she waited as he lifted her off the railing and set her feet on the ground. Then her eyes widened as he dropped to one knee on the deck. He'd had this moment planned out ever since he'd talked to Timothy a week earlier, finding out when his leave was going to take place. Both Timothy and her mom had offered their blessing, but now, staring up at Valerie, doubts mingled with nerves slamming into him.

He had no doubts about what he felt for her or

what he wanted to do, but doubts that she would accept, or if she did, would she be excited about rushed plans?

Still staring at him with her mouth open, he plunged ahead. "I know this may seem fast to many people. But I've always told you it doesn't matter how long you've known someone. It's what you feel. And what I feel for you is the kind of love that transcends anything I've ever known before. Valerie, you're the woman I want to walk beside me for the rest of my life. Seriously loyal. Deeply dedicated. Willing to take risks for those you love. I want to be a better man every moment I'm with you. And I want to be the man who takes care of you. So what do you say, sweetheart?"

Pulling the ring box from his pocket, he flipped open the lid, showing a beautiful diamond ring. Classic. Simple. Breathtaking. As soon as he'd seen it in the jewelry store, he thought it was fitting for her.

She dropped to her knees on the deck in front of him and threw her arms around his neck. "Yes, yes, yes! A thousand times, yes!"

A jolt of relief spread through him, and his arms tightened around her, pulling her even closer. Her body shook, and as he leaned back slightly, he spied tears in her eyes. As one escaped, he captured it with his lips, vowing always to kiss away her tears.

He took her left hand and slid the ring on. "I realize that women often want to spend a long time planning their dream wedding, and I don't want to take away anything from you. Quite the opposite, in fact. I want to give you everything. So if you want to wait before we get married, we can. But if you want to get married in two weeks while Timothy is here to give you away—"

Her entire body jerked as her eyes stared at him, unblinking. "Oh my God! You would do that for me? You'd agree to get married in two weeks?"

"Sweetheart, that's not a hardship. Hell, I'd marry you right now if we could. I know it's not a long time to pull together a wedding, but you have to know a big-ass wedding isn't a dream of mine. But if it's what you want—"

"No! I don't need anything fancy. Not an expensive dress, a catered meal, or tons of cut greenhouse flowers that will just quickly die. I don't need a big cake. All I need are our friends and family, Timothy to walk me down the aisle, and you at the end waiting for me. I knew the first moment I met you that you were special. And I think deep inside, I started falling in love with you then."

He wanted to remember every nuance of her face right now, knowing he'd carry the memory with him no matter where he was. "So we'll get married in two weeks?"

"Daddy always told me life is what we make it. And yes, I want to make my life with you. So in two weeks, we'll get married." Suddenly, her eyes widened again. "But that means I need to call people to start planning—"

He stood, gently pulled her to her feet, and leaned down to kiss her. Bending further, with an arm around her back and another under her knees, he scooped her up and walked inside. "Planning starts tomorrow, sweetheart. Tonight is for celebrating."

Carrying her upstairs to the bedroom, she laughed and pulled him in for another kiss. And the celebration began.

Ready for the next Keeper? Jeb's story is available for pre-order! Click on his name! Jeb

Don't miss Chris and Ian's Stories in the crossover books of LSIWC and Long Road Home!
Chris' story: Home Port (an LSI West Coast crossover novel)
Ian's story: Thinking of Home (LSIWC crossover novel)
And the upcoming story of Leo's brother, Oliver, who joins LSIWC!
Oliver's story: Time for Home (LSIWC crossover novel)

Visit my website for all updates and to sign up for my newsletter!
http://maryannjordanauthor.com

Here are all the LSIWC books!
Lighthouse Security Investigations West Coast

Carson
Leo
Rick
Hop
Dolby
Bennett
Poole
Adam
Jeb
Chris's story: Home Port (an LSI West Coast crossover novel)
Ian's story: Thinking of Home (LSIWC crossover novel)
Oliver's story: Time for Home (LSIWC crossover novel)

ALSO BY MARYANN JORDAN

Don't miss other Maryann Jordan books!

Baytown Boys (small town, military romantic suspense)

Coming Home

Just One More Chance

Clues of the Heart

Finding Peace

Picking Up the Pieces

Sunset Flames

Waiting for Sunrise

Hear My Heart

Guarding Your Heart

Sweet Rose

Our Time

Count On Me

Shielding You

To Love Someone

Sea Glass Hearts

Protecting Her Heart

Sunset Kiss

Baytown Heroes - A Baytown Boys subseries

A Hero's Chance

Finding a Hero

A Hero for Her

Needing A Hero

Hopeful Hero

Always a Hero

For all of Miss Ethel's boys:

Heroes at Heart (Military Romance)

Zander

Rafe

Cael

Jaxon

Jayden

Asher

Zeke

Cas

Lighthouse Security Investigations

Mace

Rank

Walker

Drew

Blake

Tate

Levi

Clay

Cobb

Bray

Josh

Knox

Lighthouse Security Investigations West Coast

Carson

Leo

Rick

Hop

Dolby

Bennett

Poole

Adam

Jeb

Chris's story: Home Port (an LSI West Coast crossover novel)

Ian's story: Thinking of Home (LSIWC crossover novel)

Oliver's story: Time for Home (LSIWC crossover novel)

Hope City (romantic suspense series co-developed with Kris Michaels

Brock book 1

Sean book 2

Carter book 3

Brody book 4

Kyle book 5

Ryker book 6

Rory book 7

Killian book 8

Torin book 9

Blayze book 10

Griffin book 11

Saints Protection & Investigations

(an elite group, assigned to the cases no one else wants…or can solve)

Serial Love

Healing Love

Revealing Love

Seeing Love

Honor Love

Sacrifice Love

Protecting Love

Remember Love

Discover Love

Surviving Love

Celebrating Love

Searching Love

Follow the exciting spin-off series:

Alvarez Security (military romantic suspense)

Gabe

Tony

Vinny

Jobe

SEALs

Thin Ice (Sleeper SEAL)

SEAL Together (Silver SEAL)

Undercover Groom (Hot SEAL)

Also for a Hope City Crossover Novel / Hot SEAL...

A Forever Dad

Long Road Home

Military Romantic Suspense

Home to Stay (a Lighthouse Security Investigation crossover novel)

Home Port (an LSI West Coast crossover novel)

Thinking of Home (LSIWC crossover novel)

Time for Home (LSIWC crossover novel)

Letters From Home (military romance)

Class of Love

Freedom of Love

Bond of Love

The Love's Series (detectives)

Love's Taming

Love's Tempting

Love's Trusting

The Fairfield Series (small town detectives)

Emma's Home

Laurie's Time

Carol's Image

Fireworks Over Fairfield

Please take the time to leave a review of this book. Feel free to contact me, especially if you enjoyed my book. I love to hear from readers!

Facebook

Email

Website

ABOUT THE AUTHOR

I am an avid reader of romance novels, often joking that I cut my teeth on historical romances. I have been reading and reviewing for years. In 2013, I finally gave in to the characters in my head, screaming for their story to be told. From these musings, my first novel, Emma's Home, The Fairfield Series, was born.

I was a high school counselor, having worked in education for thirty years. I live in Virginia, having also lived in four states and two foreign countries. I have been married to a wonderfully patient man for forty-two years. When writing, my dog or one of my cats can generally be found in the same room if not on my lap.

Please take the time to leave a review of this book. Feel free to contact me, especially if you enjoyed my book. I love to hear from readers!

Facebook

Join my Facebook group: Maryann Jordan's Protector Fans

Sign up for my emails by visiting my Website!

Website

Made in the USA
Las Vegas, NV
17 January 2024